The Book of the Night

Holt, Rinehart and Winston/New York

THE BOOK OF THE NIGHT

Rhoda Lerman

Copyright © 1984 by Rhoda Lerman
All rights reserved, including the right to reproduce
this book or portions thereof in any form.
Published by Holt, Rinehart and Winston,
383 Madison Avenue, New York, New York 10017.
Published simultaneously in Canada by Holt, Rinehart
and Winston of Canada, Limited.

Library of Congress Cataloging in Publication Data
Lerman, Rhoda.
The book of the night.
I. Title.
PS3562.E68B4 1984   813'.54   83-22848
ISBN: 0-03-071081-2

First Edition

Design by Elissa Ichiyasu
Printed in the United States of America
10 9 8 7 6 5 4 3 2 1

ISBN 0-03-071081-2

FOR MARIAN WOOD, EDITOR

According to the Second Law of Thermodynamics, the world will eventually die, decay, fall into drift, come to a hopeless end, burn out, slide into disorder.

According to Ilya Prigogine, Nobel chemist, under certain circumstances and within certain localities the Second Law fails. Energy increases. An organism is able to reorganize itself into a higher level of order, to transcend itself. What it is that conducts this self-organization, implicit in evolution, seems to be an inherent property of matter itself, as if, indeed, matter has mind. As if, indeed, the thrust of evolution is will.

The Book of the Night

I

T IS SOON TOLD.
I, GENEROUS, CHRONICLER, SAXON, WRITE OF THE VAST WOMAN.

August fifteenth. Dawn is far away and the night large and I small and my brothers are together and I alone on the strand in a cup of sand at the lip of the high and treacherous sea and the crescent blade of a new moon cuts at my throat. Meteors fly from the northeast. Something ice-eyed moves boldly above me through the bushes on the cliff. Stars fall and die and a vastness is out there pulling at the sea waves and my faith. Injured that vastness. Moaning it is in the shower of stars, in pain, and I wish mightily for the light and the end of night. But I wait as the old Abbot commanded me in his second sight, a marvel, for the first treasure in the morning nets. My brothers wear saffron robes and climb on their knees to the peak of Dun Hi to praise the Lord of the Elements. Their songs, sweet and fervent, drift to me through the crash of waves. That the crops blast, that the fields come rich with corn and barley, that the thighs of the mountain be berry-filled and the barn without monsters— for these things they pray. And I that I would be with them rather than in this sheephole at the end of the world.

The Abbot Isaac chews the flesh of his thumb and knows what will be. "Something in the nets, Chronicler. Something large and with great value." And so I am here and they are there.

The sea sifts through its bits of time and tosses up on our shores its waste of past things and future things, known things and unknown things, rolling, turning, mixing the harvest of articles and particles of time in its great-stemmed groves of sea flesh, of olive tangle and black wrack. Sea shells we find and bomb shells, donkey beads and crusted coins, Pop-sickle sticks from Father Time, puns from the Argonauts, argot from the Punic Wars, cargo from the nets of Naught, Naughts that are not, sea-belched they come. A whore's comb, a warrior's mantle from a battle yet unfought, shards of blue majolica and flower-traced crockery, amphorae, bullets, pelts of beasts, boxes of gold, nails, sand pails, shovels, and the dead. Always the dead.

We are only the scavengers of a vast existence beyond time. What we find is what the sea selects from all time and no time: one part to the monks, one part to the crofters, seven parts to the finder—which is why the Abbot has me here—and the tenth, the jubilee part, tossed back to the sea into the crack of the Dark Gods, into the knots of the nets of Naught.

Something flaps in the nets near me. Just as the Abbot in his wisdom foresaw, a human form. I climb from my sheephole and claim a fighting man from the Great War, claim him flesh and bones, my witness the just and faithful sky, claim him red pantaloons and sky blue jacket and silk handkerchief for his sweetheart, embroidered *France, 1918*, in red white and blue and a black hole in his head, gaping, wordless, wordless mouth in which a living sponge nests and in his eyes two Coca-Cola prize-money caps bottled in Athens and printed in large black italics *TRY AGAIN NEXT TIME.* Balloon-sausage blue-skinned, white-eyed, dreadful the fighting man and I myself, cold and tired, drag him into the sheephole so I might nap until Matins. Between the crash of waves I hear my brothers' song and I turn in the sand to find softness and comfort over the stinking foul treasure beneath me.

I saw her then, the broken God, on the night of the new moon, in the ominous month of August, on the pale sand. Bloody and blue-bruised she was, her face harrowed by the torments and the creatures beyond the ninth wave, her wings drawn under her in the sand where she fluttered to escape.

But caught she was between three brutal rocks and held through the dawn tides until, as I watched, a Splitnose crept toward her. I tried, spineless scrivener, to hide in the gray dawn as he measured her, the Splitnose did, with his rough hands, his pinch, his inch, his foot, his yard, his pestle, and claimed her by driving a hawthorn stake through her open eye, and I useless, too fat to run, too awed to cry out.

"Flesh and bones," the Splitnose tells the just and faithful sky, this low creature does, and I am witness to his rich claim.

So in this way was the vast woman come to our shore. Her length nine score and twelve feet. Six feet between her paps. The length of her hair fifteen feet. Of the fingers of her hands six feet. Of her nose seven feet. Whiter than a swan or the foam of the wave was every part of her except toes and privies. Her toes the size of saplings and painted with red enamel. The ears those of a cow, twisted, tipped with fair down silk. *The Scottish Chronicles* date her arrival in A.D. 900. As do I. *The Annals of the Four Masters* enter her date as A.D. 888–891. *The Annals of Ulster* record her arrival between A.D. 890 and A.D. 891.

The Splitnose kneels at her ear, as large as a new-born that ear, and considers how many baskets of bones she has in her, how many soup bowls and dessert plates and serving platters, considers the vat of her skull, and while he considers she speaks in a whisper that blows the sand up and against the cliffs, it does, and bends the Tree of Life backward—fat figs drop from its limbs—and rattles the windows of the abbey. And the Splitnose acrouch inside the cave of the pit of her arm in the warm perfume of her wind.

"Find Abbot Isaac," she whispers and the Splitnose creeps, stumbles, scrambles toward the crossing stones and shouts into the monks' lands and alarm bells peal and from the Mountain of God the saffron chain of monks pierces the morning mists, a diagonal across the square-rooted fields. The alarm bursts through their plainsong. They turn toward the alarm and then, informed, warriors now, run through red berries, through golden fields, through the exalted land, to the foreshore.

Poke my head out, I do, and watch the broken God struggle for air and fight with racks of pain. The unrisen sun spills scarlet on her. The waves are flames. The face of the sky burns.

What I saw then from my sheephole as the skull of the sun cut the line of carbon sea was great clots of foul blood flooding and filling the dawn sky and the boiling sea turning from gray to red in that bloody sunrise and a beast, crippled, trailing a mangled foot, tailed, terrible, born out of the loins of the broken God between the three brutal rocks. Its shadow

4

alone I saw and heard weeping over the soft parts of its dying mother.

"To the darkness," she whispered to the child, the wonder who wept as a man at birth, who coagulated into the darkness and fled the day. "Go!" she whispered and her sigh soothed the waters.

Like sea wrack her hair drifted about her. Her dark privies fields of wheat, an eye open, an eye staked, and with the open eye she blinked and a great pool of a tear slid across her temple, along the ear to its silken tip and into the sand.

The Abbot and Nicholas, Druids both, and the golden chain, three at a time, spread their arms and dropped, floating, from the cliff to the foreshore. Brother Muncas Bent-Neck carried the Abbot to the woman and, breathing hard, set him upright by her great head. "Generous, mark this well," the Abbot called, and I climbed with shame from my hole. Crofters atumble over the cliff.

Isaac, judgment without fault, nodded his grim curled head at Archie Splitnose, witnessing his claim stake and damning forever, for sure and for certain, the foolish scrivener who brought up instead from the nets not the God but the gape-faced fighting man.

With a scarlet altar cloth the monks fashioned the great woman a hat of death. Isaac held it above her head and chanted, "Cabosh, Kadosh." And the others tore at their own colorful robes and into flat square pieces they tore them and covered the holy patch work, the wise crack, the vast and tawny privies. Isaac and Bishop Nicholas, our Druids, Co'in, the Irish dogs, sharp-nosed Dogs of God, Sons of Time, Sons of Cain, Roch-el their clan, cast satires at the crofters who shrank backward into the stones of the cliff away from the savage words and thrown fruits, for fear of wizening or poisoning or toads in their throats.

5

The Abbot, coal-faced, curl-haired, his eyes painted in triangles of black and circles of cobalt, his right hand heavy with rings, his left hand of intolerable radiance encased in silver, stately he is, wise, magical, lifted his skirts over gray kid boots, he did, and stepped carefully up onto the hard parts of the woman and crossed the very bridge of her rib cage.

"From the royal race," Splitnoses whispered to their foul children. "See him. Isaac, the holiest man in the Western World. See him."

Why, if his judgment be without fault, had Isaac not told me to wait for the vast woman and reject the gape-faced fighting man?

"Write, Chronicler, write."

Isaac pulled himself upward toward the heaving chest, crept, he did, between the great white paps from one to the other and sprinkled the body with his holy waters. The fine golden arch of his waters dropped into the cleft of her navel. The rosy nipples stood waist high. Shuddered greatly the vast woman did and Isaac fell tumbling and turning himself down the precipice of her shoulder. Muncas lifted him back. She stroked Isaac gently. He closed her eye. Isaac drew out his flint knife and cut on her stone-smooth belly the circle of Heaven within the square of earth and then lay himself down in the circle and spread his limbs to touch the edges, so large she was, so brave he was. She whispered instructions to him. He obeyed.

The vast woman reached down to touch a bloody limb, licked her stained finger clean, and pointed it at Isaac.

"Take the finger, Isaac. In its digits, one to the other, is the proportion of all things good. Preserve it against change. Keep the balance."

And Isaac took that finger, the two perfectly measured digits, and with a doubly sharp knife of flint worked sadly,

6

slowly, and when the digits were in the sand he shaped them as one would dough, with his hands, until they were dense and small, the size of his own fingers, and slipped them into a golden cloth and into a cowhide bag.

Fires were lit. She raised her hand, one finger to the sky. Those close fell back shouting curses and rhymes of power. "Isaac," she whispered in the West like the sea, roaring, storming, scattering, thundering, warm, wet, perfumed, palm and jasmine, her breath enfolding all. "Isaac, listen. There is war in Heaven. The balance is broken above."

She sighed then, long, shuddering, and sweat ran along the cheeks of the Abbot as if his flesh melted. He cut and her blood flew to the sand in great sweet steaming rivers while she nodded and whispered his name to give him courage. Her last breath left her. The smells of her—flesh, hair, salt, verdure, rich—drifted over Iona and the beach that night was blood and fiery stars flashing above her holy carcass where metal met bone, and flesh roasted in fires and the Splitnoses carving and carrying baskets of bones away. Sizzling the flesh. The people greedy with fleshforks, the monks praying. Her silken thighs gave up slices the size of grown pigs. Her paps fed families. Sawing, hacking, tearing, until the next sun. And consecrated, at last, by a dark hand, with the salt of Seth. Why have I been chosen to see when others more worthy do not? Why have I not been chosen for understanding? For only I had seen how it was she was delivered of the child who wept at birth.

Fires quenched. Splitnoses gone. My brothers gone and I left to witness. The Abbot Isaac, Heaven-mandated, turned a face toward me and from his eyes the mantle of Heaven had fallen, the sweetness and wisdom gone with his tears. He walked from me and I saw, shame to say, the finger drop from the cracked cowhide of his leather bag, the cut of the digits, the measure he was to preserve against change.

When the last tear of the woman had turned into a black cloud and the ashes of her soul into an amber jewel, only then did I see in the flickering shadows the child. Between dark and shape, not yet dense, between manifest and un-manifest, dragging a foot, he was, and settled over the place of the digits, that golden measure of the Cosmos. Taking the measure and the jewel of her soul, the crippled child whistled for a wee white cow come running from nowhere, slit her dewlap, and dragged the cow to the sea and turned her loose, slapping her gently on the side, turning from the sadness in her eyes, turning her loose.

The crippled child limped away to the dark side of our island and I heard the voice of the broken God from the vat of her skull say to me, this lowly Chronicler, "Teller of things, this you must not tell until a cow comes up from the sea."

For long months the kilns smoked with her bones and wooden cases of china were loaded on the *Prince George* and one could hear the vat of her skull moaning in the wind.

So in this way was the vast woman sacrificed.

— GENEROUS

There are many endings and many beginnings and there is always between ending and beginning the very briefest of moments and in those moments change, deep volatile change, is possible. To find that moment, to grasp it, embrace it, to change within it, that is the thrust of evolution. That is the moment of chaos, of a higher order, the disorder of the Gods, but order nevertheless. And to change within that moment takes the most terrible of wills. But it is possible. And then change becomes not evolution but exaltation. Once I was in that moment, that crack between ending and beginning, but I was without will. I became, somehow, a cow. Now I am searching for that moment again so that I may become woman. Or more.

On August fifteenth, I became a cow. My father had warned me to avoid linear logic, words that began with W, and

9

August fifteenth. Cow does not begin with W, linear logic has always avoided me, and I found it impossible to avoid August fifteenth.

August fifteenth. It is a solar stupidity, a Roman specificity, wisdom suffocating in the hot furs of Aristotelian logic, in the deep deep sleep of reason. But I write of Lunar Time, the ancient time, the ninth of Ov. Ov is Ab, the month of the Punishing, Punning Father, the month of Aleth and Beth. Tishubov, the ninth day of the ninth month, the day of the letter Tet—the living cell, the number nine—the day of the crack, the nick of time between end and beginning. I write, I suspect, of the memory of the day of the Deluge, Lug's day. I write of Hebrews, Irish, Sumerians, Mexicans, Japanese. I write of them all, for in their various ways each remembers.

August fifteenth is the loosening of the deep, the day the dead return to punish the living. Shapes from the wilderness brood over Council Chambers. Wine rises in cellars. It is the moment between, a crossing over, the Old Nick of Night, a dangerous moment, a tilt in the Cosmos, the time of the Pythagorean comma in the pentatonic scale, the time irrational and transcendent, the slip up, slip out, slip in of the system that guides us between life and death, between octave and octave. Kings take to the battlefield. Meteors fly from the northeast. It is the night of the Perseids. Romans wish on shooting stars. Irish climb their mountains and pray the crops to blasting. Hebrews eat the mouthless eggs of mourning and wear no leather. It is the day of Lug in Ireland, the God of Luck himself, a day in which terrible and wonderful things may happen.

These are the Dog Days, the day of St. Siriacus, the time of Sirius rising. Crops blast or die. Victories are lost or won. Addition moves to multiplication, evolution to exaltation, the square root of two to the golden proportion, the spade to the flower, growing to ripening. This is the time of the kaleidoscope night when earth moves through the shower of meteors to the place where once was the nail, the centerpin, the core, the cube, the zauberspiegel of all this catalogued simultaneity, the eye of all the crystalline splinters of reality glimpsed now only in shadow, in vacuum. Invisible something out there in the crack. Out there, where once something moved gracefully, splendidly, augustly even, through its rounds and paused in climax and the world held its breath waiting for that something to return, to begin anew. We have forgotten the Dark Gods but they have not forgotten us.

August fifteenth is their time. It is the time when An, the Real Article, Lady Luck no less, mother of Lug, Fate, Nem-Isis, Mary, forget the etymology, was assumed. In Jerusalem it is the time of the destruction of the Temple. In Mexico it will be the last day of the Fifth Mayan Sun and the first day of the Sixth Mayan Sun. In Japan it is the day the dead return through a crack in the night sky to punish the living. It is the day of the beheading of John the Baptist (think Lunar), the beginning of the Inquisition, Custer's last stand, the day Rama Krishna died, the day Napoleon was born, the Assumption of the Blessed Virgin (see above), the day World War One began (watch the W's, forget the logic), the end for the Japanese of World War Two, and the day I became a cow.

A cow. Yes.

But why a cow? What structures have fallen away? What boundaries have I added? And why such a cow with fur sweeping to the ground, with Viking horns and white and small while the others in the monastery herd are smooth-headed, black and white pied, bald and great? What in me or out of me thought even as a cow I would be original, that I would leap somehow to the moon, across the moon, my tail straight out behind me, I would leap through the crack between end and beginning, my fur a carpet, wings, I would fly out of the orbits and orders and predestinies, out of the stories others write about me, out of interpretation and into eternity where every thing, every word, is spirit and new and without metaphor and I should wrestle with the Motley Crew of Naught, the Angels of Death, the Dark Pig Gods of Disorder, for it is they, I know, out there, Seth and Cessair, the Never-Never Gods of the alien world from which all form springs, the reservoir of Chazarei from which the future flows. I would go to them, the Gods of Naught, of silence, from which everything that ever is shall be and I would wrench meaning from them. Naming I should go, creating anew and living forever after in the Milky Way of Wisdom, unincarnated, unincarcerated in the prison of flesh word meaning, that I could leap somehow into the carnation milky bosoms of the stars themselves and there dwell in the land of Melchisedek, swimming in the milk of his wisdom, Michael, Molchu, Mocc-el, Moloch, Melech, King of the Universe, Enoch, eunuch. I would dwell in the shadows, shaddai, of the Dark Gods of Night, the why and what and when and which and who, above all who, in its cosmic august path paused in the shadows of the gates of the Milky Way while the little dog, Sirius, laughed to see such craft, when the dish ran away with the spoon. Death is too simple an answer. It is about a cow who jumped over the moon that I write and night and nicht and nacht and Naught and not and net and enough and Enoch and eunuch and unicorn. I sail over the ninth wave, an Irish sailor I am, Noe, of the great craft *Argo*. Noah, Jonah, Iona, I sail with the argot and puns of the Naught to the God Lug of the Deluge.

We came to the monastery, my father and I, he told me, I in his arms across Frankish forests, English seas, Hebridean wastes, he carrying his opera glass, a compass, my infant clothes, banknotes in his cape, two leather-bound books of architecture, his Bible, and the picture postcard of my mother and himself standing under a sausage tree in Cuba on their honeymoon just four years before he abandoned her, almost myself, and certainly most of his property, to quit the world for Iona, the farthest island in the Atlantic. I was, he told me, two. It was raining that day. He wrapped me in his cape and when the open boat we rode scraped shore at the rocky beach of the island at the end of the world, he told the split-nosed ferry man that I was his son and we were visiting the monastery. I was his daughter and we stayed there forever.

The ferry man pointed uphill into the stiff wind, up to a low wall of rough stones, and said he would take us no further, his eyes narrowing against my father's, which must have, even then, flashed strange and fiery. And turned his back to us.

I can only imagine my father arriving that first day as I have since seen him. Falcon-beaked his nose, deep-set the fugitive eyes, red his beard and body hair in large mossy clumps between his legs, on his knees, elbows, chest, and the small of his back. A ropy man, knotted. I think he had begun his weaving by then and I am certain that his fingernails, my first memory, were already long and thickened, his eyes bronze-green, with shafts of gold, astonished and frenzied at each rude light of reality.

My father peered beyond the wall of stones to a green-stained abbey of towers and roundhouses swimming now in rain. Above the abbey the island gathered itself and soared into a single mountain, lifting itself to Heaven and dropping suddenly into the sea. Plainsong drifted to us through the wind and, following the sound, my father remembered, he could see through the rain a square and sunlit field where the chanting monks reaped with sickle and scythe. At each corner of the field stood a monk in brown robes, arms high above his head, palms flat against the sky, against the rains. My father called out, covered my face with his cape, and waited for the monks to come to the stones.

I T IS SOON TOLD.
I, GENEROUS, CHRONICLER, WRITE OF THE COMING OF THE
HERMIT AND HIS CHILD.

It was I, Generous, who greeted them. He came, we thought, without a name. He would not allow us to hold the child. Brother Aidan, the Guestmaster, led them through the rain past the monastery to the Hermit's house at the top of the Mountain of God. John Joe the Amadan, half-wit, silent, dumb, followed. The new Hermit clutched the child and glanced once at our Abbot Isaac. They were not strangers to each other.

So in this way was the child brought to the monastery. Pray, I beg you, for the child and the Abbot, for their souls and pray for this Chronicler, I, Generous, poor soul so far

15

from his Saxon land, who tries to understand. Pray for this soul and for these three frozen fingers gripping the stubborn quill and this stomach agrowl and this ink freezing in this ink horn and the dull nub slipping wantonly across the polished vellum in this icehold of a scriptoire in the abbey on this our holy and beloved island Iona, Ioua, Yahweh, Jove, Jehovah, where the rock runs north and south, black, and the sun east and west, golden, and the great bright sea is all around us and the veil between Heaven and earth is thin. Pray for the chronic Chronicler whose head aches with each thundering groan of the waves below the wooden shutters, with each screech of the jackdaw and cry of the hoodie, each nuisant bleat of the lamb lost in the giant claws of the gale in the length of the darkening day and the aching clang in the bell of my belly which will feel no food until the day ends and did not feel food since the day began at eventide and will not sleep until after we are called from our work, our fields, our books, our barns, plumberies, kitchenings, offertory, our threshing floors, our mills, our prayers, called to Compline by the Holy Father the Abbot Isaac, Son of God, of Adam, of the Wise Men. Pray for me, Generous the Chronicler, who writes of the cow and the Abbot and August fifteenth. A blessing on him who would be at preserving these words against the Beast of Time and a curse upon him who would be at changing these words. Hear, O Israel, the Lord our God, the Lord is One.

— GENEROUS

And so there on the island where the veil was thin and the Other Side began west of the Mountain of God— Dun Hi they called it—my father and I, Celeste, although I was forbidden to tell anyone my name, lived as hermits on the eastern flank of Dun Hi. Below our hut, a lopsided patchwork of sea-quarry, lay the ancient abbey and the long gleaming steel swoop of monastery buildings and barns designed by my father, which was why, I understand now, we were allowed to live there, wrapped in the monks' mists, above time, watching time, beyond time, provided for, protected, and yet precariously on the edge of something only my father, the old Abbot, and perhaps the Chronicler Generous knew.

At the south end of Iona lay the machair, a long windswept plain of obstinate isolate earth and blue sheep and the mean crofts and kilns of another people in another time. Between us and the crofters was the harbor, which they owned, and the stone boundaries. Of the crofters only Archie the Ferry Man could go to Mull across the Sound. Of the monks only John Joe Amadan, who tended the camel and performed other tasks the monks could not, only John Joe could cross the boundary stones into the crofters' lands, or worse into the west lands of the island where the Pig God—Chazar, Seth, Lug, Mocc-el, his names—lives. No one from our side of Dun Hi crossed south to the machair or west to the Other Side and no one from the Other Side crossed to ours, except on extraordinary occasions. Our arrival was such an occasion.

I know now that history shapes memory and memory shapes history and how much of my father and my father's house I remember correctly I cannot judge. My father was an architect, a gentleman, and a madman. My mother, he told me, a lady. He would tell me no more. On the sepia postcard my mother—her eyes inked out and filled with yellow—and he stand under the sausage tree in Cuba on their honeymoon, she soft and small and leaning against him, round. He already dark, hollow, and rigid. As I grew older at his feet, he became darker still, a furious melancholic man with a fever of heart and a thinness of flesh and a soul that lay, as they say, in his imagination and soared with the demons—a man who couldn't relieve himself except on a sod of turf, which rested by the door, which I had to fetch for him, which went with us to sea.

Two flagstones covered with cow skins and hay lay on either side of the fireplace. There we slept. In the morning he woke me with chickory drink. At night we roasted crab claws over the turf and cracked them open against the bricks of the fire place. Tar paper, linoleum, and bark covered the walls. Handsful of fiber glass and sphagnum moss filled the window chinks. Off the common room, in a small sun-filled cubicle, stood my father's loom, patterned by a great light from a stained glass window, a relic from the Viking-razed nunnery in the crofters' lands. A treasury of silk, gold, and silver bobbins hung from nails in the rough wood.

"A rainbow of a room," my father would say each time I entered for my lessons. "And is a rainbow not light caught in its own pain?" That was my father. As he suffered, the world suffered.

Locked in a rough wood cubicle along with our supply of matches were my father's books, the old Bible filled with strange-shaped letters and the rich, calf-bound volumes of renderings and photographs of winged forms, of steel and glass, in cities I could only imagine. On the covers of the calf-bound books the letters of my father's name were pressed and gilded: Manuel. Other letters were obliterated with knife nicks.

My father was and will always be a puzzle to me. A torment. I, I suppose, to him, when he remembered me. We didn't speak often. Together in silence we ate pieces of bird, periwinkle soup, crab, handsful of grain and grass he cooked in the fire place. We spent our days, he at his loom weaving, I on a stool reading my lessons aloud and reciting my lists and strange equations. He was very tall. I can remember being small enough to look directly at his knees. "Look at me when I speak to you. Look at me!" But when I looked up into the bronze eyes, he would glance away swiftly and I would look again at his knees which were as hard as the camel's knees and his fingers near them as thick and yellow and curved as the camel's teeth.

My father fancied birds. When he wasn't at his loom or on the flagstones praying or talking mysteriously with the old Abbot on long walks, he took me to creep along the cliffs of our island and into the profound caves about the sea. He would carry a rush torch and cracked leather pouch. I, the opera glass, his fowling piece, and short strands of silk. In the winter when we crept toward a nesting cave there was a thunder of powerful wings against frozen mud and in the summer, a frenzy and a stench of ooze.

In good weather he tied a brick to a cork and on the cork stuck two hooks and a sardine on each hook and we watched from a skiff as wise gulls, made foolish by my father, swept in from the great light to take the sardine by the head and were themselves caught horribly on the hook. "The spirit trapped in the maw of matter," my father would tell me as we paddled out on a glassy sea near the Port of the Spout, out to the cork and the dying gull.

Once with a wild shot from our skiff he brought down a rare fourteen-pound Northern diver female. For days she hung from her neck by the fire, drying, the yellow webs of her feet cracking and splitting further apart each day while her mate bugled over our hut and my father waited for the spring post.

In our common room, skins and feathers were pinned and stretched to the walls. Eggs rested in flatbeds filled with mosses and raw wools. Bird-bodies, legs bound, hung over the fire place, drying out.

Even as I was torn between pleasing my father and sorrow for the birds, I also had my share of triumphs. In a clutch of seaweed after a boisterous storm I found nine dozen loon and kittiwake eggs. I waited hours in the calm for the mothers' return. At twilight, I wrapped the eggs gently in my shirt and brought them to my father who, with untrammeled delight, took the eggs, kissed me on the lips, and then drew back, leaped back, stared at me, measuring me somehow, and strode away, leaving me alone on the beach, and I wondering what it was that I was so lacking.

I came to understand that he was obsessed. He thought of the birds as the dead. When flocks passed overhead, he called out, "It is the clamor of the dead. I must guide them on. Below, souls, not above." And he would shoot as many as would be shot. Laying them out before the hearth he would say such things as "Aah, how their souls yearn for the depths." And shake his head in great sympathy or pity, I could not distinguish.

From the Edinburgh Natural History Society letters came to him from another time, thanking him for the shipments of guillemots, petrels, grebes, red-legged crows, Great Northern divers, which he sent embalmed and disemboweled from Iona each spring in gunpowder crates sea-belched from the Great War. "Edinburgh is a city," he would say, showing me the astonishing letter. "See the postdate? 1892." And laugh as crazy as a grebe lost in the storm. "1918. The First World War." More laughter as he pointed to the gunpowder crates.

With his arm he encompassed the shimmering sea and all the world I assumed lay beyond us. "Out there it is 1915. Or it was. Or it will be. Here . . ." He doubled over in laughter I could neither share nor understand. "Here it is . . . no time, all time. Here it is always August fifteenth." And somehow I would vanish from his sight.

He could not bear, he told me again and again through those years, to leave me behind in the world he so despised, of which, however, I was so painful a reminder. "So. You are my demon, Celeste, my memory," he would say as if to explain to himself why I existed. Demon, I discovered later, meant something which came from the moon. How it was I reminded him of the moon, I did not know.

I

T IS SOON TOLD.
I, GENEROUS, CHRONICLER, WRITE OF THE SPLITNOSES AS THEY
ARE KNOWN BY THE ABBOT ISAAC IN HIS SECOND SIGHT.

Noble and wonderful is the Lord of the Elements. Many are
His attributes, light and dark. Many are His names, many
are His forms, Prosecutor, Prosector, and Mercy-Giver. Dull
and mean are the crofters on the south of the island. Thick
they are. Seven faces tall, noses split to defy the nose tax.
Partly wrought of impure seed and unclean rubbing in the
ditches by the paths. A terrible low folk. In them a simple
pulse. Like fists in sunbeams they are, with low foreheads
and scabs and aprons of hide and whips of bull penises and
faces charred by the flames of the kilns and lungs choked
with the dusts of the bones they bake. Bull-like the men.

Free men, the Splitnoses, stout folk, with flowing hair and bracelets of iron on their wrists and bands of iron around their necks, withed and twisted and cysted in the fires of the kiln. Dull their eyes, milk-bleary, small. Sea-soaked their women, mean, salt-shrunk, withered, weathered, the youth bloom long gone and the stink of herring and the stink of their men stuck to their plaids.

Eels they eat with egg shells and blood they drink from slaughter. It is winter when the first sea storm shatters a clay chimney pot and spring when the cattle go to sheeling and summer when the women are ripe in the ditches and fall when the nutmeats are ripe on the trees. Four ditches of a man's life: mother, woman, potato, grave.

Little do they know and little do they need to know. Ignorant, they bless the will-o'-wisp as it blows along the path and tell each other it's the fairies on their way when all the while it's only a wisp of straw and the true fairies— the pharaohs—the Sons of Seth, dread and merciless in their judgment, sharp and exact in their cuttings, live within a sigh of us all. The crofters, Seth, John Joe, the brethren, all are in the order of things or wouldn't be. So says the Abbot, his judgment without fault, the Holy Father, Isaac.

As long as any can mind, even the eldest, there has always been among the crofters a ferry man to answer the hoarse shout when it comes flying across the Sound at midnight, to roll from his plank and his woman, pull on his oils, push off and row until his currach touches at Mull and he sits there beneath the cliff shivering at the heavy dry shuffle down the cliff. Tries to stay back, Archie does, somewhere in his sleep, as the currach comes slowly heavier and deeper with its sad royal load and then he pushes off riding low in the swells in the craw of the night in the little boat heavy with souls, invisible, in rows, and facing him, they are, and if the moon is up he might see a flash of gold from the coins

23

in their eyes but not one of the Kings has he ever seen, not a smell, not a sound, not a fart, nor caught even a corner of a rich hem but always the cold coins left in the bottom of the boat and always the light boat going over and the heavy boat going back and the boat light again as it touches the beach in Iona. And three days later, for sure and for certain, the camel comes down the mountain over the crossing stones and into the path before their low thatched bothies carrying in its wicker baskets the long, fine bones of Kings, bleached clean. Archie's wife, Erca, is rich with the coins from the eyes of the Kings and runs the store and takes the post and tack off the *Prince George* Tourist Boat. The barrels of rice and barley and bits of iron and candles and odd things for the monastery, Erca passes them on to John Joe for the camel's empty baskets. Erca sits spread out on the quay on Tuesdays, waiting for the *Prince George*, and she sells charmed pebbles from the beaches to bring good luck, such is the power of this island. For this is the land where the sun and the dead Kings, passing on, last touch earth.

Archie Ferry Man doesn't know what happens between ferry and basket and doesn't want to know. But we know, for the brains of the Kings, by agreement, we mix them with lime and harden them into Druid weapons. Our astrologers sprinkle the Kings with thyme, our Wise Men cast sage, our murderers cast myrrh. The flesh and the souls and the parts go to Seth and by agreement with the crofters, Seth returns the bones. There, among the Splitnoses, the bones are crushed and cast and baked in great fires and shaped into chalices and platters and sent then beyond to glass bowers, feather-lined, or gilded caves of ice and palaces for the consorts of Queens and the sons of Popes to dine on, and priests and holy men. Relics they are, fine bone china hidden under lock and key and stone behind Tarot and Torah, gleaming with aura in crystal cupboards or mildewed storehouses in the sewers of Jerusalem.

Cadoc once saw a great silver cylinder of a milk machine at the harbor before it was dismantled and packed on the camel's back. Large, round, gleaming, it was, and they sat, Tolua the Tall, Cadoc of the Crooked Hand, Caw Flathead, Archie Ferry Man, talking through the winter of that silver cylinder and what it meant. But about the Kings and the kilns and the bonefires, the china dishes shipped in hay to God knows where for painting and gilding and about the Dark God Seth, about that they keep silent. And do the work when it needs doing and smoke their pipes when it doesn't. In return, as long as any can mind, even the eldest, the crofters had from the monks a tenth portion of all things seacast, the May gathering and the August gathering of the seaweeds, the grains of the machair and the herring of the sea.

It is through the Amadan that the crofters are told the time to break the bones, to grind the dust, to light the fires, to add the elements, to stir, to mold, to cast, to cool, to pack, to ship. Through the year they labor at the kilns until the final hissing on August fourteenth when the fires are put out and begun again on August sixteenth. Only the monks above can reveal the times of the opening and closing of the twelve doors of the kilns and the times of the passing of the nine great men through the doors, planet after planet. Only the monks know the measures of elements, of the puffs and powders that burn the hands. The true winding course of the Heavenly year is the labor of the holy brothers, the watchers of time, beyond time, and the true course of the fiery kiln is the labor of the split-nosed crofters. For the old Abbot Isaac has said, and before him and before him until we touch the hand of Adam and the wisdom of God's heart: "When everything has been sent to dust and ash, God shall quench the fire and he shall fashion again the bones and the ashes of meal and raise up mortals once more as they were before."

But this is not something the crofters know or need to know. There is much on Iona they haven't seen and there are times, their women warn them, when you shouldn't see. Then, their men tell them, as they smoke artemisia in their crab-claw pipes and watch the blue line of sea and the purple Paps of Jura and the great sea crests beating against the sunken cities, watching it all, then you shouldn't look, for sure there's enough to be seen here and more than enough, they agree, to be done. The machair around them is blue-swept and bare. What the monks do is their mind. What Seth does, no one wants to know.

— GENEROUS

I would imagine my mother—a lady, my mother— writing a letter to me. "Dear Celeste. My child, do you remember me . . . darling?" Or to my father. "Dear Manuel," in a fine hand. "My dearest Manuel, it is time the child was returned . . ." The letter coming from her pen, from her hand, from a room someplace, across a city, forests, a long journey, sea, bay, cave, loch, crag, the Island of Mull, the Sound, and ending somehow, oh how, in the pouch of the captain of the *Prince George*, to the pouch of the Amadan, and over the camel's back across the stones and up the path to me, from my mother. Sometimes my father would sigh deeply, "Your mother," accusing me.

Except to pull a strand of hair from my head when he had forgotten his silk and needed to garrot a bird or wanted my particular silver paleness for his loom, or pull me on his lap for a special lesson, my father touched me only in blessing, once a day, in the morning, after chickory, after prayer. And even so his hands trembled until he escaped to his weaving and I dressed myself in shirt and trousers.

The vestments he wove for the Church Fathers were precious silks of the sea and the sunset, with white lilies and silver eyes, golden keys, crosses, fish, goblets, and vast great-bird wings of sleeves. And that was perhaps why, one day when he was gone with the old Abbot, I took a finished robe and held it against my cheek and slipped into it and held it up over my ankles and raced flapping down the mountainside and over the millstream and beyond the High Cross of Moses and over a causeway of boulders and moss to the beach, where I flew, billowing, a great bird along the White Strand, scarlet and gold. The flocks of ordinary birds lifted in fear and wonder and the great ancestral herd of cows, standing in the water to their hocks eating seaweed, rolled their eyes and snorted at me as I flapped along. When my chest ached as if squeezed, I fell on the sand, an angelic creature, shimmering, my wings spread, and gasped for air and from the sky, glossy and black and cold and heavier than a quern stone, a dead gull, whistling, fell and cut its shape into the sand at my head. Terrified as I had never been before, I shook sand from the scarlet of my sin, wiped its hems on my own trousers, folded it in a small square, and ran home. My heart arrived before I did.

Weaving, my father had forgotten I'd gone nor known I'd returned. His shuttle looped through startling goods: claw, stick, bone, dunged wool. And he wove equal marvels into lists: "Ark, d'ark, argo, cargo, argonaut, argotique, gothic. So. Alevai, Halloween, mistletoe, mazeltov." He saw me and stopped immediately, hand and mouth, his face flushed, and he drew out my Dark Horse Copy Book. Had I looked somehow on his nakedness? I scratched steadfastly for him my A's and B's and ice cream cones and my name, Celeste.

I do not know precisely when it was that my father began to teach me my own sets of lists. I am certain, however, it was after the gull fell from the sky, after I first heard his lists and before I learned to read. I would stand in the sun-filled room, my small hands knotting and squeezing behind my back, and recite. There was then in those lists no inherent necessity, no single assumption that what preceded gave way to what followed, nothing except my father's glowering intensity, my anxiety to perform, and his pleasure when I did well. "Nike, night, victory, victim."

"Listen, to the words, Celeste. Nike is the Goddess of Victory. Her name means night and night means not and victory means victim who is no longer, who is not."

"Zeus, Deus, juice, Jews, Yid, Druid, druse. Methuselah, Medea, Medua, Medusa, Madonna," I recited.

"Do you hear . . . in the roots? Listen. The root is the Hebrew 'why,' Medua. Why, a God's name. Why. That is the question. That is the Name. Medua—why."

"*Gaballa*, *Kabbalah*, Kadosh, cabosh, caboose," I recited.

"It is all so clear. *Gaballa* is *The Book of Takings*; *Kabbalah*, *The Work of Receivings*. Kadosh, holy; cabosh, hat of death; caboose, the last car on the train, the end. Kaput. See? Holy, separated."

The words burst and transformed themselves. They enticed me into paths and labyrinths. They bloomed from word to word without an if, without a then, without a therefore.

"Beware of linear logic, little one."

I expected a linear if-then-therefore order behind the unexpectedness of my lists and my life. I assumed that sooner or later in all things there would be intention, that the gull had been sent, that sin begat punishment.

"So. You write your name and that which means you—the I—with capital letters. And the why, and the who and the which . . . ?"

"But . . ."

"They are the names, the attributes, of the Gods. The names of the Gods are locked into the language. Release them, Celeste, and you will be a God. An, El, The, Dis, This, That. They are the pre-nouns, pre-positions, the Real Articles, the pre-possessors of the manifest. Examine any language, Celeste. They are there. Behind them of course is something else."

"All those little words that connect things . . ."

"Precisely. Now . . . I have a new list for you. I want you to find the word that doesn't fit. We begin with gelding, yes? A castrated horse. Gelding, gilding, gold, jewel, tool . . ."

"Tool. It rhymes and means the same but leads to other tools."

"Yes, it doesn't fit because it misleads."

"Now, pine, pine tree, pine for me, pine away, pangs of hell, incense, pain, death, pin . . ."

"Pin?"

"Now connect . . ."

It is true I felt dismay and fear. Perhaps I was too weak a vessel to contain all of that with which he was driven to fill me. He seemed in such a hurry and I was so small. But I remember pleasure and excitement as well.

My father would set me on the floor and spread out his most precious silken bobbins, roll them toward me or toss them at me, and when I caught them he would laugh and bounce me on his lap. He would create the Heavens with a silver spool for the moon and gold for the sun and red glowing stars and blue planets and long flaxen strands for the Milky Way. He showed me the orbits and the ellipses and the change of seasons by making silken circles of stars above my head. Before I could walk I would crawl on the ground and look up into the orbits of my father's silken Heavens, turning and turning with them on knees and hands as my father wheeled stars and planets speeding about my head. And then he would stop and the spools would crash into each other with soft thuds and he would start them on another orbit, in another direction, wheeling around my head. And he would laugh and say, in his deepest of voices, "I am the planet Saturn and I lead and you are the planet Herschel, far far out, Celeste, at the very edge of the sky and you follow." What wonders were in those orbits, what dizziness as I followed them. My father's laughter echoed, as distant from my understanding as the Heavens themselves.

And when I was older I was allowed to build my own Cosmos on the floor and sometimes I would hold the sun in my pocket for a day or keep the moon under my pillow until my father needed that silver thread for his weaving.

Once we filled our arms with bobbins and laid them on the grass before the cottage and there we waited into the night until fields of fireflies winked in new Heavens at our feet. And my father carried me about on his shoulders through the fireflies as if we were great, tall Gods gazing down upon the stars. I have never forgotten the bobbins gleaming in the moonlight nor the fireflies bursting between them like Angels nor my father's careful steps through the Universe that reshaped itself at his every footfall.

"Pine. I pine away. I pine for you. I long. I suffer. I suffer the pangs of Hell, the pines of Hell. The Messiah is at the top of the pine. Rockabye Baby, in the treetop, when the wind blows, the cradle will rock. When the bough breaks, the cradle will fall. Down will come Baby, cradle and all. The star at the top of the tree is the Messiah. Pine gives us the perfumes of death. The merd/murder/myrrh is taken from the pines for the funereal incenses. Pine is the Other Side. The Messiah rises from the Tree of Death. At the top of the pine, He is born. Pine, pang, pain."

"You are improving. The Christmas Tree is the Tree of Death. So. Here are two words. Ostrich and oyster. Oyster in Italian is ostriche. How are they connected?"

"That which buries itself in the sand?"

"Now, here are two words, macabre, meaning deathly, and merkabah, meaning the descent to the throne of light. Connect them please with a third word."

"Murky?"

"So. That will do for now. You must make your own lists. It is the only way to free yourself from language."

"Oh, Father, one more. Please. Do Anubis."

"Again? So. Anubis. B'is, son of Isis, great goddess. Anu b'is, anus of the son of Is, the asshole of the Queen of Heaven, the Jackal of Judgment who eats the dead and shits them into the Ever-After. Analyze with anal eyes and all you get is hindsight."

"More."

"You must do your own."

And one day, I might have been seven or eight, I knew my lessons would be unusual, for my father drew me upon his lap and stroked my hair and sighed. "Ah, Celeste. How difficult it is for me to say this simply. And yet it is the most simple of truths. I will place this story in time and yet I want you to know later that all Creation happens at once and we are in it, that everything is simultaneous. It is a great loom. So. Once upon a time . . . once upon a time there was the One. Not God. You understand that. Not God, that is his name. Not. And he was lonely and divided himself and created all that beyond himself although he is still himself—in the way a spider weaves her web. And all that beyond the original unmanifested became Two. It was called the scission; the One splitting into the Two. Numbers weave the Universe into patterns.

"Letters weave also. A is the unmanifest, this Not God, the great breath of existence, the One."

He blew on my neck. I shivered.

"B represents the manifest, Two that the One made. So. B is the house, the container. In Hebrew Aleph is the sign of the cow. See the horns." He drew a cow in the notebook. Then he drew an A and turned it upside down. "See. B, Beth is the name for house. See the roof." He drew a broken square. "Bothie is the Scot name for house. The crofters below us live in bothies. A is then the same as One. B is then the same as Two. Even the word be—as in to be—means that which is. A, as Aleph, as One, does not exist." My father blew on my neck again. My hair floated upward. "We are the containers. The Twos. The B's. Houses contain. Boxes and bodies and books contain. Barns contain. But *in* us"—He touched my shoulder lightly and then his own—"in us, there are large parts of the A. We are special. Now." He lifted me from his lap and beckoned me to stand before him.

"Now. Who lives in the barn?"

"The cow."

"So. And the cow is the letter . . . ?"

"A."

"And the stable is the letter . . . ?"

"B."

"Good. The cow is A for breath, the breath and the spirit of the Not God as One. The cow A lives in the stable B. Now we play with the words. That which is stable is solid and still and unchanging." He hit the wall with his fist.

"That which is unstable is amorphous, changing." He stuck two fingers on either side of his head through his hair and wiggled them.

"Cow!" I called out. I can remember how happy I was.

"A makes change. Remember this. A is change. A is unstable. A becomes stable within containers. The world is a container. A is a power, an idea, a force. And that which is stable contains, limits, and resists the force of A. But this is very complicated. A cow is an A, a force in the stable of B. But a cow is also a B, a container. Man is both A and B. Part of him limits the holiest part of him, resists, contains it. It is that part we fight against, our boundaries, our B's. I am exhausted. Tomorrow I will tell you about Three."

Only for that lesson but often enough so I knew every breath of it, would he draw me on his lap and stroke my hair. He would assure me when I faltered, "Don't try to understand. Just remember it. Someday you will make this knowledge your own."

And so I learned to count.

"So. Celeste. What One is breaks apart into One and Two. One is yourself. Two is another self, a living you, a bond with someone else. Three, though, is beyond, very, the darkness, three, tres. One is this." He hit his chest forcibly. "Two is thou." He touched my chest gently. "Three is them." He arced his arm out toward the monastery, the beyond, the crofters' lands. "One is this, Two is thee, Three is that. Two contains antithesis, like twilight, twist, Zwisto. One is unity. Two is separation. Three is separation and great distance. A is One, B is Two."

And I repeated word for word, after tormented attempts, what he told me. "One is I, two is you, three is them."

"See." He held me by the shoulders. "The, Dis, Thea, Zwis, Zue. God is only Two, only B. Devil, double, Zeus,

34

Deuce, Deva, Deus. There is something behind God. It is One, An, A, the uncontained, the breath, the unthinkable. Not God. Distance from Not God becomes evil."

"Yes, Father."

"Celeste, where is the cow?"

"In the stable."

"A is in B, but B is not in A. So, the cow, the A, is unstable. The B is stable. Yes? But A is contained by B. Now, the root of B is the same as V. B equals V, so double B equals . . . ?"

"Baby. The infant Jesus was born in the stable."

"A variation. Let us return to the truth. . . ."

And he would lead me on God knows where but what was remarkable was that I could follow. "So, then, double B equals double V and double V equals W. Then what is the name of God's house?"

"W?"

"So. Beware of W. W contains beginning and end. W is the final container of existence. W," he whispered, "is God's mouth. It is the three fingers of the Fathers—Abraham, Isaac, and Jacob."

I did not know if he was teaching me about cows and stables or about unthinkable energy and its containers and resistances, or all of it. I decided that W was the container of all that was not and I dreamed uneasily of large dark caves filled with bodies and butchers and old men and women who looked like potatoes and walked around with dried peas in their shoes to remind themselves of the dead, a great big double B cave and I would wake up with my legs numb and my blood ice and climb next to my father on his flag-stone.

One day he told me offhandedly as he was building turf in the fire place that Qu was really W in disguise. "Where, what, who, why, when, which, quhere, que, quo, aqui. So?" He drew a Q in my copy book. "Q is the unified separated into form. The circle is the One, and this little line, so? Is the circle's power descending to us." The turf pyramid collapsed and he built it up again. "See the little line? It descends to the abyss of U, double U. Qu is God's power in the abyss of W. Contained. So." I thought he was making me his container for the unthinkable. Everything meant God. Even Iona. The N he said was merely scribal error. "Ioua. Iova. Yahweh. Jehovah. The unspoken vowels."

"Father," I attempted although he hated questions and often simply fumed and turned from them. "Does everything mean God?"

The question pleased him. "A means God, actually what is behind God. Listen: A tree, A stone, A man, all are created by A, the breath, and are dwellings for A. A man is God in the container of man. A tree is God in the container of tree. Articles are the possessors, the ancient possessors, the Real Articles, the true pre-positions of reality. A, An, El, The, This, That."

"The?"

"Ah, The. Two, thee, divided, a lesser God. Already separated out from the unity." He pointed to the Q's in my notebooks, drawn in fat shaky lines. "See, this circle which stands for the original unity, the Not, the original unity has its little line. See, Celeste. It means it has sent its power down. It has split. It is really called Phi. It is a finger sign from the circle reaching out to manifest itself. It is the Two. It means further distinguished. The means God, Two, other than One. The is the name of God after the scission of the One. The more God is distinguished, the less God he is. A named God . . ." He shrugged in disdain. Then he tilted his head. "I do not tell you what I think. I tell you what I hear."

36

Since I was in the same relationship to the knowledge, I did not then find the remark extraordinary.

"And the ba? Theba? The house of God? The mouth of God?"

"So, we are back where we began. Theba is ark and the B is the container of God's soul. The stable holds A, which is unthinkable. An is the name of the Mother of God."

"What was my mother's name?"

"I don't remember."

So, as my father would say, madness is the same distance from reality as consciousness. However, the cow *was* in the stable. The animals *had been* in the ark. And the island *was* filled with dark and mysterious caves, any of which could have been the W.

And we went from numbers to cows to instability and I would go through many lives before I understood that what my father was teaching me was change, the rigidity of the scission, the measurements of God, breaking the measurements, the breaking of the containers, the feel of the breath, the Not God, the Not World, the Naught whence came, I supposed, the extraordinary Q.

There seemed then neither logic nor order in my lessons, but in our days there was a clear and dependable if-then-therefore order. "It is six, Father." "So. Then we shall have supper." "It is Tuesday, Father." "So. Then the tourist boat will come." To care for me, to teach me, to feed me, as mad and unstable as he was, to live in an if-then-therefore world for my well-being, must have been, for him, a terrible discipline.

The multiplication tables and the Fibonacci series, which I learned after the lists, had, indeed, an if-then-therefore sense about them, an imprint of pattern and expectation that was logical and progressive. In them, I could assume causes, deduce with assurance. There was an inherent necessity that what preceded in sense, followed. If one gull fell, another would. But there was always something alien, unbalanced, murky, lurking behind his teachings. The lists suggested far more than the finite mathematics, the harmonics, the faithful ellipses of the silken Heavens my father had held in order above my head.

 "Is our life strange, Father? Do other children in other places know what I know?"

"Nothing is a contradiction to the way the world is," he answered. "It can only be contradictory to the way we think the world is."

Because of the way he thought the world was, the world, for me, became. I wanted however, even then, to think for myself and create my own worlds, my own stable worlds. I had begun to suspect something was wrong with my father. "We only receive the pips and points of the waves out there and flatten them into things. Dear child, the picture has always been in our brains. There is nothing else. There is no difference between perception and hallucination. You must remember this: when you change your mind, you change the world." That was the pap I grew on. Although I must have been ultimately confused I do not remember feeling confusion, simply extraordinary curiosity, idiotic obedience, and the full expectancy that everything I learned would sooner or later have meaning. I drew W's and Q's and apples and A's and B's and boxy stables and ice cream cones and the letters of my name in my Dark Horse Copy Books and memorized what he told me and wondered about what he hadn't told me. I memorized lists and practiced my script and one day my father, examining my copy book at the light of his window, snapped the book shut, nodded, and said, "So. Now I teach you questions. So."

He began then to teach questions. He said there were no answers of any importance in this world.

"Celeste, what is life?"

"Father, what is life?" I would repeat as expected.

"What is difference? What is order? What is disorder? If something exists can it be disordered? Is order perception and nothing else? What is the cause of wind? What is the cause of form? What is the cause of cause?" He would tell me his questions and I would, when I was just learning, try to answer him with the bits and pieces I had deduced from tiny yellow texts he gave me and my father would laugh at my answers and I at his laughter until I understood he had quite forgotten me.

I would then ask questions, thinking the laughter was lightness. "Will I look like my mother? Am I to be lovely? Do you love me? Why do the monks think I am a boy? Will you kiss me goodnight?"

And he would ignore me, become enraged, or go on.

And I would weep into my cow skin because I loved him, because he was my world and I could not reach him. It was a death for me each time he turned his back in mid-sentence. The raging frightened me, but I knew, throughout the wild screams—"Why am I here? Why is this child here?"—that he cared. He raged, fell silent, and we would go on.

"Celeste, what is the principal cause of change? What carries the message of change to form?" He threaded jade silk through the eyes of a snake skull. More laughter, more weaving. I would wait for the final question of each session. He would rock and laugh and wave and then: "Celeste, why is it that all the strings of an Aeolian harp will, if set at the same note, vibrate by striking one note only?"

"Father, why is it that all the strings of an Aeolian harp . . . uh . . . will, if set at the same note, uh, vibrate by striking one note only?"

"That, Celeste," he answered, astonishing me with an answer of importance, "is how God created the world." He wrapped red silk around the leg of a tiny mavis. "By striking one note, but it must be perfect." He nodded the leg up and down. And the mavis leg became part of his tapestry. "One note and all the others will harmonize. Guitar, kythera, cithara, et cetera . . . and all the rest in harmony. Why is the note right? Why is the right note. Involute the question, you have the answer. Involute Heaven, you have earth."

"And what is the right note, Father?"

"So. That is the right question. So, Celeste, what is the principal cause of wind?"

I would repeat. "What is the principal cause of wind."

"So. Now. On the seacoast, in the tropics, the wind blows toward the shore in the day and toward the sea in the night. Why? A common-sized person bears from the pressure of the air a weight of how many tons?"

"Am I to fly, Father? Am I a common-sized person?"

He looked at me with astonishment. There was an intensity about him so great I suspected he would vanish one day. I daresay he hoped I would. "Are you to *fly*?"

And he grew splotched and threw the shuttle across the floor. "You must think about these questions. I am not teaching you yes and no. For that you can be a machine. The world is full of machines. I despise the world."

I fetched the shuttle and handed it to him and he went back to the warp and woof and the questions. But I could not contain myself for long.

"So," he said. "Of what length must a looking glass be for a person to see his complete image?"

"Father?"

"So?"

"Am I to be pretty?"

He stared at his hands and measured my fingers with his and then stroked my throat and I knew he was considering the color of jade silk wrapped tightly and smoothly about my skull. "To be or not to be. Poor binary Hamlet. Poor little pig. *That* is not the question. Becoming is the question. What to be, not not to be, how to be, why to be." He glanced up at me. "Pretty?"

"Am I to be pretty?" I repeated stubbornly.

"Pretty. So. Hamlet was the son of the Pig God Ham of Creation who was murdered by the uncle, the Dog of Time. Being, Dog, kills becoming, Pig." And he laughed. "Pretty? None of it is pretty. The dark aspects, the Dark Gods are bloody, brutal, and necessary."

I remember wondering that night how much more I could bear and realizing curiosity, not bravery, would sustain me.

As I neared my tenth year, there were more times than not that year my father worked at his strange cloths and neglected the church vestments. The old Abbot Isaac, carried up on a sledge by eight struggling monks, visited him now and then, shaking his head, fighting with him about something. I was always drawn away. My father would scream at the old Abbot. The monks, standing with me beyond the hut, would raise their eyebrows at each other but say nothing to me, except "Little Man, Good Fellow" and so on.

I think my father was recreating the world in his madness, a world of stones and sticks and bottle caps from Orange Pip and bullet shells and bits of dirty things, the sheep wool stuck with dung, a bird leg. "Who knew?" he would ask himself at his loom. "Weather? Feather? Sun? Moon? Sidewalks? Aeroplanes? A child? Who knew? Why am I here? Oh, God, I need a place to go!"

"Celeste, Celeste," he called one day. He was standing above a new cloth, hands on hips, chest expanded proudly. "So. The world caught in its own pain." In the heat of the sunlit room the cloth was already stinking. "Silver of fin from the narrows, and from the caves, guts, and pale feathers and luminous eggs and bits of you, Celeste." And showed me the old laces of my infant clothing woven in. I wept. I ran from him for this the first time, and wept at the oak tree.

The cloths remained in our hut, nightmares, hung from window and wall, horrible and beautiful and at night, the moon beams, yellow as his fingers, crept across them and then the shapes of the claws stretching and beaks screaming would slip across the stones of our floor with my father lying on his flagstone and wrestling in his dreams with a demon. "It is a demon you will never know," he promised me when I would ask him the next morning what hurt him so at night. When he wove holy vestments he slept serenely, breathing deep long rumbles as distant as the thunder over Mull. But in the nights of the days in which he had woven his Creation cloths of stolen bits, then he tore at himself and scratched and heaved and I lay awake in the immediacy of his cries, with the moonlight streaming through the cloths and drawing his horrors across the stones, listening to his nightmares and wondering what part I played in them. "Night, my darling child, turns the obscene into the sacred," he would explain after the dark turbulence and give me his gobbetroyal scraped from the piece of turf, wrapped now, to take to the crossroads below the stony face of the High Cross of Moses.

What sort of world was it that he wove with my small life? And with his own? And with the garbage of the Kingdom? What did he see? How could I know? My father spoke only in questions, Generous only in answers, and the old Abbot, when I found the courage to ask him about my father, only in principles.

 Since I was almost grown, when my father completed a church vestment, I was to take it to the millstream and set the colors in the wash of the waters. The red and purple of the silks bled into the stream. I would imagine the blood of saints pouring out of my father's hands toward the sea. Later when I saw the old Abbot dip his hands in the holy water and the holy water turn scarlet in the vessel, it seemed as natural as my father's vestments bleeding in the millstream. I would hang the vestments to dry on the single oak tree beyond our hut and later fold them, as I'd been taught, into careful fat squares to take to the Cellarer.

The delivery of my father's weaving to Hilary the Cellarer was my own incursion into the monastery grounds. I was warned again and again to speak to no one, to answer no questions, and to come home immediately. The Cellarer's room was next to the guesthouse. Aidan the old Guestmaster would nod as I passed. Brothers would pause at their work and smile benignly as if all children were innocent and pure. Eldred, a novice no older than myself, would stare longingly, smile slyly. And then I would be with Hilary in a great murky room filled with amphorae at least as tall as I, with chests, an ancient table, a calendar open to a date, although I could not find the year, slender tubes and piles of books, glass jars filled with grains and the whole of it dusty and timeless. I was careful not to stare at Hilary. He would fold brown paper and address my father's packages to Carthage, Rome, Sophia, Chicago, Troy, Cleveland, Jerusalem. His nose was without shape entirely, a sponge, being eaten by something, and his head wrapped in great white oozing cheesecloths. For the vestment, I traded flour, sugar, rice, and sometimes a bit of dried beef but not often, and Hilary would rub my hair and scratch his dreadful no-nose, call me "Little Man," ask if my father was well, and shake his own head as if he had seen something splashed and awful on the plank floor. Whatever Hilary's plight, my father's clearly was far worse.

My father brought me on extraordinary days to the Abbot to do the work of John Joe the Amadan, whom, with dread, I had only imagined. John Joe having gone off with the tasks of the camel, it was my small duty to lead the Abbot's favorite cow on the Abbot's morning rounds.

The Abbot's cow, Thirty-three, had a gentle and sociable disposition and, as the others in the herd, was a large black and white Guernsey. She alone had amulets of iron on her collar, tassels and silver bells on her horns and when she rang her little bells with a sweep of her horns, the Abbot lifted his arms to Heaven in gratitude and composed poems of love. She never balked nor stood on my feet as I led her. We would walk the Abbot's path, I pulling the cow along, the Abbot deep in prayer and his pet crane hopping along after us, often breaking into flight above us, sometimes riding on the cow's back. We sat waiting while the Abbot ministered to the sea monsters, their great snake bodies glistening, listening in the sun. Inland at the Hill of the Angels, when the Heavenly Ones descended to discourse with the Abbot, I tied a cerecloth over my eyes and the cow turned her back to avoid the shimmering lights. And when the Abbot prayed for the company of brothers at the Tree of Life, Thirty-three looked at him in admiration and then at me, sweetly, watching closely, an intelligent beast. I was under stricture to ask no questions, to speak only when spoken to, and to obey even before the Abbot commanded, and I daresay so was the cow. Bishop Nicholas was the acknowledged soul-friend of the Abbot, but it seemed the cow was his true friend.

I cannot now remember when it was I first saw the Abbot Isaac. He had always seemed immeasurably old, the way mountains are old, traces here and there of a history, but on the whole composed without a history, distant and forever. His hair was white and crisp, his nose flat, his teeth large, great, even and ivory, his skin a rich and glistening blue-black, the half-moon mark of Cain on his forehead. When angry or empowered, the curls on his head reached upward and quivered as receptors toward the sky. Triangles of black and circles of cobalt framed his eyes, blue they were and astonishing, bits of the sky in that dark face. His cassock snapped with authority when he walked. He called me CuRoi. I was not told why.

And I was, my father warned, not to ask. But I had even greater questions for I had discovered something startling about the Abbot's cow. Her sides were, as the rest of the herd, black and white, but her patterns looked more and more to me each time I was with her as the maps in my tiny textbooks. One day, having traced Asia Minor and the

Americas, and brought the tracings along and examined her carefully, I was quite certain that she carried the map of Asia on one side and the map of the Americas on the other. When I had the courage finally to question the Abbot, excited as I was, he simply dipped his head as if remarking on the weather and said, "Yes, some cows have been over the moon." Whether it was a jest or not, I had no way of telling and certainly no way of challenging. My father said the Abbot spoke only in eternal truths and I was not to question him, and further, even if the cow had been over the moon, she most likely had not seen the Gods for she was still clearly and merely a cow, and added, "Is she not?" She was still a cow.

By mid-morning the Abbot would be done with his rounds. Then we three as well as the crane circled the perimeter of the monastery sunwise, the Abbot casting poems at his cow, and later, I led the cow to the pastures above the herd where she stood majestically, queenly, until nightfall, quite set apart by the Abbot's love. I envied her his strokes, his words, his kindnesses.

At dusk, I led the Abbot's cow back to the sparkling warm barn and there waited while the Abbot picked dung from her anus and ticks from her belly and composed poems and whispered secrets and blessed her with hand and mouth and rubbed her with ashes and spoke through her to men long dead.

Except for the ominous sounds of the bull crashing against the corrugated walls of his pen somewhere far at the end of the barn, and a moon-faced clock with red bleeding numbers, the barn was a near-perfect place. I was never happier than in those twilight times with the banging of milk pails and the shine of machinery and the song of the overhead pulleys and the sweetness of the cows with their calves. An old be-whiskered Brother, kindly, ass-eared, strummed on

46

a cithara to soothe the cows. The Abbot so loved his own cow that he would forget me and I was free to listen to the music or play with the calves. But one afternoon he turned suddenly toward me. "Oh, CuRoi, and why are you not making copies with Generous?" And he leaned far down, kissed my forehead, and waited until I stood on tiptoe and kissed his cheek.

And so I was named CuRoi and soon enough I was brought by my father on what must have been a painful excursion for him to the scriptoire of Generous.

As we climbed the stone stairs hammocked with centuries of wear, my father growled: "The scribe is a fat old puffin lousy with knowledge but not knowing where to scratch." And there, indeed, at work in the long and narrow sunlit room, was Generous, at a high table, reading from great and glittering books, scratching himself, picking at himself, six-fingered, black-robed, white-haired, utterly benign, a smile so instinctive it was already fixed in the muscles at each side of his mouth.

And I was set upon a stool in the room of books over the sea while my father stood rigid at the door, eyes closed, and turned, at last, wordlessly away. And so I was CuRoi and left there to learn copying and my life in the monastery began.

Generous's scriptoire sat above the Lady Chapel and below the bell tower, overlooking the Sound of Mull. Below the single shuttered window a brook, which had descended from the grain fields above the monastery, crossed the neck of land between abbey wall and shore line. There, on the rich grasses carried down by the brook, sheep congregated, bleating, calling out to their mothers, locking heads in combat, flesh and fleece. Their joy would weight my dull tasks. I would grow to hate copying and love Generous.

The first day, Generous, licking his sixth finger, leafed through the books and then through sheets of hides spread on slate slabs. He read, shook his head, examined me, lifted more piles of hide. I burned to read what it was I couldn't. At last he found a dog-eared sheet, motioned for me to sit beneath the open shutters in a little window seat and copy.

And so I copied. "The Year of our Lord. The shining forth of a great comet as it were a sunbeam. Fearful prodigies. Lamentable battles. Duplicities, triplicities on earth and in the Heavens. Horned men in high-browed barques. A failure of bread, an abundance of nuts, a spark of leprosy. A great snow. A black sun. The dying of many cattle. A cele de bearing palms and lemons and a glass book from the Holy Land. The flooding of the spring streams from the abundance of nuts. Three Popes made quiet. The breaking of his geis by Mura, tribe of Dog, eating dog flesh. The casting up upon the strand in the net of one crofter of the vast sea-wanderer, the woman." The lists were entirely unlike my father's. They didn't bloom, one to the other. I soon understood even then that while Generous knew everything, perhaps everything in the world, he understood nothing. My father was right, Generous was as fat as he was informed but nothing, neither mind nor body, had turned to sinew.

In late afternoon on my first day, my head a plumb at the end of a long long line, heavy footsteps on the ancient stairs startled us both and into the room came Muncas Bent-Neck, whom I had only seen at a distance. His head rose from his shoulders as that of a minotaur, powerful and twisted, and his hood brushed dust from the ceiling beams. I watched as he lifted the stone slabs from table to cupboard, closed the shutters to the sea, and in greeting, clapped me on the head with a hand so large I couldn't see. Generous rubbed his own worn eyes and led me, six-fingered hand on mine, down the narrow stairs. Behind us Muncas climbed the stairs to the bell tower. Momentarily the bells for Vespers rang, I was set in the direction of my home and told to appear sharply the next morning. I ran past the working monks returning from the fields. To a man they turned to stare at me, intensity in their eyes, blood on their hands, hunger in the loose skin of their necks. Past the High Cross of Moses I ran, past the piles of reeking dream garbage—my father's shit left at the crossroads—over the millstream, and up the narrow path to my father's house. By the time I reached the cottage, my feet dragged.

"So. CuRoi. You have been given a name. Your new name means Hound of the King, the Canaanite, Canine, Khan, Konig, Cain, Co'in, Conn, Cohen, from the royal race of Sirius, Dog Star, Kion, the star of Osiris and Isis. These are the tribe of priests who watch the Heavens, whose days are the Dog Days. Dog means rach, rach means clock, clock means time. We watch time. Dog is God involuted, manifested."

"But my name is Celeste." I whined.

"So. That is a problem."

Generous told me that as CuRoi I would be a Dog of God, a slave of God as Moses was to the Pharaoh, a slave of wisdom and prophecy. "It is said," Generous told me, "that you were born knowing and one day men will call you Abba, the Holy Father, but it will take great discipline, courage and obedience, and the melting of a heart already made

49

hard." Generous sighed. My father continued to call me Celeste.

From that day on I sat across from Generous at the high table and under his eye copied strange texts, wove snakes, dragons, lions, and oxen into letters of glowing colors, scratched with fine-nibbed quills, rewriting, copying, again and again. The work was drudgery, my neck ached, my fingers numbed, but Generous told me tales of greedy blue-black presters that swam between here and there, between now and never in huge blocks of ice, who ate the souls of men, and chewed on their thoughts, about a white cow that came up from the sea and reshaped the world, about Bishop Nicholas's butterball that destroyed entire fleets. And I would tell him of my father's questions. "If Mary is the sea and Mary was assumed on August fifteenth, what was the condition of the constellation Sirius, the position of the planet Saturn, and the date of the Deluge?" Generous and I would walk to the strand, knuckles white, ears red with the cold and Generous would tell me as well as he might the answers to my father's questions.

"Now, tropical winds blow. Let us see, tropical winds blow. I will find it in a book and tell you. About Mary . . . yes, she *was* the Star of the Sea, but certainly not connected. Now, the weight is thirteen stone. Yes, of that I'm certain." In good weather he would let me hold a book upright for him and pour tea from a thermos, a drop for the rock on which we sat, a long sweet sip for me, much more for himself, and he would turn pages with his sixth and smallest finger, feed me biscuits and jam from a wondrous depth of his robes, scratch himself incessantly. "God makes change. Yes. The cause of the wind is God. The cause of cause is God. Yes." Where Generous's answers ended, nature, I knew later, began. I always felt that then at some time there would be someone who really knew, that there was a penultimate and solid truth, like Dun Hi, that I would eventually find and conquer.

It was a dangerous ground then, both of confusion and certainty. I had a monstrous self-confidence and was often terrified. My father taught me to exist between question and answer. That is perhaps why, when the time came, I could hold both suns in my mind.

Often, from the scriptoire, I heard Muncas's booming steps fall away, downward, and although I had not been aware of another level to the cathedral, I realized there must be a room beneath the Lady Chapel and indeed, one morning, Muncas paused on the steps and allowed me to follow him to the columbarium where the relics were hidden. Muncas sang our daily chant as we entered the room. Snail-smeared the walls and wet the floor and dim, but Muncas sang as if companies of Angels were about. There was, that I could make out, only one treasure in the room and that was a bright aluminum garbage can. To which, in a deep, awed voice, Muncas chanted, "Schma Yisroel, Adonoy Elohenu, Adonoy Echod." I knew that the brothers sang this solemnly five times during the day, but only in the abbey, facing the altar, lifting their eyes to the Heavens. But Muncas sang in the presence of, to, the garbage can. His chant filled the room and rose on the sour smells of the can. I pressed up against him gently, that he would know I was there. He patted my head as he sang, compressing my astonishment.

Drops of water fell through the ceiling into the can. Muncas poured bits of bread into it and turned his arm, stirring it, and his huge arm was covered with it and when he withdrew his arm, I heard a terrible sucking. He allowed me to touch what was in his hand. It was hot as if living.

"Is it alive?" I whispered.

"Yeast." He shook his head, rolled his shoulders, neckless, and bid me look into the pail. "It is known as evil inclination."

"But it is only dough, Muncas."

"Yeast," he repeated. "From the beginning."

And I shivered, from the damp or the knowledge. The pail had a living sour smell, one that I had caught sometimes on my father, sometimes, faintly, on myself.

"Wild spores," Muncas added as if in explanation, wrapped a lump as large as his head in a cheesecloth, nodded at me, and carried his bundle to the kitchenings. I was left alone with the pail. I realized later that it had been intended I discover this place. But I did not know it then and when I reached in to touch the dough and it sprang back at me my body shivered in greater vibrations. This seemed to be a thing between A and B. The next morning I waited on the stairs for Muncas. Soon I was enfolded under the weight of one arm while his other arm pushed and pulled and stirred the pail, the yeast sucking, Muncas groaning with the heaviness of it. He fed the pail holy wafers and holy water, and gave me a solemn look, almost instructive. I did not know the instruction and yet I knew I was again free to stay. When he left for the kitchenings, I myself reached into the pail and pulled up a large handful of the dough.

What was it I held? I believe it was then for the first time I used my father's methods to understand—I wove my own lists. Yeast, East, leaven, Levant, Levantine, Easter, yeaster, the rising in the East. She who rises from the East. She who rises from the yeast. Lammas Day, Loaf Day, another August time. The lump flexed in my hand and stretched. I pulled it and it snapped from me. It was existence, not yet life, but fully containing life.

There is a form, a ghost, a yeast itself, rising out of the garbage pail, drifting, promising connection, yeast, gist, ghost, gism. The ghost of the bread, rising. The mother sits in the garbage pail. Existence is in the garbage pail. The lump stretching in my hand was my first idea of what was beyond, the Other Side. The Not Yet. It clung to me, clung also to its own shape. Wrestling as if with the Angel, I scraped it from my fingers and peeled off as much as I could into the pail but I could not remove it from my hands. My fingers were webbed with it, my hands limned, and finally I ate from my hands and then took more handsful from the pail and ate of them, licking and sucking and wrestling until I heard Generous's labored breathing as he climbed down the stairs and I wiped my hands under my robes on my body, sticky with her, and ran to meet Generous who turned and led me upward toward my lessons.

"At Passover," he began through gasps as we climbed, "she is buried under the rocks of the crypt and we eat bread that does not rise, until after forty days she is ready once again. Here, give me your arm. Every day the universal spirit fills her from the crack in the roof of the crypt and every day we feed her and take what it is we need for our breads. At Easter, a new mother is begun. And while she grows we eat unleavened bread. Anything else you have heard is political or even historical, which is far worse. Our Lady is she who makes bread . . . began in Ethiopia . . ." Generous collapsed at his table, limply beckoned me to begin writing, and I heard nothing of whatever else he might have told me that day. East yeast. By noon my belly was a balloon. Gas pain unfolded through me as the yeast grew in the new Paradise of my stomach, alive, rising, multiplying itself, flowering, flouring within me, pushing and pulling the shapes of my intestines, reshaping me, stretching me as it had stretched in my hands. "I am the Universe and you are man. I am man and you are the Universe," I whispered as I copied, placating it, and bent over to hide and contain my pain which would not contain itself, and at last when Muncas came to close the day, I raced with the holy hotness into the fields, where it gurgled and bubbled and spread seismically throughout me in great and terrible waves and pulses, a sound of new seas and new continents, and I fair expected little loaves in the morning as its gism ghost grew, I prayed, incontinent. I had a night of violent pain and a foreignness in me, a quantum leap from eating the bit of wafer they gave me at the altar. I could hear inside me the agony of Creation bloody with my life. I never again ate but a bite of bread without knowing it was radiant and dangerous with existence and remembering the pain of something Not, yet ready, something Not, yet formed, something Not yet but very much so. I imagined all that I had heard about the Other Side, the place from which form springs, and when the ferment of liberty exploded in my bowels and I indeed passed my own blood-streaked loaves, I wondered if life itself were secondary to existence. I would not find out until much later. The pains, which lasted for days, reminded me that I was hardly prepared to contain the wisdom of the garbage pail. It was with great fear and pride that I wrapped my little loaves and left them by the wayside along with my father's for the dreams of the nightworld.

I soon found that I did not think altogether in ways others thought. My collections of pieces and conclusions were odd if not frightening. And so, I learned quickly not to share them. They, however, pleased me greatly for I felt, as my father always told me I was, unique. I remember approaching him with a poppy petal and asking why it looked so as the sea shells. He took me immediately to the sea and said, "Once, the world turned over and the sea shells agreed to group together and become plants because life was dangerous, dry and different. They agreed to a higher coherency. Each shell contains a creature that reproduces itself. Each flower does also. Flowers are sea shells. And if ever the world turns over again, the seas will become gardens and the garden seas, the great sea tangles will gather together and become fruit trees, just as slime molds move from singular to mass when they are hungry." I could never again see a flower as others would.

Generous allowed me to ask any question. While we worked I would call up a category. "Tell me about flying hysterics." "There have been nine on the island since records were kept." "How many breaths does a true Druid use in a line of poetry?" "Eighteen and no more nor less. Other than eighteen breaths a man speaks false." "Tell me," I would move as subtly as I could to gossip. "Tell me about Nicholas."

"Nicholas? Yes, Nicholas. Now, Isaac, you see, Osser—that means younger—traveled along the spine of Britain with the camel and the holiest relics from the columbarium to heal plague. Yes."

And Generous would be off. He was a wonder-filled gossip and couldn't separate his teaching from his tale-telling.

"Yes. Now some of us were of the blood, some only of the message. Nicholas is of the blood. When Isaac saw a young laborer he knew at once the boy to be of the blood and on the spot named him, there in the field, in the laborer's rags. Nicholas, Bishop, he named him, and took him back to Iona. Nicholas had the Druid powers and was to have been of great joy to the brothers and use to the monastery. Nicholas Osser we called him then; now Nicholas

Sinser, elder. Nicholas did not bring joy but was an excellent servant. Many years later he asked permission to journey to Rome to be named Bishop by the Pope."

"But he was Bishop already." Work halted altogether.

"Work right along, CuRoi. Yes, he was. 'No,' said Father Isaac. 'You are already Bishop by my hand. Your grace is inherent, you need no other authority. There is no other authority. Grace is grace,' said Father Isaac. But Nicholas, proud as only the once humble can become, went to Rome and returned with red robes and a ruby ring. Some thought he had promised to deliver to Rome the authority of Iona itself."

"Did you think so, Generous?"

"More ovoid. You are writing for eternity. Write clearly. I don't know yet what was promised. He returned and told Isaac that holy men could not be plucked from fields as so much fruit. Isaac answered that Iona was independent of Roman law, that our laws were those of our Fathers, the Illuminated Clan, the Initiates of the blood, the seed of Abraham, Isaac, and Jacob. Nicholas still travels to Rome and speaks seditiously about fixed dates and Sunday Sabbaths and Isaac will hear none of it, but someday, God help us, if Isaac were to be made quiet—and soon he will be—Nicholas will cause great turmoil and terrible change on Iona."

Then Generous scolded me for not working and we bent our heads to the vellum. I thought I saw tears drop on his work.

One morning as I climbed toward the scriptoire, the Amadan leaped at me, grinning, on the stairs. I had seen him, sensed him, slipping behind haystack and wall following me. As I backed up the stairs toward Generous's safety, I smiled and ran into the scriptoire, my teeth chattering.

Day after day the Amadan followed me whispering "Alleluia" as I passed him, hanging from a tree limb to startle me with a whistle, leaping from behind doors, and one day he offered me a ride on the camel and waited for me every day for a week until I finally accepted the ride and I began then to wait for him.

And so, in these ways, as Generous would say, I met my three friends, Generous, Muncas, and the Amadan, and my enemy, Nicholas Sinser.

I

‎‎T IS SOON TOLD.

I, GENEROUS, CHRONICLER, WRITE OF THE AMADAN.

Lord have mercy on the soul of John Joe Amadan, not a whole tooth in his head nor a mean bone in his body, half foolish, the Amadan, and half wise and half man and half child and half saint and for all of the halves he may be more than all of us born princeling and holy, changeling and blooded. For good is his nature and gentle is his small heart and slow are his fingers, red, rough, clumsy, as he sits at the meeting of the rocky fences the lee-long day and traces each line of each letter of each word of the psalm of the Happy Man. Lord of the Silences, of the Silence of the Silences, have mercy on the simple silent soul of John Joe, a poor man he is but all that he remembers, that much is his own.

Half foolish he came to us and dead, caught in the rocks with mussels and barnacles stuck to his elbows and the seaweed adrift in the tatters of his tweeds and a chest full of buttons and crosses and medals pinned to him and four purple cabbages tied to his feet, not a whole tooth in his head, a dark cave that head, nor a decent bit of gold in his eyes to be sent over like the others, found by the mule who licked him clean and mothered him.

There is a case against the Amadan. At the turning of time as we sing the nine great men through their twelve mansions, while we chant the harmony of the spheres in plainsong, while we tune our lips to the pipes of the Universe, here is John Joe in our midst braying like a mule his alleluias long after our song is done until someone finally hits him on the arm, so lost he is in his braying. Some of us murmured against him but the old Abbot, faultless in his judgment, punished the murmurers with flogging and reminded the flock that in the very harmony of the spheres there is always a half-something waiting outside, howling its dissonance in the Cosmos and is there not worse harm done by the dissonance of a hostile design than that of an innocent man? And so we abide John Joe when he takes his rough hands from the pockets of his tattered jacket and holds them in tight fists at his side, as a proper man, and sings out his alleluias whenever he needs. For who is to say a mule can't praise the Lord in his own way? God forgive me for those words but if it is true that the measure of our notes moves the notch of time across the Heavens, that the very harmony of our chants makes fast the foundations of the firmament and the pitch regulates the Great Wheel turning in its appointed time, why it ties this old scrivener's liver into a knot to think of the harm the Amadan does howling in the holy plainsong. But there is not one among us who dares murmur a word about the fundamental farting that follows the alleluias and the spluttering of the young monks standing near John Joe and God help me for thinking it, knowing that Seth and all else that howls in the night are busy enough . . . but a fart? A fat and cabbagy, turnipy fart rolling up the abbey's holy stones?

John Joe walks with his fists jammed into his pockets as if he has secrets in his hands. The sleeves of his jacket are frayed as the ends of the prayer shawls of holy men and his lapels are pinned and stuck with medals and amulets with the Tetragrammaton incised.

A good man, John Joe, and not a bone of his body with the marrow of hate except the hate for the camel. For sure and for certain he hates the camel but it is more true that he misses his mothering mule. And how he feels about them both is nothing against what he feels about taking the dead Kings from the harbor and leading the camel up to the brow of the Mountain of God at the edge of the Beyond and three days later, the baskets filled with bones picked white and clean, taking the bones from the Other Side to the kilns of the crofters in the village. That he hates. That leaves him worse than the camel biting at his pants and worse than the misery of losing the mule to Seth. But John Joe is the only one among us who can cross the boundaries between our lands and the lands of Darkness, and between our lands and the lands of the crofters, without bursting like a blood blister as he goes over. Necessary it is sometimes in our work that we have doings with each other— the crofters, and the Ones in the Darkness. So it is John Joe who does the doings for us. To him we feed dainties and dulce and let him go on braying his alleluias during our chantings and brush him off and smooth him out and send him each time on his awful journeys for the bodies and for the bones. A blessing on him, for grateful are his brothers.

— GENEROUS

The abbey has two towers. One draws moonlight, one sunlight. Between them hangs the lens of the great circle of glass cut into pentagons, triangles, and squares and coiled into a nautilus of growth. The lens inverts the Heavenly light and blazes it onto the seeds of the earth. Night and day the primeval patterns and crystal proportions nurture the fields. In the time of growing, the square glass panes shape addition—the square root of two, the spade in the earth. When the sun rises higher in the year and enflames the pentagons, the season for growing ends and multiplication begins. It is the time of ripening.

I too lived in the angled light of the lens and my ripening, I found, was a deep concern for my father. Very near my eleventh birthday, on Assumption Eve, the Perseids shooting across the sky, he announced that he despised the pagan ceremony of the ripening and we would leave next day to Cathedral Cave. And so while the monks in their saffron robes climbed on their knees the flanks of Dun Hi to sing the berries and grains to blasting, we readied a two-masted skiff, wrapped loaves of soda bread in bark, and stored tin cans of milk and the sod of turf for my father. I supposed Cathedral Cave would be like other places for we took with us the usual gunny sacks and pouches and rush torches and ropes and bobbins of bright thread.

In the narrows between Iona and Mull the sea was a mirror, turquoise, arctic. I leaned over the stern and dropped my hand into the sky. Shadows of inverted clouds floated between my fingers and under my fingers great sea forests swayed—groves of olive tangle and black wrack, red-inked far below the surface, purple-inked close to my hand, the colors of the dragons in Generous's books. My hand was soon numb with cold although it was August.

"August fifteenth, Celeste, Eve of the Assumption, Night of the Assumption. Eve assumed, the Goddess of Night who walks about Heaven." He pointed to the mountain. "The fools. They pray they think to the Lord. They pray to the Gods of Night."

As we passed the Isle of Errid, seals slid from the rocks into the water and swam behind us, eagerly searching my face with their bright human eyes. I thought it might be safe to seek answers. Generous had told me seals were princes.

"Are seals princes, Father?"

"Yes, yes." I think the sea calmed him. "Errid is the peak of a sunken City of the Sea and they are the princes of the Kingdom of Ys, buried when the Beast of Time was last loosed and the measure of the world lost." He trailed his oar in the water and a fine and long white hand grabbed at the end of it and pulled at it while my father strove mightily until the oar was free. "Oh, they are born in the sunken cities, maimed they are born, the half children of Seth, and they wait below for the Beast of Time to stretch his mighty maw and break the pillars of his captivity. See this." Another white hand, heavy with rings, clutched at the boat. My father beat it off with an oar and then rowed with powerful strokes away from Errid.

"And the Time Beast?" My father thrilled me. His questions sent shivers through my spine; his stories fed me for weeks; some of them, a lifetime.

"The Time Beast. Well. So. He is a greedy prester."

"More, Father. . . ."

Past the narrows, the head winds increased. The sky above the twisted marbles of the Paps of Jura deepened and the sea grew heavy. As we came upon the *Prince George*, with its three thick chimneys, red and gray, and its chorus of silver gulls, my father hid me in a skin. I could hear him wrestling with the angles of snapping sail and calling out, "And someday he will break the Great Wheel of Time and pull the pillars and return all that is to darkness. Into the mud-dry earth, iron mountain, hot bronze sea. The Cities of the Sea will be the Cities of Land. The rhythm will be gone and all things we see will disintegrate because they are only vibrating patterns and we will once again strike the note and be-thing the Universe. Once again. No bells, no hours. No thing." The sails snapped and I grew small and sleepy and slept on the sea dreaming of the Time Beast and the fine white hand until I awoke in a violent purple night, the sails down, my father tying the bucking skiff to an upright rock in a horizontal wind.

We worked our way around the outside of the cave. The stones of its sides were exact and mathematical, corbeled perfectly, octagonal. The same stones formed steps of approach, singular they were, glinting green and silver under the light of my father's torch. Over a roaring sea, over pools of brine and puddles of glowing jellyfish, we walked the odd path, my father pulling me, coaxing me, from one giant stepping stone to the next.

"Step carefully, Celeste. Come. Come." And he would stop and speak to me, holding out his hand for me to make the vast stretch across the gap between stones. "A greedy prester, the Time Beast, gaping below us in the cave. Its mouth reeks blue-black. Its eyes green-gold, rust-iron. Seething cauldrons are its eyes. Here, now, watch your step. Foul smells and seven-holed and hisses under the cathedral and swims in wide steaming circles under the sea-green sides of the cave. It will be dawn if you delay, Celeste. Come. Just a few more. Don't look down. And the prester shapes the strand and shifts the sand and echoes his agony in the underground so that the basalt columns of the cave shake and shatter as a great-toned organ—you will hear it—and shape even the jellyfish at its bottom into new forms. There. We are almost at the entrance."

I could not breathe.

"Shape even the jellyfish at its bottom into new forms, recasting them with each fierce cry. Soon he will be hungry."

I stood at last on solid stone. I shuddered. My father laughed at my fear and scratched my head as if I were a pet.

A vast-bellied animal, that cave, sucking in the crashing sea, swallowing it, spitting it out and lying silent in wait. And between pulses, far below, the Time Beast howling his eight-sided song and each note changing the shape of the jellyfish. Into a space of such greatness, such sulfurous darkness, such emptiness, a place without measure, we crept in my father's light along a slimy ledge. The vaulted echoes of the sea and the beast hammered in my chest. "Stay close behind me and be quiet."

I could not have been closer nor quieter. The more my

father spoke, the greater his distance from me. My head was the cave, my blood the sea pounding. I knew that I had to be closer to my father, that my life depended on him, and I walked faster and faster until I was able to hold the back of his robe in my perspiring hands. He felt me tug, for he looked over his shoulder suddenly, surprised, I thought, to see me.

"Rigid form has built into itself its own anomaly to break that form. See." He broke a stalactite and dropped it below. I did not hear it hit the water. "Each cause is the effect of its own effect. Everything manifests itself into complexity, or goes into entropic drift. World War One for example is the end of simplicity, also a lot of little villages. Are you following, Celeste?"

"Head of Christ," I prayed to myself. "Eye of Isaiah, Nose of Moses, Neck of Mary," and clutched the knot in the hem of my father's robe and followed him deeper into the cave on trembling knees. The ledge we crept along narrowed until we had to stand and slide along the walls slowly, seeking footholds and handholds. At last the walls of the cave met in a vault and in the torchlight we saw a smoky hole. The sharp smell of guano cut the dark.

I have always wondered since why my father had to create further nightmares. He had enough of his own. But there we were, living one out, his breath as harsh as his nighttime sounds. I held the rush torch that flickered and threatened eternity. My father filled his hands with sand from his pockets and let himself down a rope into the hole and I, in a rapture of fear, flattened against the bit of ledge, waited as something croaked in warning. And there was a terrible flapping below me where there had been only the sea breath and the cave voices. Stark and demonic shapes flew at my face, and in the midst of them my father came up through the hole and beat against the ceiling, hissing at me: "Cormorants. Hundreds." Around and above me, he beat with his blackthorn stick, brushing my very nose. I prayed he would miss me. If I had died then, I have thought since, I would have died thinking it was an accident.

After he had stuffed a gunny sack with birds, he motioned to me to take it back to the boat. Torch in hand, I pulled myself along a ledge toward the mouth of the cave, dragging the sack of stunned and dying birds on my back. Their claws clawed me and I, as some creature from the sea myself, clawed the rock face until I reached the boat, awash now in calm moonlight. Three times I crawled that dread trip and spilled birds into the bottom of our boat, but the fourth time it was I spilled, for when I returned, my father, startled, having forgotten I was with him, hit me on the head in a thunder of wings and croaks and I do not remember more than the sharp sickening crack at my temple from the black-thorn stick and waking up on a pile of dying and dead cormorants in the bottom of the skiff, rocking, my father holding forth over the sea, his arms outstretched toward the sky as the wind blew us home.

"Trace him whose way is in the sea, whose path is in the great waters, and whose footsteps are but little known."

"Father?"

"What? Who is that?"

"My head hurts."

"His true task is to ask the silence."

Somewhere, close by us in the thick dark, I heard the chains of Archie's ferry carrying the dead to our island.

My father was mad. I knew that somehow even then. Gently he covered me with cormorants that were still warm. I heard them wheeze and whistle. I slept until we scraped against the shore line, the cormorants stiff and the sky orient-red with the unrisen sun. At the Hole of the Black Cow we docked and dragged the skiff onto the beach. On the mountainside the berries were ripe, the fields exalted, and the monks weaving their way down to Matins. My father stood me before him and steadied me. He examined me. He seemed satisfied that I had not yet ripened.

 My father told me never to go near John Joe, but when my father met me with John Joe along the paths, he nodded at us as if we were hallucinations and went on. John Joe's head was empty. I've put my ear against his mouth and heard the wind and the sea and nothing else. His voice was hushed and thick as wind in the marshes, his farts long high bullet whines, or deep rolling thunder, his whistle dry. I would wait at the top of the path far beyond my father's house for John Joe, and when he appeared, tattered camel, tattered jacket, over the ridge from the Back of the Beyond, from Seth, he would lift me up and place me between the saddle bags. And there among the clean-picked bones of Kings I would clutch the stiff brush of the camel's back and ride lurching down the path. John Joe walked behind the camel.

They were innocent wonderful days. The sky was a lens of blue. Bird flocks sang in purple trees. John Joe's fool laugh ricocheted from the sides of the mountain. I would recite psalms for John Joe as we crossed meadows and marshland, climbed the causeway and walked to the crossing stones. I was not afraid for it was day and John Joe whistled through the gaping holes in his mouth.

"Oh, Happy Man," I would recite from the camel's back. Bullets of gas whined from his backside. The camel lifted his tail and dropped dung in the path and John Joe removed his shoes and stepped into each smoking clump and wiggled his toes and laughed his mad laugh, and larks lifted from the ditch and lit on the stony backs of the sheep on the ledges of the mountain and the black and white sun-dappled cattle stopped their grazing, rolled their soft eyes up at us, and bent once more to their task. And after he laid the bones of the royal race on the crossing stones and the camel's saddle bags hung empty, I would wait, leaning against the folded beast, my head resting on the bags. Later, crofters would come to the other side of the stones, rude men and women, bent and secretive, and take the bones for their pottery kilns. John Joe would paint his eyes with charcoal from a burnt cork and wrap an old cloth around his left hand and tie the stems of columbine around his fingers with the flowers for gems, and climb the altar rock and stand and become the Abbot. He crossed himself as I had taught him, and he blessed me. And then, his fists clenched tight at his side, he would speak in his great toneless words in a loud voice echoing back and forth among the rocks and over the marshlands, deep from the empty cave of his head. "Sun, Moon, Alleluia." The tendrils of his flower ring floated over his gypsy-dirt fingers.

Poor John Joe had tied four purple cabbages to his feet and jumped into the sea near Glasgow, Generous told me. And arrived somehow on Iona and every stranger is Christ although John Joe, they said, was stranger than not and John Joe was taken in and given the camel and the mule to care for. In the monastery garden John Joe would fashion cabbages into the shape of the old Abbot's head with stone eyes, and Nicholas Wry-Mouth's head with a high cabbage wrinkle forehead and slash of mouth, and Hilary the Cellarer's with his sharp little greengrocer face fringed in fat and a sponge for a no-nose and Aidan the Guestmaster with his sea-shell eyes and triangle nose and loose seaweed lips, and toss them all into the sea. They would bounce and bob in the sea as we fell about in our laughter and the gulls swooped down to rip at the heads, and as they pecked we rolled on the sand and roared with laughter. John Joe slobbered and wiped his mouth with his jacket. I envied him in many ways.

"These are the men who watch time," I would intone, crossing myself solemnly. John Joe stood, feet spread on a tide-licked rock, arms stretched to heaven, shouting, "Sun, Moon, Alleluia."

"This is the Land of Light. We watch the hours, we keep the hours."

And the heads bobbed and sank one after the other. I thought then that if the Abbot knew, we would be stilled forever. I rocked in laughter at our secret and sometimes shivered in thrill to watch John Joe make Mass of a sea shell and spit it out. And shook with dread for my own corruption.

And when we were done with the mysteries, we would leave, I lying flat on the back of the camel, John Joe leading him toward the fields and too often, sudden, Nicholas Sinser, alive and Bishop, wry-mouthed, crab-legged, the huge forehead wrinkled in anger, would appear, purple pants under his robes, and beat John Joe with a thorny stick as John Joe grinned and Nicholas raged and chased him and I slid off the camel and ran for home. But we would find each other in the pine grove and he would climb a tree and bless me and swing from a limb showering me with golden needles, flitting in the treetops, a mad gelt, and from the tree he would call, "Alleluia," and I would respond, "Oh,

Happy Man." And he would laugh and swing on the limb by his arms and drop as a squirrel to another limb, lower and lower, and when he reached the ground he waved his fists about, spreading his fingers then as we do for the blessings and then beat at his heart with his fist as the monks do when they are to be whipped on the threshing floor and laughing, his laughter rolling like stones down the mountainside and he would see that I was sore afraid for I knew I sinned and he would laugh more and I would hold his shaking shoulders and say in the perfect voice of the Abbot: "The Blind Stalker watches you every moment, Son. His knees go backward and his feet go forward and there is seaweed stinking in his hair. Watch for the man with seaweed in his hair." And then we would roll on the pine needles nuzzling and hugging each other, our foolish laughter echoing.

What I didn't know then was that in very different ways—I because I was born knowing and held the inheritance of power and John Joe because he could cross the stones without bursting, could receive the bones from Seth himself—we were indispensable to the Abbot, no matter what our mischief.

John Joe would turn to the path of the monastery, I to my father's house and I would sing out: "Blue-reeking mouth. Rust-iron eyes. Eating the bits of history. Oh, a delicate thing it is. A delicate thing to guard time. Blue-reeking mouth. Mouth." And I took pleasure from John Joe's fear as I imagined my father had from mine.

As I grew older, I would shut doors and windows for a day's time and lie on my back with a stone on my belly, my plaid about my head and my eyes being covered, I would think about the stories, my bones trembling, a knot in my liver, thinking about the bones ground down into powder, about Kings' brains mixed with lime and, afire, tossed at the high-prowed barques, about the greedy prester beneath the crypt and the end of time, about the end of myself, no more than the cabbage head, gulls pecking at me, sinking.

Of that winter before Cook came, as ominous as it was, there were still memories of laughter and warmth. I was old enough to study not only the Psalms and the Lives, but Astronomy, Hydrostatics, Mechanics, and Opticks as well. When I stumbled in my reading, my father's fingers would hang delicately in the air over his loom, and when I found my place he would smile and nod that I go on. It was a winter of great Viking storms, of hollow twilights after supper when the wind beat against our hut in sheets and shrouds, whipping and wrapping, and my father would put extra turf in the fire place, and in a north wind, on an island where no dogs dwelled, the howling of dogs through the chimney. If I read my lessons well, my father would free the two baby petrels he had allowed me to keep that winter—downy, lustrous little things with white feathers rimming their blazing eyes and extending down to the backs of their necks. I fed them drops of olive oil on a feather and they would shake their heads and clatter their beaks at me and attack the feather. When they were free of their box, their feet slid from under them, carrying them off the varnish of a tabletop, and they would fall to run about the stone floor and climb the walls with hooked beaks and claws. They would cross their wings over their backs and shuffle along the floor on their elbows, but when they reached the corners of the walls they would be convulsed with confusion and would attack the corners. I would feel their frail wings beating at my ankles and I would read on, laughter bursting my lungs.

The preserving of the birds, their joy in my hand, their very life beating at my ankles, the being of them. Oh, I was those birds, climbing the walls of the world with beak and claw, confused at the corners, trapped when I would fly, preserved for some reasons unknown to me, a story I was not told, a history I could not know.

Once I took a spool of golden thread from my father's loom and, holding it at one end, let it roll down the mountainside, connecting my place with the world, finding my way, searching for meaning as the thread wandered. But I ran after it for we were attached and I was controlling it and it twisted against a clump of nettle. I sat at that clump and waited as if I would then find my destiny, as if an angel were to visit on the spot, as if someone were to stretch out a great hand and lift me into a high place of answer where I belonged. But there was no place, just the clump of nettle and the ball of thread in my own hand, and my questions. I rolled the thread tightly as I climbed and laid it back with the other spools.

Was there nothing to follow? No great hand? No answer?

In the spring when it was time for the Edinburgh post, my father garrotted the half-grown petrels and John Joe carried them to the *Prince George*. We had word from the

Natural History Society that they had arrived in Edinburgh inutterably spoiled.

Creatures of the air and ether, spirits, those birds. Hades was my father's house with the dead hanging upside down and my father waking at night screaming, "I need a place to go. I need a place to go." And I throwing off the skins and racing for his square of turf and bringing it to him, but I never knew if he had to shit or was yearning for a place for his soul. Later I would find it was one and the same, that the waste of the world is made sacred by death. The waste of our world I carried to the High Cross of Moses and left it there, for my father said that waste is the stuff of dreams and the waste of the dayworld must sit at the crossroads so it may go three ways for the world of Naught feeds on our shit. And weren't we both screaming in our nights, "I need a place to go"?

When I was nearly thirteen and becoming increasingly uneasy about my father, I left the hut as often as I could. He noticed me less and less. One June on the strand, I came upon a thousand puffins, shaking and picking at their feathers in the sun, a black and white wave of birds undulating against the turquoise wave of the sea, interpenetrating in pulses. I curled into a burrow hollowed in the sand by sheep and warmed by the afternoon sun to watch them and make sense of the one wave of water and the other wave of bird and how they connected, when suddenly, my father, an arrow of consciousness, cut through the moment, thin, stark, beaked, red-haired, brown-robed against the crystal sands. A prowler, my father, sniffing the wind and stalking toward an innocent nest in the lap of a boulder at the edge of the sea. From the boulder, a female rocketed in terror and my father held some small thing aloft triumphantly, something beating as a heart in his hand, and he squeezed the neck once with his long yellow fingers and dropped it into his pouch, gazed at the sea, stooped, plucked something else from the sweet-tangle loom washing at the shore, and dropped that also into his pouch. Then he turned and walked toward me to the place in which I had thought I was hiding.

"Celeste. Thusly." He snapped the neck of a trembling baby plover. Its mother whistled frantically in the seaweed. "In a few seconds with very little pain, life is extinct. And isn't life simply spirit caught in its own pain?" I have since thought he was correct.

"And is that how the Kings die, Father? Is that how Seth kills the Kings that come to our island? Is that how I shall die?" Innocent I was, and calculating. I was losing my fear.

He turned and walked up the beach toward the puffins who raced to the sea. With his fowling piece, he shot into the sky above them, cracking the porcelain of blue and cloud and the thousand of them wobbled from side to side toward the water. I saw their wings moving beneath the waves. My father, his path clear, walked across the sand where the puffins had been. Above him the plover's mother cried for her stolen child. As I watched my father climb over cliffs clothed in bladderlocks, slippery and dangerous, climbing as if on flat land, his pouch swinging heavily against his brown back, I knew suddenly how he had stolen me from my own mother.

My father moved toward the abbey. The black and white pied cattle grazing moved closer to the sea, closer to my hollow, in a ring as if to protect me. Through their legs, framed, I watched my father growing smaller as he plunged into the stone-marked fields. Barley bent away from him in waves and, where he had walked, lay bruised long after he was gone. Past the glass and steel walls of the new barn, a bird itself, sprung from his head, a gull, caught on the hook of the island, ready to float into the thin air. My father became even smaller, until at last, below the High Cross of Moses, his body curved into a dark crescent blade and cut itself into the mountain path to our hut.

The final, lucid wash of sun shone on the cows' backs and horns as they waited for the gates to drop and the bells to ring. Sheep called, mother to child, child to mother. I listened with a flat cold weight on my chest and then climbed out of the hole. The cattle watched me from the red corners of their eyes, warily, as I passed between their great shoulders. Beyond them, I ran. I remember how I ran that day, gracefully, swiftly, on two legs, following the path my father took. The sun dropped behind the peaks of Dun Hi and the mountain was rimmed in flame. Above me Muncas's bells called the moon up from the sea and the monks in from the fields. Before me clouds of hoodies rushed from abbey wall to rock, from rock to abbey wall. And the jackdaws, as they did each time the bells marked the hours, flew from the crumbling arches and towers of the old abbey and sailed over me on the great golden spirals of bellsound up the mountainsides to our hut. Generous waved as I ran. The Abbot walked behind his cow.

My father was already on the floor of our hut, praying deep in the shadows. I knelt beside him. The jackdaws, a thousand of them at Vespers, tapped and scratched on the wrinkled tin of our roof in the circles of sound until the bell-ringing shrank backward to the bell tower and the jackdaws dropped on the descent of the sound to their nests in the abbey—stone, birds, and I ashiver with the power of the bells.

Cook came to the monastery in late summer from Tiree. God had somehow, with great endurance, allowed me, through my fifteenth year, to live, to obey Him and my father, to learn many questions, to connect some of the questions to each other, to prepare myself to join the monastic orders, and to bury my bloodied rags each month in the fields. My father and I were examining questions of Thermodynamics all that winter before Cook came and Formative Causation in the summer. My notebooks were filled with my thoughts. Generous, no longer able to finger his texts for answers to my father's questions, was astonished and not a little frightened by the enormity of my education. It wasn't until Cook came, however, that my education truly began.

I never knew her name. I am certain now that my father did. And more. Looking back, I know now that they must have been very young. But they seemed, that summer, that winter, that spring, very old.

Cook had lived in New York City and sinned, the monks who were as titillated as I, told me, from a time past the Second World War. Detail by detail they added to my imagination as they carried clapboard, two-by-fours, the queen post, stainless steel, drainpipes, plantings of boxwood and hollyhock and cornel from the Abbot's own garden, tables, lamps, a generator, up the path to a hillock level with our own hut but separated from us by the pine grove and a meadow land. They buried a sweet-tongued puppy hound under the queen post, and when they raised the queen post, timbers went up around and off it and the house took shape as did the woman.

"And when this house is ready, Little One," Nicholas told me with wicked delay, "the Abbot's sister will come to care for him."

"But you said a cook. . . ."

"And a cook. Yes, a penitent from Tiree. A sinning woman. The Abbot is ill."

"Death is written on his brow," someone added.

"But faintly, Child, faintly," I was assured.

"And how will the Abbot's sister cross the stones?"

Each looked at each other and beyond me and they seemed to agree on something silently. Nicholas said, "An arrangement has been made. At great cost. . . ."

"Only for the Abbot's welfare."

"You see," Nicholas added too patiently, nodding curtly to the others, "it's all been taken care of."

And I heard no more. But I knew it must have been the same sort of unspeakable arrangement that had been made for my father and myself.

The Abbot's sister, they told me as I followed them, shadowed them, until they told me more, until they allowed me to turn the garden and pass them nails, the Abbot's sister had been a dancer, deeply interested in the Vedic mysteries and was the widow of a very rich American who made packing crates. She was younger than the Abbot. Nevertheless, old, although they had seen a photograph of her in an evening gown in the Abbot's cell and she had been at one time outrageously lovely.

"And she is bringing a wireless," Nicholas who pronounced everything very carefully pronounced very carefully. I had no idea what he meant. "And bringing a violin," someone added. "Yes, a violin." And a submachine gun, we discovered much later.

78

All that summer goods arrived on the back of the camel, on the *Prince George* touring ship each Tuesday and on Archie's ferry. The dead, I imagined, held shipping boxes on their lapless laps. And all that summer I lay on my belly in the pine grove under showers of golden needles counting and calculating and dreaming that I would be a dancer, that I would wear evening gowns and marry a very rich man who made packing crates. John Joe would wait for me with the bones of the dead Kings but I waved him on. I had learned that the observer affects the observed and I suppose my daydreaming in the pine grove contributed in some way to the events that year. There were, I knew afterward, simultaneous and related calculations, localities failing here and there.

If my father's observations could create a mad and violent secretive world, perhaps mine could produce something other.

The pine grove I know now belonged to a God, a psychopomp, a Not God, who drew us all to play out our tragedies in its sacred theater. Dark and cool and still, it was so utterly bereft of light that only the skytops of the trees were alive, the rest beige and brown and golden, stem, branch, and needle, a wind-shower of needles floating silently to the ground through solitary columns of sunlight, shimmering, and a thick soft bed of needles on lacertine root networks of ancient trees enmeshed, as I was enmeshed, in the humus of ancestors. At dusk the trees lost their volume and flattened against the sky to height and width. Closer to God, they were, in their Twoness, and closer to the Oneness.

Except for John Joe, I never saw another soul in the grove, but that year, my sixteenth, the grove would be for me the very darkest heart of our lives.

When the house on the hillock was complete, a contingent

of monks came to our hut and with the same clapboard, drainpipes, wires, laid a foundation and built a small room onto our hut, the building of which my father himself directed with a lively interest. I had expected he would keep me hidden from the young monks but he actually pushed me forward to serve them bread, chickory, and cormorant soup. After the room was finished and the bookshelves and generator installed, boxes of remarkably expensive books arrived, were placed on shelves and noted against a ledger by my father. And that evening, the Abbot was carried upon his sledge to inspect the house on the hillock, its garden, its kitchen, and then to our hut to bless the new room and my library. The Abbot patted my father on his head. My flagstone, hay, and skins were moved into the new room and I spent the night seeking meaning and origins in the grand books with a small electric light. My head burst with information but at dawn a new kind of learning came to me. I woke to the blast of the *Prince George*.

I woke and did not know where I was. It was the first time I had been so without dimension and foundation except in Cathedral Cave. But, then, I had known its name. I had come to it expecting a cave of sorts, up down across, and I had come from a place I knew. In the new room I came out of the naught of sleep into that moment of being entirely unsituated, a primal moment of not knowing where on earth I was. Or indeed what on earth earth is. It must be the experience of birth. I believe it was my father's constant experience. He did not belong. I lay on the new bed that morning, I remember it well, and thought about him. He seemed always to be somewhere else and then suddenly startled as if he were waking in a new place. The fugitive eyes would widen and roll to the ceiling, floor, corner, me, even his own hands, and look about as I did that first morning in the room. Then something familiar would assure him—

his loom, the birds, his piece of turf—and yes, he was in a place. On earth. A cottage. Yes. A cottage. A cottage and . . . there . . . a child who is familiar. But he never quite gained the familiar. He came from Naught into another Naught.

The *Prince George* blasted again. Day came upon us. Night was driven out. The Cosmos in order, sea below, Heaven above, and the planets in their places and my bed on the floor of my new room and an electric light and shelves of books and two women who were once girls, who were once as I am now, two women coming to this island this day.

I dressed. The lady, the cook, the violin, crossing the stones at some great cost, with some arrangement made. Perhaps there *is* intention. Perhaps I am to belong after all. Perhaps the women hold the true thread of my life.

My father shouted in his sleep. "I have no place to go. No place to go." I ran for his piece of turf. How strange in one waking moment in that new room I should be given to feel my father's entire angst. He was truly without place.

Could the trip to Cathedral Cave have been a teaching? I had thought he wanted to kill me. Perhaps he had wanted to free me from dependence on place, space, time, to release me from matter as he had so long ago released the gull on the cork. Perhaps.

Bells announced the women's arrival. I was told by Generous, who had seen them crossing the stones, that they'd arrived with baskets of goods, that when the Abbot's sister and the cook stepped from the *Prince George*, the cook carried a wireless and the Abbot's sister carried a nasty little Welsh terrier who was as querulous and ill as the Abbot. The Abbot's sister wore tiny mauve shoes and a long leather coat the color of butter, the softness, Generous marveled, of unborn calf. She was elegant. Nobility, it was suggested. Nicholas felt there was something dark-blooded about her, but very precise, he added. And young Eldred Long-Tooth who blushed deeply, more deeply than I, declared that women should not be among us no matter the circumstances.

"Long beyond womanhood, they are," Generous assured the chattering monks gathered in the scriptoire.

But Nicholas pierced me with his eyes and pronounced ever so carefully in a voice that had special meaning for me alone, "Women are the work of the Devil. If the chickens did not give us their eggs, we wouldn't poison holy grounds with hens. Women!" And spat behind himself.

I repeated this to my father but he was not in the least alarmed by the conversation. However, there was something newly sly about his response. "So. They think you are coming into manhood and wish to warn you. That is all, Celeste. Warning you. Unless they sin or you sin, none will know. But . . ." He turned from me so I couldn't see his eyes. "Women have another sense. You must not let the women see you. Ever."

He was battling the wind.

From our separate distances, I and, I am certain, my father, watched as each morning after Prime, the Abbot's sister, wrapped in plaids and furs and wearing soft small shoes, picked her way down the path, past the High Cross of Moses, toward her brother's sick bed in the monastery. The monks in the fields turned their backs so eyes would not meet. Others also spat across her path and vanished. But each day, I, fired, crept closer and closer to the juncture of the path from her house to ours and finally one day I was close enough to see her face. It was a delicate, arrogant little face with an aquiline nose, far too large, and startling eyes very much like my father's eyes. She was indeed precise, just as my father was imprecise, and there was about her a small but furious power, much like the terrier who followed

82

her everywhere. The next morning I stood before her as frightened as I was defiant, as embarrassed as brazen. She smiled at me, licked her lips, and began to speak in a deep strong voice.

I had the distinct sense that she was struggling to be pleasant.

"Why, you must be . . ."

But that is all she spoke and all I knew from her was that I must be, with which I heartily agreed, for my father appeared behind me and drove me off with a branch to our hut and closed the doors upon us for a fortnight with no explanation except that the women were poison and evil and I was not to go near them. It wasn't until Generous, poor perspiring soul, climbed the path and asked why I hadn't come for my illumination lessons that my father relented, warning me again unnecessarily that if I were to go near the women he would beat me. As Generous took my hand, he said to my father, "There is another message, Manuel, from the Holy Abbot who is also concerned that the child has not been seen by the monks."

"What is the message, Generous?" My father was obsequious for he knew locking me up was ugly and quite against the Abbot's wishes and didn't want to be found out.

"Since His Holiness's sister has seen the boy and found him too thin, an extra pail of milk will be sent to the Abbot's sister's house and the boy may fetch it every morning."

"Never!"

"Then send yourself."

"Never."

"I shall bring that message to the Abbot then."

"Saxon!" My father turned his back on both of us.

Neither he nor I, however, could stay away from that house.

Nor, it seems, could the women stay away from us. Cook,

although we never saw her, brought wrapped parcels of food and left them at the oak tree where they remained, stinking. And the Abbot's sister, it must have been, left notes my father set afire without reading. He tossed and gasped and rolled at night, his shadow rising and falling against the wall of cold autumn moonlight while I leaned against the door between our rooms and listened, trying to understand what it was beyond curiosity, beyond human loneliness, that drew us all to each other. After another week had passed, my father indeed brought a pail of fresh milk for me and I stirred milk into my chickory and over my cereal and waited.

The next night we heard the violin. Its sound was ragged and cacophonous, not music. He flung his hands over his ears until, shaking with rage, he could bear the sounds no longer, took up his fowling piece, hid in the bowels of his oak tree, and fired into the pine grove until the music stopped and began again and continued nightly, and nightly he shot at the Abbot's sister until he was about to run out of ammunition. Then he raved impotently from the hollow of the oak that the women didn't respect the role of the Hermit. It was an odd opera—his raving, her scratching. The jackdaws fed on the stinking food at the oak tree and the violin scraped away wickedly in the pine grove and my father, maddened, with the music buzzing in his head, followed me wherever I went until I was his prisoner and I followed him wherever he went until he was mine and one day, on the beach, my father and the Abbot's sister—he on the Strand, she on the cliff—met. He had his fowling piece and shot at the puffins. She had her submachine gun and massacred them. My father fell on his knees. Waves of black and white feathers and blood washed his feet.

"Manuel," she called from the cliff.

"Tia," he murmured, weakly.

"The child is almost grown. What will become of her?"

My father stood straight, glared at the Abbot's sister, his aunt, with a hatred even I had not endured and walked between us, toward me, protectively.

The Abbot's sister stood unwavering, gun lifted, and shouted. "I will take her with me."

His aunt?

"Leave us alone," he howled in great pain and blocked me from her view. At that moment I decided, obsessed, that Cook must be my mother. I was so obsessed with that thought it never occurred to me until years later that the Abbot was my father's father. They all, except myself, had previous lives. The sepia postcard of my mother was gone. Why? There was, from that moment, no keeping me from the women's house. The moment my father left to see the Abbot, I raced toward the purple spirals of smoke on the hillock, through the pine grove, across the meadow land, and into their new garden of honeysuckle and cornel and heather and long emerald grass. There I hid behind a turf bin just beyond the boxwood hedge and watched the windows of the keeping room for signs of the women. Gourds and chives and drying corn hung from hooks and a chicken, its neck slit and gaping, dripped blood into a slop pail.

At last—my knees were nearly numb—Cook came through the keeping-room door. She carried a basket of bed linens to the clothesline and I had, finally, a full and hungry view of her as she spread sheets and beat at pillows. Wooden and stiff she was and powerful, with pale straw braids cutting across carved cheeks, knothole eyes, narrowing and hard, lips thin and straight, a bony woman in loose clothing, a sweater like my father's, heavy boots, an apron of leather, and a blanket of a skirt. But her breasts—my hands reached down to my own small teats—her breasts were astonishingly full, the final over-ripe fruit on a winter-stripped tree.

Could she be the same woman on the card? She returned to the house. I crept closer. In the kitchen she wiped her hands on her apron, took three eggs from the basket, cracked them, let the whites run through her fingers, drank the yellows, beat the whites, and piled them onto a cake, yellow and red with fruit. Although I had often watched the monks bake, I had never seen the likes of that cake before. Sliding it into the oven, she leaned against the wall to rest and splayed the branches of her fingers over the stove's heat. Her body didn't ease nor did her eyes which slid pale and dangerous across the keeping-room windows, over the drying herbs and seeds and cornstalks and bleeding chicken. I trembled, holding my breath as her soul burnt into my memory. If she was my mother, who, what, why was I?

Very carefully, I unlatched the keeping-room door and pulled it open slightly. It was then, for the first time, I heard her growling. It may have been that she hummed from the far reaches of her throat. I thought though that she was growling, softly, as a wild beast broken and trapped and dying behind the scrubbed panes of glass.

The cake was out of the oven. When the Abbot's sister entered the kitchen, Cook dipped her finger into the cream and the Abbot's sister licked Cook's finger and then kissed Cook full on the lips, caressing Cook as Cook caressed her, and then Cook presented the cake to the Abbot's sister who seemed exceptionally pleased. Without her furs and plaids, the Abbot's sister was indeed old and fragile but lit somehow from within. She, with Cook's kiss on her lips, carried the cake out of the room into the depths of their house and Cook followed with a tray of tea things, cups and saucers and a teapot covered with a plaid and lace cozy and I made hot notes of every detail of their lives until Lauds rang and I knew my father would be coming up the path and I ran home, pausing for a moment in the grove. I half expected

Cook to be there already, for something I had seen in Cook belonged somewhere else, in withed and twisted forests, impenetrable places of pilosi and woodwoses and wizards— a place very much like the pine grove.

I suspect the enormity of our fascination for the women overwhelmed our imprisonment of each other, for my father began to leave me alone. It wasn't more than a week I was crouched again behind the turf bin and spying on Cook as she stretched sheets over the lines, as she swept out the floor of the keeping room. And when my father arrived to fetch the milk pail and stood, bent and ashamed somehow, in the keeping room, she offered him with a gesture a cup of coffee. But he shook his head, his face a stone, and picked up the milk pail. She put down the coffee cup and stood by the open door between the kitchen and the keeping room, where my father seemed nailed to the floor, and ran her hands over her breasts down to her hips showing the outline of her form under the loose clothing, the leather apron, and the blanket skirt. It was the way my father rubbed his eyes and temples and forehead when he was exhausted. Although her eyes were half-closed there was an energy in her body that even I felt and I'm certain my father must have felt, for he froze, half bent, stared at her with piercing eyes, straightened up, and turned on his heels, awkwardly. She stood in the doorway and laughed broad and lewd, her cheeks flushed with enjoyment at the sight of the proud Hermit scuttling away from her and I began to laugh and stood up and she stared at me. Her face stiffened, flat and hard.

"Shame! Shame! You break the rules."

I pointed to her breasts.

"Go!" She thrust her broom at me, her arm toward the fields where I buried my rags each month.

I stared at her breasts and touched my own in a mute

question but she didn't understand and with an ample swing tossed the chicken's blood and coffee grounds and egg shells at me and as the miscarriage of slop slid and the sweater I wore clung to my body with the blood, she saw my shape also and covered her mouth in alarm.

"Run!" she shouted. "And be dry in the wind before he finds you. I know nothing!"

I ran. Who it was who would find me, I did not know. Nor did I know whose shame was on me. His, hers, my own? I did not know. Somehow she was deeply and terribly involved in my life. I sat in the grove as the blood dried and hardened and thought about what I had seen and then I ran in the wind toward the beach, cutting across fields where no one would see me, and threw myself into the sea.

For many days I was ill with a chest cold and kept in my bed and when, within a fortnight, I could leave my bed, my father sat at his loom, I wrapped in cow skins at his feet, and we did our lessons together as we had forever, clinging, I thought, to each other in our odd way because change, terrible change, was in our bundles.

 I wrote in my copy book. "Flower petals are sea shells in agreement who have cohered in a plant for survival in a new niche.

"Seeds are whole numbers. Through the power of their roots they can be increased and multiplied, transformed, into other numbers beyond themselves. The sign for the square root is the sign of the spade mark in the earth. It is through the root sign that the power of the Universe is planted in the soil which feeds us."

"Celeste? So?"

"Coming, Father."

"So. Now. What is the quantum sense of the word not?"

"What is the quantum sense of the word not? Would you include the word and in the question?"

"You may."

I repeated the question.

"So. What is the relationship of non-linear thermodynamic dissipative non-equilibrium structures to evolutionary theory? And to the seed? And to war?"

I repeated the question.

"No. You must write these things down in your copy book."

"Why?"

He looked out the window toward the oak tree soaked in chill solstice moonlight. "Write them down."

I wrote.

"So. What is the effect of the uncertainty principle on the fugue?

"So. Does intuition follow the constitution of objects or does the constitution of objects follow the constitution of intuition?"

"Father, if the latter is true, then the structure of physics must indeed be consciousness."

"Write the questions down. No ifs and thens. So. If the human body is a conductor of frequencies and these frequencies are the only knowledge the body receives, what then is the nature of form?"

"Father, you just spoke an if and a then."

His fingers hung over the loom. He stared longingly toward the oak tree.

"Is Cook my mother?" I was a desperate child. Pain flashed across his face.

"Is Cook my mother?"

"No." He didn't look at me.

"I see. Thank you." It was not what either of us meant.

"Let me see what you have written in the copy book, Celeste."

He read out loud and I was ashamed of my scribblings.

"I am from this man's seed but I reach, must reach, to another pattern. Material form is transmitted and regulated through frequencies perceived by the mind. Everything then is frequency, not form. Perception creates form. If I were to increase my perception, I could see higher frequencies of form. If I were to increase my perception, I might be able to change the form I see. Doesn't this all mean that I can create my own world? That I can create my own shape? My own future? Instead of merely growing, of merely adding to myself, can I create the sort of change that creates a flower from a seed, a disconnected non-linear change in which the plus sign is replaced by the multiplication sign, a quantum change? One strikes the perfect note and all the other strings vibrate. What is my perfect note? How can I image myself to a higher being? What form might I take if I were to increase my perception?"

He sat still and stared again at the oak tree.

"Father?"

"Puerile thoughts in your book."

"Father?"

"So?"

"Are you leaving?"

And then, that night, at lessons, after he had read my copy book, my father, in answer to my question, with two bright spots on his hollow cheeks and the torturous twitching of a smile at the corners of his mouth, placed two pieces of the red and yellow fruited cake on our table. I could not eat any. He ate my piece as well as his own.

Although I did not know my father well, then or now, I do know from my own soul that we both have poisonous streaks in us, visiting demons. And although he vowed never to look on the face of a woman again after he had closed his eyes to my mother's eyes, I know, because I know my own self and my agonized passions fired by my dreams, that he somehow would find that growling woman with the squinting eyes and the full-fruited breasts hanging from her scapular body and share her cutting bones and her hatred, as if, in some terrible destined way, he deserved it.

I slept. The jackdaws danced on the roof.

Weeks passed. Great storms raged around Dun Hi, frozen rains crystallized the fields and branches, a heavy dew, a new-fallen tree, a cow died, was roasted, eaten, bones were laid out on the crossing stones, the passing bell rang for the dead souls. A crack appeared in the rose window and it was said we might have an odd crop in the fall. "Or worse," others said. "It is a crack in the pattern of Heaven." We will have monsters in the herd. Nicholas said it was only a crack in man-made glass and a craftsman would be brought in at winter's end. The rose window rattled in the winds and anyone who heard crossed himself. Generous and I drew half-uncials and human heads interlaced with cats and mice and letters. My days were filled with lesser initials and sweeping curves on thick-glazed vellum, serpents, entwining birds, distorted men, acrobats swinging on the letters of the holy book, blossoming ovoids and trembling copies of Generous's noble script. My nights were filled with my father's questions.

When there was a moment in the day I wandered into the pine grove, raced to the house on the hillock, and watched the women. My father allowed his tonsured hair to grow longer and longer and combed it with his fingers.

Finally, inexorably, I came upon my father in the grove. I had never seen him there before, yet there he was standing still as a tree trunk with his fists clenched at his sides and the skin on his cheeks wooden. Soundless, I came up behind him on the soft needles, and before him, across the grove, Cook walked toward him and when they came to each other, he held her and they sank to the ground and he fumbled in a fury at her skirt and at his trousers and I saw in the cold duskiness the startling flash of hot orchid, gleaming and wet—his instrument, hers, for a moment a single thing, bursting the monotone, gaping, hungry, autonomous. I understood then, if not sexuality, at least the unyielding willfulness of evolution.

In that stillness in the pines there was something pre-existent, anaerobic, something of another kind of nature than the man and woman who surrounded it, a wild nature enclothed only later in time with bone, flesh and form, sympathy, but there, the wounded creature panting and growling, my father and Cook its lesser creatures.

They were caught as in an ocean wave and at the same time they were the ocean and within them were the answers to wave field frequencies, to mutualities, to the lattice of structure and the light-packets of energy, to so much, and then I looked away because I was not part of the ocean and could no longer bear the intensity and above them, looking at them, not seeing me, was the small moon-white aquiline face of the Abbot's sister, her mouth agape, her hand clawing at her cheeks and screaming stop. She looked like the clock in the barn. Numbers bled from her cheeks.

"Stop!"

I shall always remember the three of them frozen in the pine grove, my father, Cook beneath him, and the Abbot's sister, standing above them. As silently as the needles falling, my father stood, Cook shook her blanket skirt and leather apron to her ankles, and the Abbot's sister turned, head high, and Cook followed, her head bowed, across the meadow land while my father stood in the grove with his fists clenched at his sides, his cheek skin twitching as if plucked, and his trousers unbuttoned. I slid away into the pines.

With me, forever, the shell-less orchid creature. Having witnessed it did not help me to understand my father, certainly not Cook, but after I had examined my own now fleecy pubic self with an alarmed curiosity and sympathy, I asked my father if we could not study evolutionary theory, particularly its microbiological aspects. I needed to know, I told him boldly, how the fracture of the Eucharist relates to the square root of the numbers of growth. He smiled. And how seed relates to the humus. He looked to the ceiling. And how the child relates to the family and how all of these relationships relate to each other.

"Evolution," he answered after a long delay, "is quite beyond me." Since the day in the grove he had become entirely vague. I began to study Cook and the faces of the young monks and then the older monks, and wondered with whom among them I might myself be one day called upon to recreate the Universe, which I knew in its beginning could not have been innocent.

My father, I suspected and was proved correct, would continue to see Cook. And there would be more between us all and I'm certain now that what was to happen my father had expected from the day the first clapboard was carried to the hillock.

It was in March, a storm-blown night, that Cook, shamefaced and red-eyed, rapped on our door and my father, upon opening it, was greeted also by his aunt and her submachine gun.

My father's face flushed dark and bloody. He pulled me in front of him, took up his fowling piece, and, howling, attacked them. I suppose it was my safety and his true madness that made them both turn and run toward the grove. Cook ran, shouting, "No, Manuel! No! Don't!"

My father kept me before him, and the Abbot's sister kept Cook behind her so that my father would not shoot. They were of the same cut, this family of mine. And then we stopped, my father's arm around my shoulders, gripping me, panting, howling. And in the woods I heard Cook scream and shout no. And then she ran past us down the path for help. My father released me and ran after her. I heard her shouts ripping through the fields and the warning bells ringing for the monks and because everyone was gone, I took a rush torch from the hut, lit it, and ran to the grove where the Abbot's sister lay on pine needles in the root networks of the old trees as if this moment had been known a thousand years before. She lay as with a broken wing. I had not heard a shot nor was she bleeding. She had fallen on something. Her breath in the cavernous air was white and her lips were gray with pain and red where she bit through them in pride and as I came up to her a single ray of moonlight cut through the pines onto her face and her skin was translucent. Her terrier lay garrotted beneath her.

"Who is it?" She twisted but could not move.

I moved to her face.

"Celeste?" she whispered. Her eyelids fluttered. She lifted her hand to my face. "At last."

Her breath unfurled in ragged cartouches of pain and yet I pressed on. I was perhaps in as great a need then as my father.

94

"Tell me about my mother."

"Your mother?"

"Tell me!"

"A princess."

"More!"

"Paris. She lived in Paris. Her rooms . . . leopard skin . . . oh, God, leave me be."

"What did she look like?"

"Walls, floors, her clothes . . . all leopard, her bed, her gloves. Lovely. Everything was leopard."

"Am I lovely?"

"You? Yes, lovely." She was struggling but I had to know. I took her hand.

For a very long moment she did not stir.

"Celeste? Are you there?"

"Yes."

"I am too late to help. I am sorry."

The monks were climbing up the path. I gathered her in my arms, for in some way she was my mother, laid her down, and sprinkled her with a handful of pine needles. I ran from the grove.

Leopard skin. I wiggled fingers in the moonlight and imagined them paws. Exotic furs fell from my shoulders as I crept through the night, green eyes gleaming, tail straight, graceful, leaping, bounding, until my father found me, took me home by the hand, and, without a word, sat at his loom and beckoned me with my copy book. He waited, his face inutterably serene. I sat at his feet.

"So. What are the principal stars of Canis Major and Canis Minor?"

"Sirius and Procyon."

"No answers, Celeste. No answers." He wove a shred of the lingerie I had seen on the line of the Abbot's sister's house, lacy and silken, into his pickings. "So. What time of year does the Dog reign?

"At the rising of the lesser Dog, the great heat of the summer is most extreme. Why?

"So. How many moons has the planet Herschel? You are not writing?"

"My hands are shaking."

"So. Why did the lesser Dog laugh when the cow jumped over the moon?"

"Father?"

"So?"

"I don't understand the question."

He collapsed over his loom in laughter and the grid of the weaving rose in waves. "Oh. So. Hey, diddle diddle, the cat and the fiddle," my father laughed. "Cow, dog, cat, moon, sun, stars, who knew?"

He was clearly finished with the lesson but I was not.

"What did my mother look like?"

"I don't remember her," he answered sullenly.

"What do I look like, Father? Do I look like my mother?"

"You look like an insolent, persistent child."

And I stood before him, my eyes half-closed, and did for him what Cook had done with her hands and growled as either she or my mother might have.

He tried to be light-humored. "Why, you must look like your mother." And then he laughed like a grebe caught in a storm and I believe he suddenly remembered my mother for he pulled me up by the arm, wildly, dragged me across the room and outside, and sat me upon a stump so hard the force split upward into my neck. He squeezed my neck and held me still while he cut and whacked and hacked at my hair until it was as short as the down on a young bird's head. Then he pulled me back inside the hut, threw my trousers and shirts in a bundle, and dragged me out the door.

His face was a black knot. He dragged me down the path so hard the socket of my arm ached and I began to run after his large and awful steps down the side of the mountain down to the High Cross of Moses to which I clung and then he released me and sank to the ground. I gave him my hand, lifted him, led him back to our hut. At the oak tree, he swept the lengths of my hair into his palm and put them in his pocket and then, weeping, crept into his bed and I into mine.

But near dawn, he pulled me from my bed, down the mountain once again, down to the High Cross of Moses to which I clung, but he tore me loose and took me on across the fields, to the Street of the Dead, to the Abbot's Tor, to the door of the Abbot's sick room upon which he crashed with his fist.

"Father!"

The Abbot's servant, Eldred, dropped open the hole in the door and light streamed through. When Eldred opened the door, my father threw me forward.

"Herewith I dedicate this child and all his belongings to the Holy Mother Church."

"Manuel," the Abbot called weakly. "You must not."

But the door had closed and my father was gone into the night and the Abbot's servant, no older than myself, hovered about me and finally wrapped me in blankets and I slept out of numbness.

They laid the Abbot's sister out on the stones. John Joe brought me the pair of mauve shoes and a tiny pair of cow ears, twisted, with tufts of silk at the ends of them. I spread my hands in confusion. He pointed to her shoes, his feet, the ears, his ears.

"But these are beastie ears, John Joe."

He pointed again to her shoes, his feet, the ears, his ears. I wrapped them in hay and stuffed them inside the shoes. I still assumed then that there would be an explanation for everything in the Universe.

The chief duty of the Chronicler, Generous instructed, is the register of the genealogies of the men of Erin, the recital of battle, of courtship, voyage, cattle-spoil, siege, slaughter, death of Kings, letters from Popes, visitors from holy lands, and other moving incidents of flood and field, fleece and flesh, the calculation of the cow-tribute and the synchronization of remarkable events on earth and in Heaven. These I copied. Endlessly. And when I threw the quill in impatience, Generous would look up from his work and say for the hundredth time as if it were a new thought, "Surrender yourself, CuRoi. God will save you. Give Him your mind. Give Him your reason."

Copy I did. "Then is every thought of man God's cliché?"

"Oh, CuRoi, God help you. What lurks there in you that will not surrender? He is the Creator. You are only the creature. Copy."

I would copy until the language exploded into magic figures and danced across the pages. "I want the word to be mine. I want to make it meaningful. I wish to be original."

"Copy, CuRoi, and let God dwell in you."

It was an angry, impatient God indwelling, if God at all. I copied the events in my less than noble half-uncial script for Generous and my mind danced in the spaces between them, looking for meaning. If three Popes were made quiet in the Holy City and a stream were clogged with rotten nutmeats for three seasons, what, if anything, is indicated? I could find nothing indicated from the events, no meaning, no connection, no prophecy to gain, only the expectation of a sudden event, a sudden howl of event at my back that would throw all the other events into other shapes, that would throw me into other shapes as the eight-sided song of the Beast roaring in Cathedral Cave reshaped the jellyfish in the abyss below. If three seasons a stream is clogged and three Popes murdered and a black sun is seen in the Southern Vault, will I soon see my father?

"Has he yet asked for me?" I would pull at the sleeve of Hilary the Cellarer, the other monks, John Joe. "He must have asked for me," I would insist, weeping.

They blessed me, except John Joe. "No, Son. Bless you, CuRoi, you must be staying away from the poor raptured soul."

John Joe would smile and the wind would blow through the stumps of teeth left in his mouth and he would whisper, "Sun, Moon, Alleluia," and I knew my father was alive.

I began to wait, not to ask. Surely I would glimpse him. By day I prayed he might send me a pillow of the silks and wools stuffed with feathers. By night I dreamed he had sent me a pillow stuffed with his beard and his body hairs. I received nothing and yet I waited and copied.

The old Abbot, even older now, attributed my wrong-doings and my hotness to the Spanish blood on my father's side. Sometimes in Chapel, he looked at me as if he knew, in the way my father looked at me, a great unpleasantness, the bearer of bad luck, a boil on the nose. He would sigh. I could see his chest rise and fall heavily. And sometimes, most times, he looked beyond me. When I passed him and knelt for his blessing on the path, he would warn me of myself.

He would say: "Virtue lies in the center between two opposing poles of excess, CuRoi. Beware."

"Thank you, Your Holiness."

When I led his cow about the monastery grounds in the morning, he would say to me: "CuRoi, afflict the flesh, overcome lust, resist avarice, triumph over the world."

"Yes, Your Holiness."

And then he would shuffle after his be-ribboned cow. I would bring him full milk pails to bless and he would tell me that my prayers had been caught in the thatch of the roof, that they ought to fly to Heaven as sparks, that I was not sincere, and then command me to confess my sins twice as often as other novices.

"As a floor is swept, CuRoi, with a broom every day, so the soul must be cleansed. Especially yours. And about your poor father, CuRoi, Eldred has told me that you weep for him. Sighs are permitted. Nothing more."

And I took his blessing on my knees and confessed to him four times a day although I had to compose my confessions from my imagination. Sometimes I deliberately neglected to bless a spoon before I ate so that I would have something to confess other than my true thoughts. An error in the script, an alleluia where there ought to have been an amen, neglecting to kneel, sleeping during office, all of these errors allowed me privacy. Both the Abbot and I, I think, were betraying each other as we needed.

I soon learned that the senior monks, whenever they were with the Abbot or had just been with the Abbot, spoke as he did, with the same careful phrasing, long breathy pauses between short sentences of eternal truths and the falling away of those sentences at the end as though the phenomenal world of words and ideas were of little interest, rather a necessary task. I dared not mimic the Abbot, although I found an affinity to him which I couldn't define, a recognition which terrified me. But the others I mimicked for I found that if I became like them they found me agreeable. I listened carefully to their speech habits and repeated to them in different phrases what it was they had said to me, what it was they seemed to feel important. With Justus I spoke softly and talked of the numbers and notes of God and how a cow's milk for a year was called a note and he laughed, worked his ass ears in half circles, and patted me on the back. With Nicholas, as fervent as he was inflexible, I spoke of Rome and I spoke in a hushed voice of enormous humility because Nicholas with his dry thirst of ambition held himself as the representative of Rome here on Iona and it behooved me to be seen by him as his servant, recognizing his imperial desires. With Hilary No-Nose the Cellarer, I spoke of the quality of cord and paper and rice as if each of these items were ultimate to my life. No one seemed to understand what I was doing and I was subtle enough so none overheard me speaking with another in the latter's tone. I knew it wasn't a matter of words, but of vibration of phrasing, which is just beneath mimicry, something of a song beneath their words that I simply began to sing when they spoke with me. It took me a while to be able to speak with more than one person at a time and I tended to whisper to each of them, which was lauded as an effort toward golden silence and admirable in a young boy, they told me, but in truth it was part of my deception. While they never knew me, I came to know each of them intimately. Muncas Bent-Neck, though, was silent. He would cuff a surly novice or lift him in the air by his feet. But when I lost my chrismal in the fields he came to me. Long after he had searched the fields, long after I had given up and was prepared for a year's penance on Tiree, he came, clapped me on the shoulder, opened his big paw, and showed me my chrismal but turned away gruffly when I fell on my knees to thank him. A simple man, not intellectual as the others. At planting, the plowshare broke. The crofters too were planting as were the penitents on Tiree and we were without and in sore need. And poor Muncas over anvil and fire struggled to fix it. Sweat and tears rolled from him. Then the Abbot came to the smithy house and said to Muncas, "Give me your hands, Brother." And Muncas put out his big hands and the Abbot blessed those hands.

"O, Ancient of Days, O, Lord of the Elements, bless Thou these hands. Bless Thou these hands to make us a plowshare."

And Muncas then fashioned a new plowshare from piping in the barn stalls and ship logs washed up on shore and we all thanked God for giving knowledge to the hands of Muncas.

It was Nicholas whom I didn't like. Nicholas did everything crablike, his walk, his hands, his head shaking side to side and always nodding. Up and down, sideways, so when one spoke to him, one had to shake one's own head, nodding up and down, sideways, in order to look into his eyes. I learned Nicholas's manner quickly and nodded so enthusiastically when I was lectured or admonished that my teacher, who indeed tried to look into my eyes, would soon be dizzy and lose his train of thought and never know why. And I would assist the dizziness by saying: "I agree completely with your first point, which, as the body of Christ, is both mystical and adorable," blink rapidly, and if my teacher wasn't yet ready to end his talk, I would add something from the lists. "Yes, yes, merkabah and macabre. Your points have the very same relationship. Of course. Brilliant, Holy Father," and thank him profusely and leave. Other novices were lectured endlessly while kneeling on a cold floor. I was not. No one looked into my eyes.

I parroted them. They found me agreeable and I was unknown. Someday perhaps I would find someone like myself, who might be parroting me, but the likelihood was that if I were to find someone like myself, aach, God, he would be parroting me and I would never know. The truth be known, except for John Joe and Muncas and possibly Generous, I trusted no one. Generous was loyal to me, but he might have become unintentionally disloyal because, sad to say, he was stupid.

For each of my brothers I was a different person. For myself, I was CuRoi, still curious, hidden, too smart, too informed, rebellion burning, dreams, obsessions burning, not brave, chosen, bitter. While I walked I kept my hands behind my back. While I reaped I prayed loudly and at meals said "Deus in adjuctorium meum" between every two bites. And yet the Abbot would stop at my table and say to me before the others:

"CuRoi, the chastity of a monk is judged by his thoughts."

He knew as much or more about myself than I.

Compared to the logic of my father's teachings, the simple rationality of my studies was child's play and I not only excelled but found great amounts of time for my own wanderings. It was in those first long months that God, what I thought was God, grew in me. And surely with the glowing rapture and titillating pity and passion, with the enthusiasm and confidence of my few and silly years and my need to be safe underlying it all, I gave myself to the labors to rid my body of its earthly passions which, aside from lust of study and fear of father, I had not yet felt but fully expected

and imagined hopefully in every pulse. I gave myself to
God, such as He was. I lived by myself in a small cell among
cells of other monks in corridors, and while I now lived in
far greater comfort, my loneliness for my father was a bed
of nails.

Each month I buried my bloody rags in the fields and took
those days of ill humor for retreat to a stone cell beyond the
lettuce garden. I asked no questions, invited no friendships,
and avoided Eldred of the Long Tooth who always blushed
and added extra honey to my bread. My father had said no
one would know unless I were to sin or they were to sin.
My retreats were thought to be an excess of devotion, my
blushing an excess of sexuality, and the purity of my boy's
voice, continuing far longer than the other novices, was a
welcome and agreeable sign that I would sing without a
quaver, unpubic, innocently. We all had our passions and
confusions and what we thought was God growing within
us might well have been the swelling of that orchid creature
I had seen in the grove. I knew nothing yet that would
establish one or the other as different. There were novices
who were slim, gentle, shy. I followed their ways. My breasts,
though, strained against their bindings, my mind against
the rote, and, too often, my tongue against my brothers'
subservience to the fathers who knew even less than Generous. I put aside my questions, my lists, my A's and B's
and Q's and W's. Against that my heart strained heavily.

And I copied endless event upon event that were somehow in their disconnectedness as deliciously mysterious as
my father's lists. In the closeness of Generous's narrow
scriptoire, I would listen to the powerful and happy blasts
of the *Prince George* coming down the Sound, the bleats of
lambs playing under the window, the slap of waves against
the green shore, and the waft of thyme and clover. And
when I could no longer bear copying, I would beg Generous

to allow me to go off in solitude. I think now he knew it wasn't solitude I needed so, it was freedom. But we both needed to term it solitude and so I went off with his blessings. Solitude, suffering, and wilderness were the ways of the monks. My wanderings on the island were accepted, even praised.

My body bloomed with the freedom. Thermos and cakes on my back, I walked over the monastery lands with my hands behind me, deep, it would seem, in thought. But over the rath, I ran. Past the Hole of the Spout, past the Beach of No Return, past the Port of the Cow, past the Hill of the Angels, around the wave-washed stones to the very edge of the Other Side, for what did I care, to the Bay at the Back of the Beyond, where seals fled at the sound of me, where Seth, lonely and terrible, I'm certain, watched me, measuring his territory, marking out my path. And once, alone, I walked in moonlight and cried and often, to foolish songs, danced in pools of green-black sea-water, low and warm at my ankles so that I was without feet.

At Giant's Ground I leaped between citadels of rock twice my faces and raced about in their monolithic maze, in and out, and measured them, I did, with my body, my arms, my feet, for their alphabet, the circle, the angle, and the name of God so placed. And I sang to the waves, my joy rippling and spilling over into song and tears, my moments filled with a beauty beyond words. Down the warm flesh slides of sand dunes I rolled, over and over, head and hair and mouth filling with sand, dizzy at the bottom, the sky out of orbit above me, and then I rolled naked in the gorse and let it tickle, scratch, and tempt. And caught snowflakes in the cold with my tongue, and when the weather was warm I tore off bindings and robes and swam out beyond the ninth wave to the crests of the great slow waves and allowed them to take me, rolling and tossing me in their harmonies and throwing me toward the shore. Gravel and shells and sand scoured my belly and breasts, and the beasts of the waves, as I lay exhausted, licked my feet, calling me out again. And once, when the sea was spellbound and clear, I floated face down and looked at its bottom and saw beneath the sea-tangle heaps and hundreds of high crosses, broken at their stems, like corpses in the rocks, their essences rising in volatile bubbles to me. For hours, until the light changed and the tide moved faster, I hung over them. I read inscriptions that were strange and powerful. "The sun returns, time never does." I traced the worn lines of carved faces of strange Gods and wondered whether an act of savagery or concealment had spilled them into the sea. "Blue and reeking mouth, blue and reeking mouth."

And then a sound. A sharp deep voice. Undeemously naked as I was I thrashed in the water toward the shore, raced to the pile of robes, and struggled into them. Although there was no one about, the voice commanded again without words and there on a rock not ten meters into the sea sat a great shining seal who barked once again at me. He was without question looking directly at my shivering self and I at him and then he barked a last time as if to assure himself of my complete attention and somersaulted into the air and dived into the water and I thought him gone, for no seal stays where man is, but then up he came, spitting sea salt in an arc like Typhon and clapped his forelimbs together and barked again and leaped into the air and down to the rock and somersaulted into the water, forward, backward, lasciviously, a perfect entertainment and I transfixed, laughing. And then with a final sharp bark, he somersaulted into the sea, flipped his tail, and he was gone and I stood there on the beach knowing, as if a thunderbolt had graved my name on the brass doors of destiny letter by letter, that the entertainment had been for me. I waited but he was gone. And so, lifting my arms for the wind to dry my robes, I turned toward the monastery. At the water's edge, I came upon a cluster of jellyfish, globular and viscous, and looked at them as the seal had looked at me and felt them as I had felt the seal, in my center, their presence in me. And I walked home, ran home, danced home in such a way that the ground and the cliffs and the sharp stones and the slippery bladderlocks and the nettles under my bare feet must have made way for me, for I never broke my pace, never looked down nor ahead, never considered this way or that. I was connected to everything in the Universe in a way that man dreams. For lateness I was unremorsefully targed by Justus of the ruddy face and ass ears and sent to cell with neither bread nor porridge.

The crosses ought not to have been at the sea bottom with their stories. The seal ought not to have spoken to me as he did and the jellyfish ought to have turned my stomach.

And that night I had my first vision, a pillar of fire, and within its center, a great raven hung and blackbirds flew in and out. It was Eldred of a cunning and prying disposition, adoring me, who drew down my eyelids. I thought I had been dreaming. He whispered to me. "No, Brother, it is a vision. It is the second sight."

I

T IS SOON TOLD.
I, GENEROUS, CHRONICLER, WRITE OF THE VISION OF ISAAC
AND THE CONFESSION OF MUNCAS. THESE EVENTS I RECORD
FROM OBSERVATION AND SECOND SIGHT.

Noble and wonderful the Lord of the Elements Who maketh
the stars go around in their appointed seasons. Noble and
generous the Abbot who welcomes to our gates all strangers.
Noble and zealous the brothers who fight for the eternal
crown.

The sterile depth of winter, it was, the time of the visions
of Father Isaac of the traveler from the north of Ireland. The
calling by Father Isaac into his cell of the novice, CuRoi, son
of the Hermit, and the bidding of him to travel to the Druid's
Altar at the western edge of Dun Hi, and there to set himself

overlooking the sea toward Tiree, Isle of the Penitents, and wait there, for within three days' time a traveler would arrive. So said the Abbot in his second sight.

"Go, my Son," said the Abbot. "For I have seen a worn and weary traveler. Take with you bread of withered barley and water of clay and prepare thyself by such fasting this night and next day and then go and recite the psalms, the Song of Moses, and the Creed, and when you do that begin again and dwell on your sorrow. After the hour of noon on the third day a traveler will arrive carried by the force of the winds. Spent and weary and at the end of strength, he will fall beside you on the coast. Take him up kindly, CuRoi, and bring him as a guest here for three days and three nights. For God Himself is received in the person of each stranger."

CuRoi, his mind attuned as no other, glanced sharply at the Abbot's countenance, but wisdom holding, asked no questions, made no challenges.

Later, he came to me and asked if man could speak to beast. "It is a beast coming. Of that I am certain."

"Saints speak to beasts," I told him.

"How is it the Abbot knows a traveler will come?"

"It is a second sight, CuRoi. The Abbot's mind moves through time and space in such ways that he is in all places at all times." Together we searched the *Annals* and found moments in history when men spoke to beasts and listened to bees. I asked CuRoi if his own father had the second sight. He looked away from me. But I already knew CuRoi had the second sight from Eldred's tale-bearing.

"I am afraid," CuRoi told me and reached for my hand.

"Ah, we shall all rejoice and drink thick milk and wild honey if we have a guest and guests are rare, are they not, here on this island?"

"What manner of guest might be carried by the force of the winds?"

"Any sailor."

"The Abbot did not mean sailor."

"You know more than the rest of us then. Go, Child." I took him in my arms although he was no longer a wee boy, but a tall and slender boy, a sapling, sweet, and told him: "Prepare thyself by fasting this day and night. Make your three days of prayer in the wilderness good. Cling, CuRoi. If you become frightened, cling to God, for He alone can reproduce the likeness of Himself within yourself. Cling to Him."

Because Father Isaac so valued this child, he sent behind him Muncas Bent-Neck, strong, silent, and watchful, who cloaked himself in a grove of boulders below the Druid's Altar and waited also.

Confessions of Muncas Bent-Neck, made to Abbot Isaac, taken by Generous.

On the first day at the edge of the great-waved sea, CuRoi shivered with anticipation and fear and as the clouds opened above him and he was struck with the rays of power, he prayed, prostrate on the ground. Once he stood and leaned over the cliff and saw Your Holiness's boat traveling to Tiree to minister to the penitents thereon and in it he recognized his own father for he cried out: "Father! Father!" and then jammed his knuckles into his mouth until blood ran over his chin. A good boy, as he had been commanded, he stilled himself and mortified his sorrow, a true martyr. He returned to his seat on the Druid's Altar and prayed and wept and watched the clouds and so labored.

The next day, the water being calm, a pair of grebes ran on the water as they do when they court, red-eyed, silver-backed, lifting their necks to the sky and dancing on the water, mating. And as he watched I saw him caressing himself, rubbing his hands along the curves of his slender boy-body and I called to him, as if I were discarnate, "Beware lust, CuRoi. Beware lust." He looked for me but I was well hidden and he prayed on his knees for forgiveness. But still he leaned flat over the cliff and watched the grebes and I made note. And on the third day, something strange. An owl here not seen before on this island, screeching with pain, attacked by a swarm of crows, almost brought down, drops of blood falling on the rock of the cliff and the owl suddenly swooping into the sea, and, as true as the legs of the stool I sit on, the owl struck out to swim in strong strokes, one wing after the other stretched above its head, and the crows, confused by the great wisdom of the owl to change from a creature of the air to a creature of the sea, flew off. CuRoi began to move his arms as the owl had and then stood, and it wasn't a great work to imagine his head, for he thought if an owl could swim as a boy, a boy could fly as an owl and, facing the sea, he began to flap. For fear that he would leap, I caught him by the hems of his cloak and pulled him from the cliff edge, for his character is still unformed to have him in the air as an hysteric. And I sat by him, holding him, while he, delirious with visions and nightmares, lay in my lap.

And that day, shivering under a chill and futile sun, he dwelled on that owl aswim, until the torpor of noon overcame the both of us and we dozed and sure enough and sudden, the crane arrived and fell beside us, and the boy removed his outer cape, wrapped the crane, gently, as you know, as you see it here before you, and brought it here. And I, Father? Watching the boy was watching a flower blooming. And when he called for his father, I wanted for that moment—when the hordes of evil descended and clouded my heart—to smell the honeysuckle of his sweet soul and for that I wish forty lashes minus one by your just hand.

— *Muncas*

The Abbot granted the forty lashes minus one to Muncas who bent his neck willingly, for that is his name, yet they were weak lashes and then the Abbot sat with the crane and read the psalms to him and the brothers came and sang, each of them, praises, and adorned the visitor with garlands of bog flowers and played music and followed as the crane strutted about the monastery grounds, turning as he turned, singing songs, and Justus brought his cithara and for three days we celebrated and drank thick milk and wild honey until the crane, strengthened, was taken to the rath at the edge of the monastic lands and set aflight.

The Abbot clapped the boy on the back and the boy asked, "Where is my father?" And the Abbot's countenance knotted and he told me, Generous, to make note, that the boy's next lesson would be that of silence.

And upbraided him, the Abbot did, on the limbs of a tree and let him hang without his cloak till dawn. And when he was come down, poor little soul, the Abbot, judgment without fault, commanded him to the foreshore for the night to wait for the morning and claim the first treasure in the nets of night.

— GENEROUS

My days as a novice were interminably long; my years short. I had been there for what seemed a lifetime but had in fact been three or four years when, walking one day on the Strand of Slaughter in prayer, I looked up suddenly and saw an invitation of smoke rising from the chimney of my father's house. Perhaps I had not been ready to look before nor dared break my promises to the Abbot. Perhaps a tree had fallen or lost its leaves and, in doing, cleared my vision. I remember feeling blessed that day and full and, I suppose, safe because safety then was the queen post of my decisions.

And so I climbed the path toward the curve of smoke, toward my father's house, thatched now with the snow-white breasts and silver wings of thousands of birds, and looked into the window of his weaving room.

His eyes were distant, his beard white, longer, his hair a

tangle, his skin nut-brown, darkened somehow, his fingers yellow and deciduous as they carved through the wools on his loom and he sang his lists as the wind sang in the pines behind me. I think he may have been at peace.

A dozen times I turned from the chilling fingers but finally I tapped on his window and directly, with eyes jewel-hard and round, under the falcon beak, he looked up at me and lifted a hand to wave me off. Twice, slowly his hand moved as if I were an insect. When I tapped more insistently his eyes narrowed, focused, blinked and then he banged with his fist in din and fury and demon on the corrugated wall between us and rushed at me through the doorway. I fled to the grove. He climbed the roof. There he hammered with his shuttle, evoking the great beast wind of the mountain Dun Hi, which howled at my back as I ran to the safety of the monastery, past Eldred, whom I knew then to be my spy, and to my stone cell beyond the lettuce garden where I held my knees and shook with the fear of what I was to become.

The old Abbot reprimanded me. "You will kill him yet. You must make yourself unknown to him."

I had, until then, thought that I, for my virtues and my strengths, was a more precious being than my father. It was I who had given myself to God to become His warrior. But it was to be my father protected, preferred, for his weaknesses and sins.

And I was sent with Nicholas Wry-Mouth to the strand whereon I was to lie and beg penitence and make genuflexions until perspiration came if not tears, my face in the sand, until Nicholas released me and I did lie there and beg not only penitence but guidance and wondered mightily about the thatch of feathers on my father's rooftop, and when the face of Heaven blazed in its final anger and the tide licked at my feet and the bells had rung the monks in from the fields, I lay there still and wondered when Nicholas would come for me and wondered, when I had to lift my head to avoid the tide and finally, given the choice of drowning or further punishment, inutterably disobedient, I slithered higher and higher on the beach away from the tide and it was only in the moonlight when I was in the safety of a sheephole on the ridge, that I saw Nicholas approaching slowly the spot he'd left me in. He turned away, satisfied, I suppose, that I was drowned. What part the Abbot had in Nicholas's absentmindedness I would never know. At Prime, the stars still bright, I intentionally sat next to Nicholas in the chapel and I felt his body stiffen. Neither he nor anyone else spoke of my punishment. Certainly I would not go to my father's house again, and it was arranged that I would be found and warned by Eldred when my father went wandering. John Joe it was who watched my father's house and would run flapping his tattered sleeves to Eldred who would then take me to sit in the pickup truck given so uselessly by my aunt's estate to the monastery—my prison when my father was, as Eldred would tell me with a shiver of excitement, loose. I believe Eldred was sent by God to test me.

And so one day, so led, I sat with my hood covering my face in the pickup truck, listening to the radio with Eldred whom I had begun to hate and who had, for reasons he was unaware of, begun to love me. I let Eldred choose between the music we were allowed and, when none was near, the screams and shouts of the soccer match we were not allowed.

It was neither music nor soccer that interested me in the truck and certainly not Eldred. It was the mirror. I had at last seen with a shock my own face, my own lovely face, as my aunt dying had told me. As if being denied my father, I could see myself. And when Eldred bent to search for the shouts of the soccer or the music of the Beatles, I could look quickly into the mirror and stare into my own eyes at my own self hotly with all the swelling passion and curiosity of a lover. My cheekbones and jaw were my father's and his aunt's, ivory, thin, carved, but my eyes were not their eyes. Mine were soft in the way a cow's eyes are soft. My lashes long, my nose not nearly as sharp as my family's, my brow wide and my mouth full. And then one day through my own eyes, past my face, into the corner frame of the mirror, my father came threading his way up the dirt road, threading his way into my eyes like the scarlet silk he passed through the eye of the snake's skull when I was, so long ago, his child.

I closed one eye. Still he came, wearing his velvet cape, ragged and shapeless, dragging one leg, the flapping soles of his torn shoes two mouths eating dirt and stones. I closed the other eye but he was already looking into the window of the truck. Eldred turned off the music abruptly and the moment I had clung to was next to me, with me, and stunk.

If three Popes and three streams and one black sun in the Southern Vault . . . will my father know me?

Now we come to the relationship between quantum logic and the fugue. My father may have known me, may have not known me, may have suspected it was I, may have decided not to know me, and anything in between for he stuck his head into the window of the truck and said, "God be with you, Brother." I imagined from his breath that his organs were rotting.

"And with you," I murmured.

And then I opened the door and stepped down from the truck, away from Eldred's hot scrutiny.

"And see my fine bag, Brother." There is no relationship between quantum logic and the fugue. My father opened his gunny sacks for me. He and they smelled of the urine of his own universe. All those years I had wept for his touch or to touch something he had touched, and now he opened his reeking sacks and he was dirty and his breath stank and I shrank from him and the sacks were filled with feathers in luminescent colors and claws and shells and tiny bird skulls and mice and, to his shame be it spoken, excrement.

"A breakthrough in my art," he whispered, stunned, it seemed, by his own antediluvian inventiveness.

"In his bowels, CuRoi," Eldred whispered to me, for which I never forgave him.

And then my father fell at my feet and clutched my knees. "So? Forgive me? Forgive me. I hate her as I hate myself." His feathers spilled and lifted onto the wind, drifting in dozens of probabilities, vectors beyond the planes and forms of what we know. We ran after them, my father, Eldred, and I, grasping at them with empty fists. Some descended into the lilies, some into the cabbages and the marigolds, some would never, as my father, be caught by anything.

"I have sinned. I have sinned, Brother," he called to me as we ran. "I have found her and sinned."

Perhaps if Eldred hadn't been there standing at my shoulder, running beside me, I might have said, "It is I, Father, Celeste." Perhaps not. As a monk I tried to reach him and touch him, to comfort him, but there was no comfort in me. He stopped, looked at my outstretched hand and then, as if I were a mote in his eye, looked through me to his feathers drifting in the sunlight, and he ran off stumbling after them. Bitterly, I watched his diminishing shape.

Eldred put his arm about my shoulders and asked me to be his amhara, his soul friend. I refused, giving him as much pain as he had given me by his hounding presence. If he had not been there, I might have followed my father.

"You wish to be my judge, not my soul friend, Eldred. I must be my own judge." My father had disappeared.

Astonished at the sudden cruel sharp center I had finally exposed, his face turned red in alarm, disordering his features. He tossed his hood over his chagrin and, as I realized when I was summoned for punishment, made straightway to complain to the Abbot. When I arrived after the evening supper, the Abbot sat staring at the peat fire, his back to me.

I kissed his hems. He spoke so softly I could barely hear him.

"CuRoi, you must, for the love of God, love all men." Was he weak? Was he embarrassed? Was he using his illness to cover his embarrassment? How much did he know?

"Do you mean Eldred or my father?"

"All men." His head dropped onto his chest. I kissed his hems and backed away but at the door a blood blister of anger burst. If three Popes and three streams and one aunt and one brother . . . the Abbot is my father's father. Does knowledge like this come only when one needs it? God help me. My father's father. This too in the humus of my grove. The magic and the powers, the curses, coursing through me also.

"Why do you keep me here? I know you. I know who you are. You know who I am. It is your selfishness to have me here. To keep me from my mother, to keep me from my father. You know what animals they had inside them, my father, your sister, and you . . . and you put them . . . all of us . . . in the same cage for your own reason. You know why I had to be cruel to Eldred. How can you punish me for what you've brought me to? Eldred loves me. Something natural in him recognizes that I am . . . that I am a . . . a . . ." I could not believe the sound of my own voice filling another stream with rotten nutmeats of my own. I covered my ears.

"Huh? Huh? What's that? Who is it?"

I left. I shall never know if he heard me or not. With the

vagueness in his sleepy eye and the spittle on the dry lips, I suspect he had dropped off to sleep in the center of my curses. So much for the eternal. In this my father was right. There are only questions.

Copy, CuRoi. Let God be original. Hey, diddle diddle, the cat and the fiddle, the cow jumped over the moon. Compare the force of consciousness to formulate itself with the orbit of the planet Herschel. Hey, diddle diddle. My father had taught me so much. And I had found no answers in the monastery, none at all. At last my father sent me a gift. I was eighteen. I carried it to the Abbot.

"Father, I cannot bear this."

"Your father is a great artist. His works hang in palaces and museums."

"It is not a gift. Do you not see? It is a scream. I cannot bear it."

"Shame."

And soon thereafter, the hanging, for that was what it was called by the brothers, a hanging, and indeed it was, appeared on the wall of our cell retreat against the coarse white bricks of the inner wall near the library. It was grinning and gothic, archaic, with its claws and feathers and rags and, in its center, as the foreskins and nose bones of the saints rested in the reliquary of the columbarium behind the crypt, the ghastly long nail, yellow, deciduous, embedded in the pickings of the Universe, rested. No one else recognized it as human. Later I thought the paper-thin curls beaded onto threads were pieces of his skin. And I could not rest from the terror of my father's work.

Very late one night I woke Eldred and confessed to him. He told the monks of the flayed skin. No one told the Abbot. The monks prayed for the soul of my father and I slipped off to Cook's house with the desperate and regrettable hope that she had an answer or a cure or a clue to my father. I ought to have known not to look for answers. Nevertheless, I went, intolerably curious, wondering if he had taken little shavings from her. She was, however, whole and un-harmed. In fact, much fleshier. Day after day I slipped to her house and tried mutely from her garden to speak with her, my arms outstretched in supplication, but when she saw me, she would clang an alarm bell and I would race shamefully as a thief to the lettuce patch of the stone cell and hope it was not known where I had been for it would never be understood.

Winter passed quickly. We shed our seal-skin cloaks and our gloves, ended our trips for peat moss for the fires, burned our pallets of heather and bracken and renewed them. My footsteps in the snow to Cook's house melted under a high sun. Soon a yellow carpet of St. John's wort and belts of yellow iris led the way. Still I pleaded silently from Cook's garden for her word. What did my father know about the world that he would flay his own skin, rip out his own nails? What had he not told me?

John Joe whispered, "Sun, Moon, Alleluia," when I asked after my father. By late spring Cook would rock her head sadly, which I thought to be a sign of communication, and then would ring the alarm bell. Buds came to the trees, browned poignantly, and dropped to the ground in the dryness. New grasses yellowed in vast patches and the cows were taken to sheeling far up on Dun Hi where snow streams were caught in pools. And I was of age.

My father had taught me that the world was random and terrible, a butcher's feast. Generous, that it was safe and given, and the Abbot, because I was to be his heir, began to teach me the eternal abstractions mixed with the spittle that slipped from his mouth.

"Someday," he told me, "it is your destiny. You will have my powers, the second sight, the satiric curse. As sure as the planets in their orbits. As sure as the stars. As sure as—" I wept, interrupting him. He dismissed me and I left wishing my leaving would leave his words.

One morning, when July parched the green on the island and I stood watering the surviving turnips, eight monks passed me carrying the Abbot on his sledge, the Abbot seeing something in his second sight, croaking, "Faster, faster!" His eyelids were arrested and his eyes staring and he reached out to me and touched me so that I would see his vision and I saw my father climbing into the hollow of the oak tree, and then they left. "Faster, faster." Eldred it was once again who drew my eyelids down over my eyes and broke the vision for me. And then, too quickly, from the hill of my father's house came the eight monks and the sledge and as they passed I saw the Abbot's face changed, his soul altogether gone, his eyes eclipsed by whatever my father had shown him. And that evening after I had washed new cabbage in the kitchen and stood outside swinging wet leaves in a cloth above my head, round and round, I watched smoke rising from the field by my father's house. There ought not to have been smoke. I told no one. Instead I spun against time and space, enflaming that tree, swinging the leaves of cabbage about my head, spinning until the fields swarmed and spun with me and I could feel the world moving in my head because I knew the oak tree was afire and I knew that he had climbed finally into it and set himself aflame.

Father? Is this not a rite of Seth, of Pig? Is this not what St. Patrick's father did, Molchu, the swineherd? Your immolation, it is not a rite of Cain. My name, CuRoi, then is false. You are Ham and Pig, aren't you? Am I?

Is this my inheritance then, Father, that I inherit my powers not from Dog but from Pig, not from Cain but from Seth? Is that your message? That I and you are from Molchu, Mocc-el, Michael, Melchizedek? Are these my ancestors? Mucc, much, muck, the riches of Pluto, the treasures of Hades, the Chazarei of the Chazar God? What have you left me? Why are you leaving me? Am I to be free and with power?

So I spun, enraptured, and spun enflaming that tree, firing it with my turning, a simple stick rubbing against its own destiny. The smoke pillared. Escadrilles of crows flew through the pillar. The battle-raven, Badh Catha, hung in its center. I was not surprised. By sunset a mighty fire had crept, climbed, and claimed the fields stretching away from the hut. Nicholas, his face wreathed in joy, arrived breathlessly, fell on his knees, said he was witness to a great vision, a miracle of the fields in holy flame, and rose from the ground above the heads of the other monks who, ignoring him, formed a sea brigade and passed pails of water through the fields, up the path to my father's pyre but he had already burned, I knew, and his eyes and heart and tongue rolled out of him and the top of his skull blown off and vanished in the pillar of smoke. And I went to the flagstones to say the ordained words for the soul of my father, and the words of my prayers stood on end as did my teeth and then toppled, scattering as pebbles under the feet of mountain sheep into an abyss of inertia.

Kadosh, holy; cabosh, the hat of death, his skull cap bursting into the pillar of smoke; cabbage, the leaves I swung to enflame his pyre; Kadosh, cabosh, caboose. Is this the end of the train? And I am to disembark from the family tree? Separate, at last?

I had considered, romantically, prostrating myself on his pyre. Instead I watched the grass fire, listened to its roar and crack and thought about minor fluctuations in the bifurcations of evolution that bring about major change. This was a major change. Would heat dissolve reality or cohere a new being? The flames were aqueous against the night sky, a sea of flames, an ocean of fire, a juncture of elements. Through them came Cook—Madonna, Medea, Medusa, Medua, Why—stumbling in the ruts, her locks loose and wild, flames themselves, and in the great heat, wrapped still in her loose clothes and aprons, trails of smoke and hair and flame smoking about her and two of the sea brigade caught her up by the arms and helped her, holding her above the ground as her legs tread the air. Her head was turned to the fire behind her. The three of them passed me. She did not see me behind the chicken wire. I wet the fields with a hose. So. Medua means why and I am to beware of W's.

When at last the Abbot was roused, in his last act of power, he called down the rain, but the fire had already of its own accord contained itself just as it had organized itself. Who knows what inertia, who knows what internal intelligence had brought it about and brought it to its own end? And why? If three streams . . . there is no prologue. To understand the match is not to understand the fire. The real question, the true mystery lies in the Why.

The Abbot begged his monks to carry him up the path but they would not. Something had happened irrevocably, a moment had changed and would never return. I found him sitting crying in the field I was watering, his cow Thirty-three beside him. In the dark field I had watered the Abbot.

"Huh? What is it?"

"Father, I am sorry."

"Manuel?" His voice rang with hope.

"No, not Manuel. Celeste," I dared.

"Manuel?" One eye was black steel, the other milk white.

I dried his head and face with the hems of my robes and found a brother to help me take him back to his cell and his cow to the barn.

When dawn became day the monks searched smoldering fields, four abreast, they searched for my father as if he were a lost child. My father's house was untouched, only the wall nearest to the oak was singed. The oak was ashes and stump. I and the Abbot knew his bones were in the oak but I dared not go there. All that day I heard them calling, "Manuel? Manuel? Manuel?"

"Lost in the fire," the monks reported to me and looked at me queerly, Nicholas Sinser who had given up his vision, Eldred who studied me with hooded eye and long tooth. Others. Sympathy, respect, astonishment for the very colors of my life, the Spanish blood, the reds, the blacks, the madness. They wondered, I knew, when I too would claim an event. Nicholas had become impure for his sin of parablepsis and I had become questionable. That week was a dreadful week with hawks and a dry scorching heat, a desert week. We fasted.

The elder monks sat with the Abbot and the poets cast poems about the event. Generous repeated the event of the lost bones. The Abbot nodded his head at the explanations, smiled.

And because no one watched me, I walked to Cook's house, which was, strangely, leveled. Had a cinder from my father's fire caught on the roof? Cook's house had burned in its own fire or in my father's fire even though the fields separating the houses had not burned. And hadn't Cook walked by me without seeing me, with wild eyes, and climbed into a currach at the strand? The murmuring that the Cook had sinned swarmed like bees around me, but when I neared, the murmuring settled and prayers began. Generous came to me.

"The love in your heart," he said, humbly, "is torn by hatred. Forgive your father. You alone must forgive him. When you do you will be able to love again. When you are ready to pray, pray with us. We will pray for you."

I

T IS SOON TOLD.
I, GENEROUS, CHRONICLER, WRITE OF THE DAY THE HERMIT
WAS MADE QUIET.

O Ancient of Days, I ask Thy blessedness that whosoever holds this book in his hand may remember Generous and the terrible day. Here on this remote island where the veil is thin and the Abbot Isaac so great that he links earth and Heaven, here the tower of fire stood in the sky for five hours and black birds innumerable flying into it and out of it and one great battle raven in the middle of it, Badh Catha for sure and certain, the red-mouthed raven, ravener of flesh, and the wee birds flew under her wings when they went into the tower. They came out and lifted up, moreover, into the air, a new-born calf which was without its mother in

126

the field and let it fall down again, so that it died immediately, and they lifted up three of the vestments of the Hermit and let them down again.

There was great fear, and Nicholas Sinser, volatile, and the rest of us, Dogs of God, Co'in, wealth of God, barking at the moon in praise. Men of the Dog God, Roch-el, praising the Pig God, Mocc-el, Cain honoring Seth, for it was his time of death and change, and we, lepers, taboo and holy we were, ate the flesh of swine and drank sows' milk in his honor, our brother Seth, known also as Ham, I am.

And the Amadan dispatched he was to the Hermit's shack to fill it with pine nuts for we pined and had not coffin nor bones nor body to give up to Seth, nor could we pour sows' milk on the threshold for the funeral feast.

Our heartaches, a thousand tortures, woe and pain together for our brother Manuel, and his child by name, CuRoi, left an orphan, as us all.

Stout-ribbed and ass-eared Justus took up his cithara and seven strings and two swan shapes fixed thereon and stilled the cows and comforted the grieving mother cow and the novice CuRoi with the songs of Hyperborean Apollo. For death is a time when all things unite.

— GENEROUS

What at one given moment appears as an insignificant deviation with respect to a normal behavior, may, in other cases, be the cause of crisis and renewal. Rules are associated with events and those contain an element of chance. Certainly near August fifteenth.

In the Dog Days under the face of Sirius, the blossoms had withered on the almond tree. Six weeks to the night of the fire, on the day before Assumption Even, I pruned the almond tree's lower branches to ease its plight and looked up to see Cook returned, carrying a bundle of rags in her arms and a shapeless black purse. She was dirty and ill, shrunken. She had come on the *Prince George*. The aprons and loose clothes were gone, the braids cut short in ragged lengths, the hems down on the blue cotton dress, and frecked she was with great spots and stains of color on eyelids, cheeks, lips, nails. The outline of her fruited breasts pushed against the thin cotton of her shirt. I could not look into her eyes—the brightness had turned to chafer-black bogles.

"So. Where is your father?"

To run, to leap, to fly, anything. The heartaches, the thousand woes. I who perform so well my chores, my Latinity near perfection, my singing voice clear. I who am humble, do fast, obey the vows. But she held me sharply by my arm with one hand. I shall never forget her hot touch, her black purse and the bundle which was an infant swinging before my eyes.

"God help him," I said in my lugubrious monk's voice. "He is passed on."

"Where?"

"Dead. The fire."

"So. He is the lucky one." And gave me a final and quick nod of the head and pushed the bundle and the black purse filled with baby bottles into my arms. "Your brother."

I heard the doors of the chapel grind open.

What is the cause of things? How can one predict in time?

Why do events notch into each other, vectors cross, morphogenetic fields meet, enfold, unfold? A few minutes more, a few minutes less, a few words, perhaps, but I knew. My father had woven, drawn my fate through his loom, as if I were one of his threads—and was I not?—and the Fate, Cook, Nem-Isis, came snipping at it, cutting off what length she had assigned to her, what he had designed. I would escape neither of them, I who prune trees, they who pruned me.

"Yours," she said as the shadow of Eldred cast itself on the ground between us. "Yours."

"No." I howled at her back and she ran and I never saw her again except in each tree I cut.

I thought if the singing of the Hours hadn't ended as it

had, if I had not clung to the woman as answer, if she had not rung that alarm bell giving solid sound to my spying so she and my father could sweat and wrestle with their orchid demons, I might have woven myself from my own pattern. And both she and my father, to hide my secret and their secret, made me somehow sinner. Madness. In a twisted way, she must have felt she was also protecting the secret of my womanhood. Perhaps that was her rationalization. Perhaps that was her evil. Some say there is no evil—there is only good intent by stupid men. Perhaps.

Trembling, I lifted the cover from the infant's face. A smooth and lovely creature it was, a sweetness, cooing as St. Columba's dove, neither mad nor stinking, no shuttle, no submachine gun, no second sight.

Eldred pulled the cloth over the baby's face and pointed at the chapel for there, framed by the stone-faced saints carved in the doorway, the Abbot, amid all that rocky strength and eternal power, saw Cook give me the child, heard Cook give me the child, saw me take the child, burst from the shell of his senility, pointed his miter at me with the forming of a dreadful curse on his lips. The blue-black skin blacker, bluer, glistening and the white curls on his head straightening upward, trembling the hairs were in the very frequencies of the powers of Heaven that he called down as he invoked the Goddess Sin upon me in a rhyming death. And I knew the words:

"Canadh, Esnadh, Sin without blemish.
Gaeth, Garbh, Gemadhaigh
Ochsadh, Iachtadh, a saying without falsehood.
These are My names in every way."

"Sigh." He stood there, the miter shaking at me. "Music, Storm, Rough Wind. Wintery Wind. Groan," and fell groping, the miter still pointing to me but he had not finished the last of the death rhyme—Lamentation, the true name of Sin—and it was his own death upon him. For his judgment, only I and God knew, was unjust.

Receiving his own curse, he clutched at his robes and fell groping at the ground. I might as well have been cursed. He died that night, not serenely, in his bull's skin, his crane upright on his shoulder, the cow, Thirty-three, by his side. At the dying, I held the child in my arms. It cried with us. I shall not forget the sweetness of that child weeping. The Abbot screamed as if he were being burned with my father and we crossed ourselves in his room and kept vigil and the wind beating without us and within us was cold, deeply cold. No one of us slept for his pain. Ring-eyed we were. Winds of fear blew in our own empty hearts and we prayed while the old Abbot covered his mouth and bit on his fingers as if to keep something from escaping and we chanted him to his peace. I regretted every cabbage head John Joe and I had tossed into the sea. God knows, the Abbot fought and cried and wept with a greater clarity than any of us had seen all these months. And he looked at me, pointed at me, pointed to the sea and to me and I knew he wanted the child tossed in the sea. I had hoped and not hoped he would tell me what it was I needed to know about myself, why I was kept on Iona, and indeed his eyes fell on me at the last moment, flicked with an anguish so terrible I thought, shame for the telling, that he was seeing Hell, and rolled back into the sockets. "Forgive . . . new Abbot."

He died with my secret. Was I a Seth creature? I alone now had the burden of myself and truly it was great for it had killed my aunt, my father, and my grandfather, but now at least, it was my own.

Nicholas it was who declared him quiet and put the red cabosh over his head. Hilary it was who crossed his hands, one on each cheek. Justus it was who covered him with spices of the pine and sage and thyme and the Sin of Amon, and Aidan who wrapped him in white linens to deliver him to Seth. Nicholas, at the last wrapping, turned to me with eyes as blank as empty bowls and became my enemy. Generous put his arm about me and led me from Nicholas's stare, which fell as the black gull on my back, on my soul, led me to the barn where we took milk from a fresh cow and Generous told me that I must sleep in the barn, with the baby, in the hay with the cows. I would be safe and he would see that I had food and we must wait until the new Abbot came and he would decide my fate. So. It is Seth who shakes the child from the pine tree. Pain, pangs of Hell, the incense of the Tree of Death, and I understood the grove/ grave/grief of the pines. Seth was the Not God, leading us on, the stern of the great Craft, the Saturn of our orbits.

"A shame," Generous said, "and you were to be elected, but you have sinned. You were chosen. Now you will be excommunicated."

"Generous? I . . . this isn't my child, Generous. Dear Teacher, I am *not* its father."

"Then give it to me and I will send it to Seth with the Abbot whom it killed. It is impure and cannot stay."

"It is all I have."

"You have God."

I could only look at the child.

"Is this too not God?"

And then Generous, who had all the knowledge in the world collected, looked at the child, at myself, at the child, and said very sadly, "How can that be? I do not understand."

He had to turn away from me. I knew then what troubles I had brought onto the abbey.

Nicholas came to me, his head nodding up and down. I

fixed my eyes on the moon-faced clock behind him so it would not seem I was agreeing as I followed his words. The letters of the clock were red. They flashed, bled from the clock-face, 10:22, 10:23. Nicholas gave me words of sympathy. I barely heard him until he was somehow, suddenly, speaking of Christ, of Seth, of conversion.

"Through Christ we will bury death and do away with Seth entirely, CuRoi. Nothing will be seen or known of Seth any longer. There will be no death, CuRoi."

"Leave me alone, Nicholas."

"No death, CuRoi. Join me. Join Rome. Turn your powers from this—you need not suffer. Come, let me baptize you."

"Father Nicholas . . ."

"I will be Abbot soon. I will let you stay. Join me, CuRoi. Defy Death. Deny Death."

So. That was his promise. I held my hands over my ears. He shook his head sadly up and down, sideways, and waited for me.

"No," I whispered.

Nicholas shrugged. "You choose the path to your own damnation."

"At least I choose that much."

His face showed no understanding.

"Oh, Nicholas, you are wrong, Nicholas. Seth is not damnation. Seth is change and chance and choice. . . ."

He did not stay to listen.

I

I, GENEROUS, CHRONICLER, WRITE THIS LAMENT FOR ISAAC.

Noble and wonderful is the Lord of the Elements.
The Great Abbot was made quiet this day.
It rained a shower of honey upon Tiree, a
shower of Silver upon the Marsh and a shower of
blood and a hundred prosperous chieftains died and
along the spine of Britain nine persons that flyed
in the air as if they were wingéd fowl and above
us a thin and tremulous cloud on the fourth watch
of the night of the fifth day, stretching as a
rainbow east to west in a clear sky and the moon
was turned to blood.

— GENEROUS

134

I remember my father's silken Heavens wheeling above my head. "I am the planet Saturn, Celeste, and I lead. And you are the planet Herschel, Celeste, at the very edge of the sky, and you follow."

Is the planet Herschel easily distinguished? How large is the planet Herschel and what is the distance from the sun? What is the length of the year and how far does it travel? What is the difference between the orbit of the planet Herschel and the ability of consciousness to create itself? Where was I to go? Where had my father gone? Who would help me? John Joe, who alone could speak with the Other Side, who alone could cross the stones, came to me, pariah that I was. He laughed at the baby and the baby laughed at him and he farted in his long gassy whine and the baby curled his fists and gurgled and we fed him milk from the old

Abbot's cow who looked over her shoulder at us, and the baby fattened and thrived.

And one red and dewy dawn after Lauds, before Matins, the baby sleeping peacefully in a pile of rags and clean hay, the abbey silent, I took a milk pail and ran to the beach to wash myself as if cleansing could renew me in the hearts of our company of souls.

It had been a long and mild month. The uplands burned with buttercups. I had just dipped my pail into the sea when I heard shouts. At the beach, a terrible sight. Three of our brothers bloody on the White Strand of the Martyrs and our bull roped and riding on a log float toward a high-browed barque of the foreigners and then it was I wanted the powers of my grandfather and then it was I, neither child nor man, girl nor woman, stood on the edge of the water and shouted curses at them and prayed for a Druid mist to drown them and return the bull and twisted myself for the powers but they were not yet strong in me and the foreigners shouting in derision, brandishing bloody swords and insults for it was the manhood of the herd they were raiding and suddenly the mist fell over them, a great black noxious cloud rose from the sea over their barque, and there on its prow stood their Druid, the Pale Shouter, cursing. I thought my end was within the hour but he was shouting beyond me to the cliff, to a stranger who stood with the mark of hero on his brow. He, one man alone, repulsing the savages, thrusting them from our isle, and in a crashing of waves and hideous demons and flaming fires thrown upon one another, I watched as he, this new stranger, was flung sideways into the sea. As the bull was winched onto the barque and the ship made way, I tore my clothes from me and swam to the spot of brightness and found the man, near dead, and he clung to me as I swam, body against body, the wind ripping my lungs, his arms around my waist, the sweetness of him against me filling my heart with strength, and when at last I fell with him on the shore and opened his trousers and his velvet jacket to ease his breathing and kneeled beside him to examine the half-moon tattoo of Cain on his brow, I saw his beauty there on the wave-washed stones. His face was white and ghostly, with a fine scar on his cheek, the hand I held in mine limp, the other silver-cased, his bones long and thin, delicate, and his earlobes in the morning light transparent as sea shells. I looked too long on his face. It was gently shaped with darknesses of intensity, carved with pain, not from violence but from sorrow. Pearls of sea-water lay on his eyelashes. His lips were parted slightly and I leaned forward to feel his breath on mine. So gentle was the line of his jaw and so elegant, I reached to stroke the pale hairs of his cheeks, but as I did he opened his eyes and glanced at me once, saw my nakedness, saw my womanhood, my breasts, my hair.

He whispered. "Are you human? You look human."

Prologue is an epistemological net we toss over events afterward. What were the three main causes of the First World War? For me, that is.

For others, events are the results of long courses and looms of determination . . . my family, my father, his aunt, my grandfather. And for others—the church, the monks—we are perfected beings standing outside time, watching the unfolding, guiding the unfolded, living in the eternal, everything in orbit. Now you are a man, they told me, but what you shall become, you shall be forever.

But I see no unfolding, no determination. I see bursts and splashes and rudenesses, singular moments. No orbits. The joy I felt dancing at the shoulders of the great rocks at Giant's Ground, the revulsion at Cook's hand on my arm, knowing that hand had touched, enflamed my father's tortured body. The attack of his heart upon the Abbot. Was I to blame?

Name the three causes of the Abbot's death. CuRoi, the novice; Celeste, the Hermit's daughter; and the cow. No.

These are singular points of events, localities; they are not trajectories written in the stars. They *are* the stars. The stars burst, vanish, are born. A rigid star falls from the sky and we have a desert. My father said, "Sun, moon, stars. Who knew?" No one knows, knew, or will know. What is the cause of the cause of the cause of the cause? There is none. I am that terrifyingly free and that terrifyingly connected with every other star, cause, jellyfish, cow. We are in the present and connected, moving in bursts and spurts, sometimes sluggishly, sometimes dazzlingly ourselves in our own Universe. We are. I am the Universe. And he looked at me and I at him.

Trance-fixed, I watched his eyes follow the curve of waist to bush of belly. His hand reached up to touch me. Somewhere between waking and dreaming in the sheen of summer sun, he knelt at my feet. Just as I pressed my face into the silk of the cow's side and wept out my pain, he pressed his face against the hair of my belly and held me, pressing and weeping and I could feel the waters moving inside me and then I felt him licking me, tasting me as if I were victual. Victual, victim, victory. For a moment I was frightened but waves of warmth and pleasure rolled over me and the red sun rose over the sea and fell into my mouth. He lifted me against a rock. Waves of his hair and his breathing and the twitching of my legs. I could no longer stand. Enduring sweetness and weakness and part of me thought this is what killed my father and another part of me knew it was the first time I had been held and loved by anyone, any creature at all, and while I didn't understand the licking, as if it were a mother cow grooming her new-born calf, surely I understood the pleasure as he lifted me and pulled me onto himself and entered me as if he too were the red hot sun rising within me, two suns suspended within me, thundering together, and when he was still, he took my hand and rubbed it along his cheek and then his hand on my cheek and fell back into the sand. How is it that that which is most prohibited is most creative?

I fled to the sea, to the loom of tangle where the limbs of seaweed became his limbs, wrapping, holding me, and I lay suspended, hidden, hanging in the loom as a spider caught in the rapture of a moment I would seek for the rest of my existences.

Generous and John Joe arrived with the camel and I watched from the loom as they threw the bodies of the bloodied brothers and the near-drowned man over the camel and led the camel, and weeping, led the sad and sorrowful load to the safety of the monastery as John Joe sang out his fear, "Alleluia! Alleluia!" and Generous stroked the head of the new Abbot, the fine and lovely head dripping a trail of sea pearls into the sand and I slept in his seaweed arms and wept in my rapture.

Generous and John Joe had not seen me. The new Abbot would think he had dreamed and even that dream would be for him and myself a sin far worse already than my own. The warriors would be healed in a great vat of milk.

I T IS SOON TOLD.
I, GENEROUS, CHRONICLER, WRITE OF THE ORDINATION OF THE
NEW ABBOT, THOMAS.

In the name of God, the Mighty One, the Wise One, the
Compassionate One, the Merciful One, Lord, make smooth
the way by Thy mercy.

Then at the mouth of day, at the hour of birds, my brothers singing, was the Ordination of the new Abbot, Thomas.

"Deep is his counsel, the comeliness of Kings on his brow."
We walked to the great-waved sea all but CuRoi, impure,
excommunicant, sitting in the barn. We walked to the wave-
washed stones and sang, the old deep voices answering the
young sweet voices, and at the stones they led a religious
turn round it, the Rite of the Rock, and pronounced, we

did, a rhetorical panegyric setting forth auguries and pedigrees.

"A warrior for God, he is. Dog of God. Roch-el."

"His cheek like porphyry."

"His brow like the hero's light."

"A fragrant strong apple is he, the comeliness of Kings."

"Intolerable the radiance of his silver hand."

"Of stature great and graceful. Of family royal. Cain, Co'in, Conn, Cohen, Khan. Of battle fierce, in speech gentle, of pedigree ancient, of valor great, of liberality greater, an athlete of God. Dog of God, Roch-el."

And then Nicholas harangued him, taunted him, and cast rhyme and satire at him, but firm he stood, this Thomas, not young, nor old, but worldly, a hero of many battles, a man familiar with the courts, a man of passion and impulse. Firm he stood until he was given the sword, the bull's skin of Ordination, the miter, and with his sword he struck the rock. Rock, dog, roch, clock, Time, Tammuz, Thomas, O Cur, Occur. One fine voice singing the taunt and then still. A mouth-lock on the birds. The floodtides of the sea swelled and filled the bays.

They sang, the brothers, and they returned, the new Abbot leading them, and they came to CuRoi and as a company wept sorely as women, not in anger as Manuel on his roof, and not in weakness as the old Abbot in the field, but in bitterness, they wept, for his fate, and CuRoi wept bitterly also, he who was born knowing, and flung his arms around the neck of the new Abbot whose cheek muscles twitched like harp gut. He stiffened, Thomas did, lifted CuRoi's arms away from his neck, and drew back into a shadow.

And read the sin. "Ruina Maxima." And read the punishment. "Seven years in a foreign land without bread or water. In the morning you will leave. With the child. It is all I can do." Others took the sinner's robes and gave CuRoi

141

a rough cowl and a plaid and a seal skin. And left, singing the praises of the new Abbot who followed slowly, solemnly behind them.

"His father's name is God, O Siris, Ysir, sired, of Isis, Sirius, Dog Star, all that Is, Son of God, Son of Adam, Son of the line of the Gods of Being, not the line of Elohim, not the line of Justice, but the line of Mercy, not the line of Seth and Noah. He is of the wise men who treat and heal and know the properties of all growing things and the movements of the Great Wheel and the paths of the power through the living body of the earth. He is of the clan of the man whose name is God, the man whose plot is the Eastern Paradise, as this man's plot is the Western Paradise, the island Iona, dear to our heart, the man and the island. . . ."

Great thanksgiving and feasting that night in honor of Thomas, and Thomas, secret and quiet, burdened, he told us, by the knowledge of what he must do, by the lives and destinies placed in his hands, and he held his hands up to us, the one cased now in silver, the other long and graceful, and blessed us and we bowed on our knees for his blessing and prayed thereafter that the community be preserved in peace.

— GENEROUS

And at Matins with mist on the rough meadow and black clouds on the mountain, John Joe, bawling, led me over the rath to the stones where I sank with the child who cried out in hunger. It would be through his furious hunger they would force me into the village of the crofters. John Joe turned and led the camel away. The crane flew overhead, watching me, and I feared it would pluck the eyes from my child whom I wrapped tightly in my plaid, and behind me, over the stones, the crofters, rustics, one a lowly sorcerer, drew milk from a bull and I rocked the child until my breasts filled with new milk and then I fed him in a rapture and he slept and I with him. Because I was filled with the miracle of the milk, I walked back to the monastery and knocked brave and loud at the gates of the chapel. There is nothing contradictory in the world. And Aidan the Guestmaster looked out at me from between iron bars and grimaced. The crane, within, stalked up and down the corridor and at Vespers my brothers walked by me, faces pinched as candles.

I lay that night obstinately in the barn. The cows complained, rolling their eyes at me, and then I became of them, quiet and harmless. When the bells rang for Lauds I rose, wrapped the child, and sat with him on the steps as my brothers, sleep-struck, walked past me.

The Abbot halted before me, looked down, a man both inflexible and ambivalent. His spirit moved across me and even in the dread of his presence, I pulled the limbs of seaweed across me and held fast.

"Where might I go, Holy Father?"

"Away."

"I pray, Holy Father, a little more time, Holy Father." I hugged his legs.

"Until Samhain, three weeks. Find work in the barn. Take a stall."

And the doors swung closed behind me. But I sang the offices with my brothers and ate grass on the steps and wept and pleaded with each of them as they walked out, Sinser and Osser, Muncas, Nicholas, Generous, Hilary. They stepped around me as if I were already dead.

"Give up the child." The Abbot Thomas came to me one evening as I sat under the Tree of Life with the child. "Give up the child and I will allow you penance on Tiree."

I shook my head. He walked away, his shoulders tightened and narrowed, protecting himself from me. My heart followed him. My legs—between them a tingling.

As the air before a cloudburst, I was so with Thomas. Everything I was and knew and felt was filtered through his being. I was heavy with him.

I would hold the child and watch the clouds losing and

gaining form above us, dancing Gods, a roaring lion, enormous white storm clouds after a dark rain, always clouds but becoming, becoming, becoming. What would I become if Thomas reached out to touch me? Sin? Storm? Lamentation? I remembered my grandfather's curses.

My labor was to say a blessing over the empty milk pails and when they were full and sloshing with new warm milk, to carry two at once to the Abbot's cell, where he would reach out, quill in hand, as we were all laboring, and bless the milk. My arms trembled with the weight of the pails and the sight of him. He would lean out, mechanically, make the sign of the cross over the pails, and I would return them to the barn and pour the milk in the holder. Beyond, Justus played his music and the baby slept. In the round stainless curves of the holder my face was long and misshapen and bright with two red spots for having looked on Thomas. I would pour slowly, examining myself, eyes, nose, mouth, imagining what it was he saw, smiling at myself as I would at him. And then there would be new pails and I would return with another cast on my face. I looked to him I suppose either holy or in love. When one is expecting holiness, one sees holiness. Whether he saw love or holiness I do not know but he had powers and he must have known what was in my heart. And if he did, might he not drop me at a stroke? Or did he want me somehow to have these thoughts in my head and in my heart and in my parts and in my limbs and in my fingers reaching out to touch him?

I crept after him on his rounds, picked up leaves crushed by his feet, left bunches of clover and lavender in his path. Once I wrote "I love you" in the sand but added "God" afterward and watched the waters lick as he had me and then I drew his profile with the sloping eyes and long fine nose and the fine scar of Cain and the strong chin and the hollows in his cheeks which I pressed with the heel of my hand and then buried my face in the warm sands that were alive under me and wept and at last understood it was the orchid creature moving within me that I felt. Not God, and God . . . a quantum logic.

I slept each night with him, with my head against his shoulder and his breath gentle on my face and his lips . . . I dare not. Yes, the orchid creature. How I dreamed of his limbs, the silver hand, ungloving it, the eyes, the long leanness of him. Outside the world withered. Trees were naked, the sky lower and darker, sterile, all the harvest stored and I was as my father had been—afraid and ripe.

When I thought of Thomas's face in the darkness, it would fade, but I would find him again in the day and memorize his face, each line, each proportion, and form it again in the darkness of the barn. I touched myself as he had touched me and felt the great sweetness and the weakening and wept for him as I had wept for my father and pressed my face against the side of old sweet Thirty-three, and wet was her fur when I had confessed. I kept him with me always. When the baby sucked, its lips were Thomas's lips. Thomas looked at me sadly when he caught me behind him on the path or waiting with the child on the steps or under the Tree of Life. I could see God behind his eyes. Dissipative non-equilibrium thermodynamic self-organization. I was re-organized, indeed, through his being. Now a new being, a being in love I was, but not through self.

Once, indeed, forgetting, he reached out to bless me with his silver hand, then retracted his hand as if touching fire. "The damned also need blessing," he assured both of us. Later in the barn—and I was not surprised that he came— he sat on a milking stool by my stall, held his head in his hands as if he ached, and said, "CuRoi, Dog of the King, Watcher of God, how terrible it is that the community will lose such a nobility as in your line. I too have been weak in faith, and carnal. I too have done penance for wantonness, for kin murder, for terrible battles. Carnal, CuRoi, and I have done my penance for it. I too fight a demon of wrath within me. If you will give up the child and go to Tiree and there labor for your soul . . ."

"And what would you do with the child, Holy Father?"

One knows when a man has a secret. The lens darkens, the jaw tightens, the eyes slope downward. So it happened there in the stall, in the half light. I had the keen knowledge that I was again touching on the wound, the burden of the entire community, with which I was somehow inextricably involved. He said nothing. I shook my head.

One day I forgot to bless an empty pail and banish the demon from it and when the pail was filled and I carried it to Thomas and he blessed it, the demon, unable to bear the blessing, was wild and the pail shook as if to break. Its lid flew off and half of the precious milk spilled to the ground. The good fortune of it. For Thomas threw his arms about me and prayed against the demon until the pail subsided and mysteriously was filled again. And I became the vessel in agitation. I barely heard his words.

"Shame, for you didn't bless the empty pail to banish the demon, CuRoi. But I cannot punish you for this, since you have already sinned and are not of the company. But know . . ." He held me tighter and I was without breath. "But know when you leave here to join the world that on the edge of everything there is danger and evil. For everything sunlit there is shadow. You must not lose courage." Then we stood quietly together, my arms around his waist, his around my back, and I was very small and very safe and there was shadow nowhere. How distorted were our perceptions.

He looked up to the sky and spoke in a different voice.

"I see you again in a new time, CuRoi, I see you returned. Have faith." And then broke away from me.

It was three weeks I was allowed to stay in the barn. The Lord provided milk and mild weather and Archie's wife sent blood puddings and custards on the camel and my brothers with stony faces and sorrow-filled eyes walked around me to the chapel where I sat on the steps and ate grass six times a day. I called out to be forgiven, to remain, and promised anything except the child in exchange.

On the last night, a dreamless sleep I slept in the dry hay with the infant next to me and he did not wake for milk but slept without a noise. A barn cat purred softly, the infant breathed softly, the night stirrings of the cows were rhythmic again, and I slept. And at the end of my sleep, washed by my sleep, I woke to electric buzzing and thought I was in my own cell and safe. But, no. Nicholas was shaving the brindled hindquarters of a milking cow, and I turned on my side and looked at my infant and there was no infant, no gurgling sweetness, no fat arms and legs aswim in the air, no angelic cheek.

"Nicholas!"

He turned stubbornly to his task. He knew.

"Where is the infant?"

As a beast I clawed through the hay to the cold of the concrete floor and found nothing except wet blood in a clump of hay and took the dreadful hay and pushed it to Nicholas's face. He turned off the razor.

"We are under oath not to speak to the excommunicant."

"For the love of God, Brother . . ."

"The will of the Lord." His voice dropped, his head hidden against the soft flank of the brindled cow. "I will speak to the cow. Who hears, hears. Those who speak to the excommunicant suffer his penalty. The cow Twenty-nine loosed herself last night and stepped on the infant. I found

it this morning and buried it in clay. She rolled it away,
licking it for the salt. I am sorry. The blood is all our blood."

"Nicholas . . ."

"You have God."

Malice and envy burned in his eyes.

"You let him die. You let the cow loose!"

"It is also possible that Eldred did, to save you."

"Eldred?"

"It is possible," he told the cow. "Anything is possible.
Except the excommunicant staying, that is impossible."

And he left.

I sank into the hay, holding the bloody pack of straw to
my mouth. When the Abbot came, yellow Wellingtons shuffling under his robes, I could not speak. He sat heavily on
a barn stool at my feet.

"Hear, O Israel, the Lord our God, the Lord is One, Lord
of Justice; Lord of Mercy. Hear me, Lord, and give me the
power to help the tormented. Give me a light to guide him
to a new life. Save CuRoi from the Devil within."

We sat together many hours. I prayed silently. I prayed
to have the child in my arms. My head was hard and heavy
and fell often.

"You tremble with guilt, my son."

"Not guilt, Holy Father," I dared.

His lips barely moved as he prayed. My tongue cleaved
to my mouth, my jaws locked. The cows, untended and
swollen with milk, complained. He looked at the floor or at
the roof but not in my eyes, and when he did, at once his
prayers stopped. His hands clenched the rough wood of
the stool.

"Your cassock, why is it wet?" He spoke, this man of
belief, with disbelief.

"Tears."

"No." He shook his head slowly. "Your cassock is wet

149

as my mother's shirtwaist when she nursed her babies. This
I see." And he leaned forward shuddering and reached to
me as he had on the beach and one eye was filled with
sweetness and the other with fear and he touched the spots
wet with milk on my cassock and very gently he placed his
hand in the soft hollow between my full breasts and looked
at me. I could feel his soul to my roots.

"It was you then on the beach?"

"Yes."

He leaned his head against the flank of the old Abbot's
cow who stood watching us, the sweetest cow, and stroked
her and wept into her flesh, buried his sorrow in her side
as if it were I.

"Ah, God, I owe you my life then."

We prayed until the cows howled and Justus came to the
door, but the Abbot motioned him away. And the brothers
sang around us beyond the barn and the bells rang on and
on and the jackdaws screeched and the cows moaned and
I at last told him.

"I love you, Thomas. I shall always love you."

"No," he shouted in all his power, powerless. "Away.
Away from me. Come no closer." Cords and knots swelled
on his neck and behind his eyes and he knew my truth and
his own and he leaped away from me and flung himself
against the wall of the stall, his arms spread. Cows bellowed.
He flung himself with such force pails and ropes, orches-
trating the immeasurable disgust, fell from their hooks and,
I know now, but I did not know then, the longing he felt
for me. All of my soul drained. My bones loosened from
their sockets, my liquids seethed without course, I came
undone, as empty as the infant's rags were empty and sank
to my knees to the hay. In the fingers of a moon beam of a
larger lunacy than I had ever imagined, I crept toward his
Wellingtons as he beat his head against the wall. He tried,

I know, to touch my head, to comfort me, but he couldn't comfort himself. A faltering, a thrusting of hands. He could not. Blinded by the darkness of my own tears and his disgust, I turned and ran from the barn, past its flower pots, past the workshop, far into the fields. He called to me, following. I could hear as he called "CuRoi, CuRoi," his voice breaking in the wind. It was not my name. He called long into the night for me as I raced over the sharp-edged stones to the back of the island, to the beach where I heard the vipers whistling for female eels and the females sliding from the sea, sliding across the sand to writhe as I writhed but I writhed alone as he called into the night and I writhed in pain as my bones and my skin and my spine and my self and my hands and my fingers and my heart hardened in agony and I bit my lips so as not to call out to him or any other and I crawled into the cave of an uprooted tree trunk as if it were an empty skull, its nerves and brain torn, as mine, from the matrix of its life, and I felt my jaws stretching, my eyes rounding, my nostrils spreading, my teeth digging at my gums, my tongue pulling and pulling until I was myself, at last, a cow, and I could stay. With a cry I answered Thomas on the night—a long deep howl.

What grief is this upon the land? What grief is this upon me? I, black-mouthed and club-footed with foul juices on my tongue and dung streaming from my beyond, see the world now, strange, misshapen, from new eyes stretched

151

out of my terror and the world is terrible, deformed, and I from tooth to tail deformed and the sun. And the skull of the sky threatens and each cloud shifts in the cut-glass light of the dying sun and in my new bones a heavy foreboding that I am to be swallowed by the night. How long shall I be a cow?

I know only that I can remain in the monastery near Thomas. I will not leave. The I, the Cow I, the Not I, the esse and non-esse, all of us will remain, the new pattern of patterns, whatever is left of me, pattern upon pattern, two suns, two worlds suspended. And I alone on the lonely shore.

I howled and the last light fled. I howled for Thomas. It was John Joe who answered.

Silver-plumed and angry and deep the sea as John Joe climbed, braying his alleluias for his fear, beating whacking at bush and boulder in the sable cloth of night, tearing the dune grasses as he pulled his way up the cliff, the grasses shrieking and I crashing four-footed along the ridges and finally he found me, not Celeste, not CuRoi, all he found, dear fool with his fool's laugh and his farts and his dirty fingers, was a cow collapsed in a bloody thicket and he crying for his friend CuRoi and tearing strips of wool from his ragged jacket and braided a tether with his gypsy fingers, he did, and led me, on the night, not Celeste, not CuRoi, with my new horns ripping the thickets in anger and my new fur tangling in burr and burdock and my new legs folding and I, weak with fury, weak with loss, leaking and weeping stones from every part of me, my language gone, my fingers gone, he led me over beach and bracken to the monastery lands and tether-pegged me to the dry limbs of the Tree of Life. And ran off, I suppose, to tell someone and forgot.

So. I who was a woman and yesteryear a child, who wore

feathered slippers and skipped along paths of shining blue stones and danced in the red silks of my father's loom and rhymed and laughed and dreamed, I have made of me, somehow, a wee cow, a white cow.

My body rises as a wall eclipsing my sentences. My ideas huddle behind me. My words limp after me. I am silenced. I have no fingers. I have no toes.

"Surrender yourself to God," Generous said. "God will save you. Give Him your reason, give Him your mind. God help you, CuRoi. What wickedness lurks there in you that will not surrender? *He* is the Creator. You are only the creature."

And my father said, "Celeste, my child, there is no truth but your own. There is no ultimate but yourself. You are your own poem. Write, Celeste, sing. Sing your own song."

Sorrow hums in my head. The sky threatens and each cloud shifts its shape into one more terrible than the last and cormorants form swarthy equations on the limbs of the Tree of Life and even they fly off in a large black trembling triangle. And I tethered to the Tree, caught up in the curtains of Highland snow, I who thought I was a miracle, am not. Rough mead and mountain are deep in mist. Archie's chains clink in the fog as he ferries the dead Kings across. I turn on my tether around the Tree. I spin and unspin. I, Heaven, beat a circle into the earth. It is perhaps why I have become this cow.

I

LT IS SOON TOLD.
I, GENEROUS, CHRONICLER, WRITE OF THE COMING OF THE WEE
COW.

Noble and wonderful is the Lord of the Elements. Noble
and wonderful the creatures of the deep. Good and blessed
our brothers. Comely the cow led down from Dun Hi.

The grebe sounds its bugle note, breaking loud, gleeful,
clear, high in triumph over the uproar of blue-black wind
and angry sea, exulting in the storm. Close-gathered, the
company of brothers sings meekly from their flagstones in
the abbey. Melt the Heavens they do and move the Great
Wheel in its place. Their psalms rise.

And through the beaded curtains of snow, the young

Abbot, Thomas, on his rounds, a cone of flame in scarlet wools, Thomas comes. Tall he is and holy and twisting he is against the wind, stiff-necked, flowing, a hero's brow, radiant, strong, open-faced, dark, lean, a man of royal blood, long his Druid line, great his gentleness. Along the cobbled Street of the Dead he walks between stone walls, low below the thrust of the Mountain of God. The scarlet hems of his robe lift puffs of snow over dull black shoes. He stops under the Tree of Life, kisses the hem of his sleeve, and touches with the blessed cloth the Tree. He climbs to the Hill of the Angels and holds discourse there with Those descended. He prays for the souls of the departed Kings at the Ridge of Kings and turns again onto the bitter white strand to watch against the high-browed barques in the great angry sea. How he watches the night for us, that there should be not one extra portion of dark. How he counts the hours that there should be all the promised portions of light. The Abbot bends his heavy head, lifts his head, spins in the wind, his warrior palms support the very Vault of Heaven. Spins, his elbows bent and the scarlet hems of his long sleeves dip in great curves to the snow, painting runes. He stretches his arms east and west, north and south, a spinning Tau, he is. He takes the wind with him. He is flame. The spirits of rocks, of trees, of plants come unchained and dance behind him.

The curtains part. Thomas looks up sharply from the White Strand of the Martyrs and sees a shape. Lord, Lord. He looks up to the ragged ribs, he does, of Dun Hi where the cow stands. Thomas sees the woman, naked, flowing at the shore. He looks and covers his eyes. He turns back and sees her shaggy whiteness against the sudden violet of the sky, the gleam of stars in her Viking horns, the silk of her long hair drifting in the wind. The sheep complain of a stranger.

"Is it you?" he calls. The sky closes in answer and he, with a fist, hits his own forehead. "The Devil swallow you sideways!"

Pebbles cascade.

"You are a woman!" he shouts in a voice to raise even the yellow-backed sea monsters. "The Devil does battle with holy men by means of woman!" And crosses himself. "May he make a night's work of your foul neck!"

"Alleluia!" answers the Amadan from the peak. "Sun, Moon, Alleluia!" His voice, as the grebe, triumphant, exultant.

And a silken-haired, shaggy beast, small, with fine proud curving horns and the veil of cow hair falling between her horns over her eyes to her nose and fur to her feet, a long sullen tail sweeping snow behind her, her belly star-speckled, emerges, slips down the mountainside, snorting white, hot bread clouds of fear, turning again and again to look behind her at the moon and the Amadan dragging her down, doggedly, laughing with glee.

A fragrant strong apple is he, Thomas. Before, a hero he was, in stone-casting, in lifting the race ring, in battle. Now, the Abbot falls on his knees and thanks God for deliverance from temptation.

Noble and wonderful is the Lord of the Elements and let no man change what has been written.

— GENEROUS

In the night, the wind was shining and wet as a bird's back. Petrels whistled and clucked and the night cleared and the moon at last spread before me and very late, Thomas came. He carried a bale of hay and a pail of water and tied a green-gold tassel on my horn. My moon shadow and Thomas's moon shadow and two of us under the moon. Oh, Thomas, the word for moon is Sin and Sin means All-Embracing and Lamentation and One, the Other of the sun. Sin is the name of the moon. Our shadows fused on the sand in a new corpus.

He stroked my side. His breathing was hard. His breath subsided. His stroke slowed. At last he spoke.

"Well, now, what song can I sing to you?"

Do you wait for an answer, Thomas?

"A song for a woman? For a girl? For a cow? Something

behind your eyes, something in the sadness draws me. How is it a beast is sad? Does something yearn in you as it does in me? Can souls be wounded?"

He held his fine head against my back. Yes, Thomas, sing to me of your wounded soul and I shall tell you of the orchid creatures we share and my own longings.

"Is it some ontological given, a wound in the soul that reaches to the core of the Cosmos? Have *I* violated something in myself? A yawing slash of impurity . . . or is it a slash of the pure in the bedrock of impurity? I love this cow. Yes. I love this cow." His voice was at a whisper. I heard despair.

"I lust. I desire. Am I wounded in such a way by my passion—a wound that flies deep to my center and reaches out to some sort of metaphysical depravity? Is it the Universe wounded? Well have I fornicated, murdered, decimated clans, stolen cows, holy books, relics . . . yet this troubles me more. I know it is sin and I know it is not sin."

Sin is knowledge, Thomas. And the moon is wisdom. It reflects in the darkness of Sin and shines on the night. Poor Thomas. You are thinking in opposites as I must now walk. In straight lines and balances. The Devil flies in straight lines, Thomas, which is why we build mazes to keep him out.

"And there is some knowledge in you, isn't there?" His stroke quickened. He looked at me.

I turned my head away.

"From what mysteries do you spring? And so oddly at this time of schism between monastery and Rome? Have you come of miracle to lead the way to free will? Have you come because I need you? Will you reunite Church and monastery or split us apart?"

I may have come to bring the circle of Heaven into the square of earth. I may have come because I have been dreamt elsewhere. I may have come because I have been punished. I who wanted to be Creator have become more creature. I know not why I'm here, Thomas. I did not choose.

"You reach for me, don't you? I feel that. Even now as you turn away. How can we break through the veils of consciousness between us?" He stood to leave and I dared to turn and look at him.

He stood rubbing me, he trembling in hand and thigh, and then caressing and brought the orchid creature alive in me and I felt him gripping the hairs on my side and pressing the knot of himself up against me and into me and moaning in terror and ecstasy and I howling in the pulse of his body. Behind me on the sand his head rose between my horns as a lunar disc and he calling, "No! No!" And he sinking to his knees, clasping himself and rocking in pain on the ground and there was nothing I could say to him. Finally he moved away into the night, back to the peat fires of the abbey and his world, and I was left with mine. Why was it so painful for him and my father? And why so sweet for me?

The sunfires fell on the sea as silk, on the strand, on the pastures, the abbey, and then the barn. It fell, the sun, on the flanks of Dun Hi and on the Western Sea at the Back of the Beyond and it was day.

"Hey, diddle diddle." Sweet and gentle Justus, saintly Justus. I wake to his voice, singing on the morning. "A diddle, a diddle, a diddle a doo, cum wi me my loving cu." It is day and the face of the sun is deformed.

And I a cow.

And now John Joe, braying on the morning, comes down the path leading the old Abbot's cow. The same Thirty-three, the same path, and yet the face of the sun is deformed, but for sure and certain, as Generous would say, it is the Amadan and the old Abbot's cow and John Joe drops the bar of the monastery gate as he does every morning and leads the cow over the meadow to the sea-shore where she stands alone, her head hung low, the tassels on her horn torn and faded, her body collapsed in the center as if her heart had dropped through. A sad shadow of herself she is. The sun shines through her bones.

Sin/sun. Sin is the name of the moon. And sinser means older, the old man in the moon? And osser means younger. Osiris. Where are these thoughts coming from? They feel given. They fly into my head from the edges of things. Sin is Seth. Seth is One. The sun, Osiris, day, that is Two. Is this how cows think?

Things—tree, sky, cloud—are different, hot-blooded they are, many-colored, many-shaped, immediate, shimmering without boundaries. Yet all familiar, not deformed. And the face of the sun deformed. And I a cow. Did I strike the wrong note on the Aeolian harp? And become this form? Frequency creates form, does it not? My father taught me that if I struck a tuning fork with a 440 frequency, the A strings on a piano would vibrate and the A strings on a piano in the next room would vibrate as well as a 220 string and an 880 string. All the octaves would take note, and if my tuning fork were large enough, there might be resonances and reciprocals all over the world. I wonder if I am such a resonance created from such an original pluck of a string or ring of a tuning fork, of an ineffable A? *Have* I been dreamt elsewhere? Or am I the result of an event that is a result of me that is a result of and so on across space/time, always attached, always reacting, never an event myself, never a locality, never my own story, never my own tears? Or am I my own maker, autopoetic, self-organizing, Creator, not creature? The right note, Celeste. And all the others will harmonize. If I have been determined, who plucked? And if my will is free, what am I to do with it? The herd is coming through the bar now with the largest cow leading. They move over the meadow toward the shore and they come closer to me.

John Joe looks up to me, peg-tethered, and comes to bless me as I have taught him but there is nothing now in his eyes that knows me. Yet he stands with me as the dragon chain of cows crosses before us, sluggish, rolling, insolent, stupid, gigantic, coiling, dappled, thick. A single chain of flesh, hoof, horn. A beast, this oneness, this herd, they pass me under the Tree, sniff at me with suspicion. Their snorts bellow on the morning cold. Steam rises from their backs as they pick their way down the narrow path toward the White Strand of the Martyrs.

John Joe drops the bar and runs off as if he'd forgotten something. From the abbey tower a cloud of hoodies unfolds, arranges itself in couplets and triplets on the backs of the cows, and the cows, their hooves buried in the low tide, their tags tinkling in the wind, bend their heads to fatten their great selves on the fresh dulce and tangle of ebb tide. How strange they seem and yet, for now, I am one of them.

One note on the Aeolian harp, Celeste, and all the rest will harmonize. I raise my head and lengthen my neck and call to the herd below me. Stiff with disdain, they turn at my discordance and examine me. It is clearly the wrong note. "I, O," I call. Io, I, O. I have changed myself. A ten, the last note beyond the ninth. Io equals jo, Jove, a name of God, the word joy, yo is I. Crows laugh above me, raucous and insulting. Haw, haw, they scream. This cowness is neither joy nor jubilee. But if it has something to do with I and O, with the end, it may also have something to do with a beginning.

I wonder if Adam once plucked such a wrong note and made us sinners forever, mooning for something we only half-remember? Am I a sinner? Have I fallen? Was Adam a mere bad example in the zeitgeist? Am I?

I repeat my call and the herd climbs the sandy cliff toward me. If you castrate the words, cut off the first letters of words, enlighten them, you will find inner secrets. Sinner, winner, inner, dinner, WWW, wictim, wictual, wictory, die and dine. I cling to my knowledge as they approach. I am surrounded by gargantuan meats. And surely, frightened of me, the cows close the circle, touching shoulders, a solid steaming line of equipment. Their eyes enlarge and whiten and roll. The largest one, wearing the number Twenty-nine, heavy and mean with muddy eyes and an International Harvester body, solid gears, chains, axles, fenders, valves, pistons, tyrannical, her face fixed with muscle and bone, blocks the morning sunlight. I turn toward her. She moves toward me until our noses touch and our horns interlock and she presses her forehead against mine. Eyelashes brush each other. Brutally she presses until my head hurts.

And I remember waking under the pile of dead and dying cormorants. "Father, my head hurts."

"The true task is to ask the silence," my father answered.

I ask the silence. Why a cow? Why a descent? From one end of me shit collapses, detaches. From the other end language thuds into the soil, absorbing itself, absorbing metaphor, this metamorph, ridding myself of words which fix, of sentences which sentence, of stories which imprison. In the silence I hear them fall. Words collapse, sink, intensify, grow dense. The beast of a cow presses against my head, squeezing them out. Categories disintegrate. Language trembles. Words remain but the webs of their meanings drift away.

This can't be God's mind any longer, he who fixes orbits and proportion, who sets seasons, the means, and the measures, galloping about like this without structure. It is a new mind for me and I cannot remember what mind I had before. The cow pressing against me wears a tag. It tinkles in my breath. Her son, a sleek black bull, presses against my side. At last, the great cow Thirty-three comes down from her lonely spot and stands next to me, facing my adversary until both son and mother back away from me and turn to the dulce and sweet tangle at the sea edge. I am a cow and I am not a cow.

I

T IS SOON TOLD.

I, GENEROUS, CHRONICLER, WRITE OF THE SEARCH FOR THE OR-
IGIN OF THE WEE COW.

The Abbot called us to himself and blessed us and assured
us that the stranger, even the cow, is God Himself, and the
monastic rule is celebration when a guest arrives. And indeed we feasted the next day and drank thick milk and
honey. And as the brothers worked joyously in the field
and I in the scriptoire, up the narrow stairs came the wee
cow, in a great tendehary of a noise, came into my library.
Dust rose. Slate slabs crashed to the floor and shattered.
She lay her head on my very lap and I shouted for the others
and four of us could not turn her about and finally we
greased the beast with butter and pulled and pushed her

164

backward down the narrow stairs, so stubborn, so determined she was. Altogether a strange and unlikely beast. Where her head had lain on my cassock were wet spots as if she had wept. Nicholas denied this and said it was the dust of the ancient books burning her barbaric eyes.

Then she approached the altar and so horrified the brothers that she was beaten with the backs of holy books until she galloped out and stood before the abbey, head hung low and, one might think, in shame.

When the three days of the guest rule were expired and the abbey itself nearly so, she was led to the edge of the rath, but we could not drive her off. We turned away and each time she followed us and each time we beat her with our staffs. The Abbot's eyes remained gentle as he pushed her over the rath, but his lips were thinner and tighter as if something needed to be said, but could not be. As hard as he pushed, well-matched they were, the two of them, Abbot and cow, the harder she pushed back, and at last, close to Vespers, we left her standing there, the golden rays of the sun lighting her and some of us were sorry. And some of us were not. She watched us depart and followed after us, daintily, and Thomas tied with her a rowan-wood fetter to the Tree of Life below the abbey.

Thomas himself tied two young wethers to the Rocks of Ordination and there stood in cross vigil, arms outstretched, and called, he did, to Seth. Diarmat, novice, was sent by Nicholas to spy. Shame to say. But when the clouds covered the sun and the land trembled, Diarmat fled. The Abbot returned without explanation, without the wethers, and it is said that he did not sleep on his pallet again but sat up through the night. As for Diarmat, the Abbot cut off the novice's hand for a fortnight and then, controlling his own warrior reactive character, sained the hand and it became whole once again.

The wethers were devastated and flattened as the patches of lichen on the rocks and neither beast nor fowl would take from their flesh or their bones, for the smell of Seth, of Life-Death, surrounded them. An offering refused was an omen of dread. Nicholas as Bishop sat with Thomas and in discord harried the fate of the cow. Thomas felt the cow must join the herd and begin a new line with a bull soon coming from Spain. But Nicholas most steadfastly did not. I, Generous, spoke for the ancestral lineage of the herd.

"It has been with us for a great thousand years. As ancient as the brotherhood of monks, as ancient as the camel given us by Simon Magus, as pure as the purest among us. A noble line. What nobility has the new cow? What father, what mother?"

"Perfect proportions, she has," argued Thomas. "We can begin a new line with her."

"A cow is as good alive or dead." Nicholas was overly opposed and one could not imagine why. "I insist we query Rome. This is not a simple matter of white cows, small cows, large cows, milk production. If the cow is supernatural . . ."

"Why do you say that, Nicholas?"

"Do not play innocent with me, Thomas." Nicholas stood, clasped hands behind his back, and walked to the narrow cut of window. "To know if the cow is supernatural, we tie it down with stones. If she is supernatural, she will rise. Then we query Rome. I myself will travel."

"Rome. Rome. Rome. You give them your mind."

The cow was tied down with stones and rubber tires just as hay mounds are secured against wind. Good rope was slung over her until she stood beneath a net. Neither rise nor escape she did but looked at us with eyes that struck more than one of us as amused.

She was not supernatural, but surely, we all argued with

each other when we could, low and hidden, she is not an ordinary cow.

After Matins, the most holy Father Thomas, sad-faced, clench-jawed, his eyes painted in triangles of black and circles of cobalt, his right hand heavy with rings, his left of intolerable radiance, encased in silver, climbed as he did every morning, fair or foul, to the rock knoll of the Hill of the Angels and there held discourse with those Angels descended on the Light and then carried his staff to the great boulder at the Hill of the Seat and ministered to the monsters, yellow, wan and wide-mouthed, in poetry that calmed the waves. And from the Hill of the Seat, he descended with the peplum of care about his eyes and saw indeed in the light of morning the cow tied to the Tree of Life and eating its old figs, and sent Nicholas to find the Amadan. Went quickly he did, Nicholas, always obedient without, disobedient within, found the Amadan and when the Amadan was brushed and straightened about, Nicholas led him directly to the Abbot. The Abbot leaned from the half door of his rock cell, sained John Joe in iodine with a swan quill, and instructed him to journey to the crofters' lands and inquire after a white cow and trade ointment of healing for bags of lentils from Archie's wife and carry back the papers from the tourist boat. John Joe rolled his eyes in fear.

Why John Joe felt fear for the journey was this: the ground between the monastery lands and the crofters' lands was freezing and a thin tablecloth of lineny snow lay over the Marsh of the Dog, and by nightfall of his return the Marsh of the Dog would be frozen and too dangerous for the brittle ancient ankles of the camel and so John Joe would have to lead the camel in a circle about the edges of the island, along the edges of the lands of Darkness, at the edge of the Valley of the Black Pig, into the wastelands on the western side of the island by the way of the Beyond. But a good man, John Joe, awful as it would be, he buckled the leather bags around the camel's middle and took the blessing of the Abbot upon his head, a blessing for the safety of the camel, for the safety of the Amadan, for the safety of all wayfarers. He left the yard of the monastery in a bright morning and, climbing over the rath, turned himself to the south end of the island. "Poor John Joe. Run, John Joe. Have bowels, John Joe," the brothers called as he left. "Have bowels and run while you have the light of life lest the darkness of death overtake you."

Brother Nicholas went to the noble stones of marble in their basins at the wall of the old abbey and turned the three ancient ones into the course of the sun, the rising sun of Osiris, deaseal their direction, to bless John Joe. And then he turned the three noble stones tuathal, against the course of the sun, the setting sun of Set, to stay his dread hands when John Joe passed near him. And then, when no one saw, except I, myself, Generous, Nicholas fell on his knees and prayed to Christ, for in Christ only, not in the Old Ones nor in their Ineffable Father, was the true and narrow heart of Nicholas, friend of the Pope.

— GENEROUS

I have gone where neither my name nor my language will follow me. Wherever I am. Oh, Thomas.

With my tether trailing behind me and my ideas limping after me, I go where I dared not go before. From the rath, across the cobbles. My hooves clack like a mill. I hush my ideas. Along the Street of the Dead. How does one tiptoe? How does one smile? With my nose I push open the door of the Abbot's cell and stand still quieting my stomachs, snuffing my smells, feeling my power, sudden and raw in me, and I hear his deep exhausted breathings and find him on his pallet and lie down beside him in the dark and in his sleep he turns to me and flings, as a drowning man, an arm over me and buries his head in the long fur of my neck and, restless, turns further into me, becomes smaller, holds my head in his hands. My legs are tucked under me.

I have made some kind of leap. For I lie in Thomas's arms as a woman. I have created this idea and made it flesh. I love him. I am comforted. Hear, O Israel, the Lord is One and His name is One. Not one God but the number One.

Night, Not. I listen to him breathe through the night. Night is Naught, is None, is Not. It is the darkness from which all form springs forth into the day, Thee. The necessary darkness, radiant. There is None before Thee. Deva, Devil, Deus. Enlighten the D and there is Evil, Eve. And Eve is Night. Day and Night. Night and Day. There is One and there is Two. Day is Two is du is thee, the sun of God. He stirs. I breathe on him evenly and softly and he sleeps again. There is only One and Two. Everything exists between One and Two. I exist more than I have ever existed before because I am close to the darkness which is Sin, which is One, which is Not-One.

At Lauds he opens his eyes slowly and looks into mine. There are golden flecks in the blue and I look into his and watch the flecks and it is wilderness, the first day in the garden when One became Two and Two became One and he sees identity, me, not distortion, but then he blinks and is out of Paradise.

Identity is gone. There is distortion—horror, disgust, shame and sin. It is the moon, Thomas. You are jumping it with me. And he leaps upright, gropes for a black shoe, and beats me about the face. Sin is the name of the moon. Sin is a word for One, Sin means all-embracing. Embrace me! And I step down hard with my hoof upon his naked foot until he calls out in pain and there is blood on his foot and on his shoe but I will not release him—no more than either of us will ever be able to release ourselves from each other. He shouts and shoves at my heft until Eldred and Muncas Bent-Neck arrive in the dark with torches and beat at me with the holy rod and staff and I lift my foot from Thomas's blue foot and go after Eldred but I am beaten off with the staff and Nicholas arrives. Thomas holds the torch before me as one does to frighten a beast. I don't offer him a blink. He is astonished. He knows. Somewhere he knows.

They are all shouting. "Hoo! Hoo! There. Hoo! Out of here. Hoo!" Watch the W's. And I am delirious with love and identity and I with my horn drill Eldred through a rib to the wall of the cell, wounding him like the Christ. "Hoo! Hoo!" For my infant brother.

Thomas lies. "She came into my cell at Lauds."

"A devil of a cow. . . ." They are dodging my spreading horns and I am tormenting them. Oh, Thomas, see me again. See me. Violence is the other side of language, Thomas, the other side of God. Thomas, see me. Look into my eyes again. I speak to you. Look in my mouth. I cry out. Look and see if the name of God is written on my tongue as it is written on the side of Adam and on the wings of Gabriel and on the seal of Solomon. Smell of me and tell me if I reek of musk and speak to me of my holiness!

Muncas and Nicholas have my tether. Thomas beats my rear with the rod. Shit drops. Eldred drops dead. Words drop onto the flagstones of the Abbot's holy cell. Deva, Devil, Deus, Two. Thomas has wisps of my hair, white and silken, twisted in his hair, black and thick. He pulls one from his mouth and Generous with blowfish eyes comes running and takes the tether from Nicholas and I, who am about to run Nicholas through, am relieved and allow Generous to take me into the faint and startled starlight back to the Tree of Life.

He takes me and I follow dancing. Olympic, O limbic, O limbo, limp on. My fingers, my language, my reason is gone.

I am near the Other Side. And I dance in the moonlight among the boulders. Four-footed I dance twice as much. There is a new wakefulness in me, a large understanding in my long bones and thicknesses. Conductors of myself listen, listening in the electric night to all the things that are not yet.

I

T IS SOON TOLD.

I, GENEROUS, CHRONICLER, IN MY SECOND SIGHT, WRITE OF
JOHN JOE'S JOURNEY.

Down the Mountain of God came the camel and the Amadan, down over the hidden causeway, sedgy now in the
morning dews and easier, over marsh and meadow and
millrun with the camel wheezing, dragging, swaying, and
John Joe prodding and pushing. Cold were his feet, John
Joe, and heavy his thoughts but it was light walking and
the sky china-blue and a mavis singing her unbroken song
from a boulder and sheep with slack faces and golden eyes
calling insults from their ledges until John Joe stopped to
sing his alleluias up at them and leap away, they did, and
the alleluias pirouetted and echoed back at him from all the

173

rocks. Over the spillway, he came, over the crossing stones. When the camel eased herself on the path, John Joe tied his sandals about his neck and hopped from steaming warmth to warmth behind her haunches as they went along and John Joe forgot about the night ahead because his feet were warm and the sky was china blue and he was sure to get a blood pudding from Erca Flatnose and the blood pudding always smelled just as his auntie in Glasgow smelled.

A decent man, John Joe, he washed his feet in the icy waters of the mill race and followed the village stream down past the dead winter-brown gardens, through the gates of the ruined nunnery where the stubborn camel pulled at dry nasturtiums that snapped "Hurry, John Joe, hurry," as they came loose and John Joe tugging at the tether. Over the stile they went, along the path to the harbor, to the poor thatched bothies, to the husbandmen and the husbandmenwives, to ask after the white cow.

But when Archie the Ferry Man told them John Joe was coming down the Mountain of God with the camel and that the bags were empty of bones, Tolua the Tall, Caw Flathead, Cadoc of the Crooked Hand, Archie the Ferry Man, and Archie's wife, Erca, leaned their blackthorn sticks against the low frames of their doorways, put a rock at the kick wheel of the grinding quern, tied a knot in their looms, took their big hands from the pockets of rough trousers and hide aprons, and watched in the distance the Amadan and the camel picking their way across the stones from the monastery on the Mountain of God.

The Amadan's hee-haw had sailed down the path before him and when he came upon Tolua the Tall and Cadoc and the rest of them, a dumb crambo they were playing, on their fours, braying like mules, teasing, and John Joe dropped to his fours mooing, without sound, mooing with his lips pushed forward, the crofters braying, laughing and kicking at him and each other. Crawl, he did, between the thick legs of the crofters, displaying for them the silkiness and length of the cow, but the men hee-hawed even while his hands drew for them the lovely turns of the cow's legs and delicate feet and how her belly was high and firm and didn't slope back and forth and the haunches, high, splendid, upright, and the waterfall of hair between the sharp horns. A wee cow, he showed them with his hands, with a comely, sullen little face and horns like a new moon and pointed, he did, to the whiteness of their raw wool stockings and thrust his moos at them while they poked dirty fingers into John Joe's fool chest and fool belly and brayed like mules and bounced John Joe between them, cruelly, and John Joe, pleased for the fun but hurting to remember his own mule passed on, he wept against the ragged hocks of the old camel for his silver-gray mule.

It was Erca who kicked her man, Archie, in the ankle. "A cow, Archie. The fool's telling about a cow."

They stood upright. "A white cow?"

They looked at each other. "Ginger, they are, John Joe. The cows. Ginger."

Caw pointed to the machair where their own hardy cattle stood ginger, cut out of the late wine sky.

Archie, who had been across the Sound, said, pointing to Mull, "There lives not a white cow. Here lives not a white cow."

John Joe looked into each of their faces, scrutinizing with his half brain. The crofters shook their heads. They knew nothing of a stray cow, nothing of a white cow. But Archie's wife gave John Joe the blood pudding that tasted as his auntie's flesh smelled and Caw and Cadoc took the ointment of healing from him and spilled lentils into the wicker saddle bags and Erca made notches in her accounts and gave John Joe a bundle of papers and tied a rag for luck on the camel's tether.

"Unborn," added Tolua. "A cow unborn is the start of the evil."

"Oh, and couldn't she been swimming over from Mull?" they asked Archie. Archie looked out at the weave of turquoise and purple waters.

"A good swimmer, Archie. Aye? Maybe she came over in your boat." They laughed at Archie's fear. "With the others."

Archie shrugged. "Cows on Mull are ginger. All of them. No such thing, a white cow in the islands. Strange things what happen with cows coming up from the sea. Ah, but wouldn't that be a fine thing out, a white cow with long hair and horns like a new moon. A beauty of a cow. A fine thing out."

Erca spat on the ground between them. "You don't be crossing those stones. You don't even set your mind to crossing those stones." And turned to yell over her shoulder. "You do the potatoes yet, Archie?" The husbandmen were already chewing on their pipes and dreaming as John Joe pulled the camel to her feet.

"Four ditches," Caw, sighing, told Archie. "Mother, wife, potato, grave."

"A white cow, a beauty of a cow." Archie, bowed with gout and stained with tobacco juice, hobbled off to his square of soil and sand crossed by washlines and draped with the quilts and the rough linens of the croft come out in the clean cold wind. He bent to feeble rows of potatoes.

"Mind, John Joe," Caw Flathead and Cadoc Crooked-Hand called to the Amadan. "Go by way of the Dog Marsh in this cold and you break the legs off that ugly beast."

"Off with you, John Joe," Tolua the Tall called. "Off to

the monks we cannot see and tell the holy brethren that to them we cannot see belongs the cow we cannot see."

"And everything else what we cannot see!" Archie shouted from his potatoes. And for that he had good reasons.

Coaxed the obstreperous camel, he did, John Joe, past the graveyard nasturtiums, over the stile, and along the winding of Nut Creek. Across the belly of the island he went, and with one hand he ate blood pudding and with the other threw lentils at the sheep. Down he went over the middle moors, over the low moors, around the four brave Rocks of Ordination. Slow he went for slow is the foot on an unknown path and slower still on an unwanted path and the sun was already an hour above the western sea when the camel and the Amadan crossed the stones into the west and entered the thin collar of strand circling the western shore. On John Joe went, witless, throwing his lentils at the shadows overtaking him, around the Port of the Dead Man now and the Cave of the Seaweed Woman. Closer and closer to the Other Side he came with each step and the Seaweed Woman calling to him, weaving her tangle of arms and hair and the sun drowning in the sea, going to Set the sun was, and blue shadows slipping over the cliffs. Sheep with golden eyes leered at him from the blue shadows and leapt with sudden springs and tumults of stone that froze the poor soul's heart. And dismal John Joe reached deeper into the camel's bags and threw large handsful of lentils at the golden eyes of the demon sheep who laughed wildly at him, blinked, folded themselves into the shadows, and clattered off into the new night only to spring forth from other places. And when those sounds were gone and the golden eyes gone and the dear sun drowned in the vat and the pudding in his stomach billowing in waves of terror, the fist of fear gripped his heart and he ran. Breathless he ran, toward the sea. Witless he ran, toward the Beyond. He prayed deep in

177

his head to the Lord of the Elements and squeezed his hams together against the high tight whines behind him for if the Blind Stalker heard but a white breath in the wasteland, the whine of a fart, the murmur of a prayer, he might do to John Joe the same as done to the mule.

Dismal John Joe to have skipped in the camel's dung and thrown stones at the sheep and played the dumb crambo with the crofters for it is darkness now, the sun has gone to Set, and it is their time, the Dark Gods, the men of myrrh and merd and murder and shit and seat and Set, the Fixed One, the men of cutting and the men of the Lord of Privies, of Parts, of Underwear and Underworld, of strangling, the men who mete out the judgments on the souls. Closer and closer with each awful step came John Joe to the strand at the Back of the Beyond until he passed the Port of the Whirlpool and was on the Other Side. There, where black sea meets black sky, sea beasts, lamenting, rise to grapple with the demons and only the red points of their eyes and fiery tongues mark the horizon of hiss and howl. Only the light of his fool's heart had he to bring him across the land where the Blind Stalker could rouse a sending and strangle him, could carve out his tongue and his parts, his heart and his rectum, and turn him inside out. With his fancies on the outside—lungs, stomach, delicate things—and his hide on the inside. And hadn't John Joe seen the sending once at his own shoulder when the mule was killed? Terrible close and came like a living cheese, the sending from the Black One, a violet vapor, the horror that froze into form and sat on a man's face and gripped and grew there and sucked him inside out.

Cold was the sweat on John Joe's back, white his knuckles on the camel's tether, his toes gripping for balance on the slime of the rocks, and the rocks rollicking with him, unsteady beneath him, rolling him backward when he went forward, forward when he went backward, an endless thing, this place of imbalance. All sponge and bladderlocks between his toes and his chest aching while the sea groaned at his shoulder, blackening, loosening, swallowing even the poor prayers of John Joe. Dismal John Joe, alone but for the pounding of his fool's heart.

The Other Side drops away dark and deep-spined into the sea and there is only the narrow path of sand and rockfall for the wayfarer and John Joe throwing his lentils at the darkness and the camel snorting, pulling John Joe back on the tether and in the blackness from the camel's nostrils fear in white balls and a last pair of golden eyes watching them from the tip of the crag above the Back of the Beyond.

A shadow of a shadow of a breath John Joe felt and the moon gone in a gulp and for sure and for certain something was sucking the feet of the Amadan into the sand and the golden eyes watching. Lost the toes. Lost the ankles. Lost the knees. Ah, God. John Joe hurled his head into the neck of the camel and clung to her but the camel was sinking as fast as the fool and he could feel the sending, cold and thick and flying about the two of them, closer and closer, tighter and tighter in circles, cold and silent, and then stopped with John Joe up to his chin in sand and there before him, clear as a black moon at midday, stood the Blind Stalker for who else would it be, hooded, wrapped in the great domino of a cloak, smoking with fires and spices? And grasped the twig of John Joe's arm and John Joe frozen to the spot, looking up at the fiery eye and the black temple and the arms like tree roots notched with the welts and cuttings for the dead and the scarlet bag of tongue tips tied to his belt and the flaming blade smiling at his side and the mouth a grim slit with long and curling teeth and the neck bent and

179

the eyes of him flashing red and gold cinders of cinnabar, the Dread One. Seth.

"Raise thou the stone and find me there. Cleave thou the wood and there I am."

Frozen and the spittle turning to stone on his lips and rolling his eyes. "Moon, Sun," John Joe croaked in that wind of a voice. "Alleluia?" he whined.

The God turned to his voice, blind. And then, the God pulled his domino up about his thighs, huge hams of thighs, dark red flesh pulsing with heat, and crouched, he did, in the sand before the voice of John Joe. Threw over their heads a blanket of black felt and cast a light within and the irises of his eyes cinnabar and hot and John Joe frozen to the spot with only his head and his hands free.

And snapped from his long knotty strangling fingers ten cubes of gold. Nine of them he laid out on the sand before John Joe, three cut red with crackles of fire, three cut blue with whirlpools of sea, three cut green with reeds of music, and spread out the cubes he did, as well as the tenth cube cut only with a brown knot.

And waited for John Joe.

"Alleluia," John Joe whispered.

The Dread One threw the jubilee cube, the tenth, over his shoulder into the sea. And waited for John Joe.

"Alleluia, Alleluia, Alleluia," John Joe shouted as he did at the hours. "Alleluia!" bravely, forcefully, manfully, until the God laughed in rolls of thunder, a great tendehary of a noise it was, a vast, lonely laugh of solitude and up he swept the cubes from the sand, pulled a cerecloth over his blindness, and said to John Joe:

"Tell Thomas the balance is breaking." And swept himself away in the blanket of black felt and John Joe up to his chin in sand and the camel up to his hump, and John Joe sucked sobs of the darkness.

There they were, the holy company at the long table, eating the Sunday stir-about to take the hunger off them till the morning and all their shoes off under the table when Thomas visioned John Joe in the sand and alarmed the brothers. So fast they answered the alarm that none of them put on their shoes but all ran barefoot, hobbled barefoot, on those smooth fine feet of the holy, across the icy rough flags to the oratory, the flock of them, ringing the bells of the brooch and the bells of the hours against the Dread One and the satirist casting curses and the poets casting mists and broke the night, they did, with a sudden, sharp, charming chant for the Amadan stuck in the wasteland, coming through with the camel and stuck there before his appointed time.

A blessing on the hand who holds this book and a blessing on the young Abbot who in his wisdom and his second sight saved the camel and the Amadan and on the brothers who in the fervor of their bells and prayers brought him back to the monastery, a man dead almost from fear, saved he was from a swift and sorrowful spoiling.

They sang plainsong and cast about the camel and the Amadan the White Light of the Christ and freed the bodies from the sand. Even so the living cheese of the sending brushed John Joe's face with its fearsome coldness, circling, until the full power of the prayers was on it and the sending shrunk backward winterward, into the Land of Seth and Saturn, into the land of the judgment. But it may be that the Black One himself called off the sending. The powers of darkness are always about us and we must be always vigilant.

As John Joe watched, the camel's legs folded beneath him in the glamour of the poet's power and grew small and glossy and blue-green in the curtains of the night. For the letter lammed is contained in the letter ghimel and the lammed is a snake and the ghimel a camel and such is the magic of the poets and the wonders of the Word that the camel becomes snake and the snake becomes camel. And when it was done John Joe flung the snake about his neck and the snake wrapped itself on each of the fool's arms and off they went along the edge of the sea northward across the rock where three streams meet, over the Spouting Cave, into the Cairn of the Back of Ireland and over the boundary stones. But still John Joe ran until at last he fell against the heavy oaken door of the old abbey. The snake slipped from his arms, clung for a moment to a pillar, and then slid into the night.

John Joe, good man, washed in the bowls of the kitchenings, washed disorder from his skin, face, hands, feet, and crept on his knees to the cell of Thomas. Behind him, he heard the camel moving along the cobblestones, ungrateful, toward her shelter. The Abbot opened the half-door and sained John Joe once again with the quill, noble and fine, the sign of the cross over John Joe's pale fool head.

John Joe sat on his haunches and rocked on his heels and stuck a dirty finger into the keyhole of the Abbot's cell, into the holy light streaming out in the shape of the Holy Queen, and then sucked his fingers and rocked for a long time.

"And the cow, John Joe?" the seniors asked him in the morning and he tried to tell with his hands that which he could. The Abbot Thomas did not ask, for he already knew.

In the darkness of the cell it was, the conciliatory retreat, lit by candlelight, bread baking on a flat stone, mede in two-handled jugs, far distant from the abbey, the three of us praying together and fixing simple meals and the talk. Thomas stirred his honey and crumbs into a circle on his dish. Nicholas, nodding up and down and sideways, wore his Bishop's ring. I listened. Thomas continued, softly. "Black cows, white cows, the dates of the calendar. Let us discuss these things, Nicholas."

182

"Yes, Your Holiness. And the white cow."

"And change, Nicholas. That is the question. How is it that things change? How is it that we change? By rewriting the law? What is the thrust of evolution? Will or balance?"

"According to the church and of course St. Augustine . . ."

Thomas waved the idea away. "Change, Nicholas, internal transformation." He hit his own chest.

Nicholas nodded up and down and sideways and his tongue darted out, and as he nodded his grin was sudden and sardonic, a twitch of a grin. But he remained silent and respectful.

"Think on this, don't bother me with calendar dates and who appoint Bishops—all your politics, Nicholas. The black cow eats green grass. The green grass becomes white milk. The white milk becomes yellow butter. This is an odd world. An odd world where a break in order may be a rule of life just as order is. Perhaps higher." Thomas lifted his hand half in blessing, half in command. "Tell us, Good Scribe Generous, this holy Bishop and myself, tell us of disorderly things from your books."

"In the annals, a woman births a dog, a child is born with the head of a donkey, a herd of cattle vanishing—"

"Yes, cattle. The Abbot wants to hear about cows," Nicholas said.

Thomas lifted his head sharply. "Yes, cows."

"Of cattle then. A cow grazes on the roof. A cow changes colors. A cow eats men and is imprisoned. A cow licks a stone and finds the relic bones of a saint. A cow is born with silver horns. A cow keeps the Sabbath. Cows speak to each other at Christmas. A fairy in the form of a cow—"

"Take notice!" Nicholas interrupting, set his mouth as if he himself had found the relic bones.

"Shall I go on, Father?"

"Fairy cows . . . have they not red ears, Nicholas?"

"Yes, Father. And often one horn."

"Brothers, what if among us the white cow is a creation of something else, something new?" Thomas asked.

"The fact of the matter is, the white cow has murdered a brother and should herself be killed."

"You speak forthrightly, Brother Nicholas."

"I despise ambivalence in myself."

"And in others, I suspect."

Nicholas looked away. Shake his head about as he would he could not hide from the Abbot's wisdom. I filled bowls with warm mede and the three of us drank solemnly and slowly. Thomas rubbed his chin in thought. Nicholas held his ring to the candlelight. The ruby and he had many faces.

"Are you not curious about the cow, Nicholas?"

"No."

"Nicholas, Nicholas." He berated him gently. "No curiosity? Perhaps she was hatched from a cheese, Brother Nicholas?"

"You make a fool of me, Holy Father."

"Hardly a fool. It is Rome makes a fool of you."

Nicholas's ambition locked his mouth.

"Our work is to win the eternal crown, Nicholas. To perfect ourselves. To change. I have no time for new calendars or the politics of hungry men in Rome and Carthage."

"Can this beast help us in our work then?" Nicholas looked with deep malignity into the Abbot's shadowed face. "Is she easing *your* path?"

There was no answer.

"She reeks of sexuality, Thomas, reeks."

Thomas looked up sharply, then rubbed his neck at the back and I could hear the crack of tension. "I feel she is not ordinary. Not in the order of things. I feel . . . that she is a woman."

Nicholas folded his hands and his head was finally still.

"A woman become a cow? It is not in the order of things. It is a mere bad example, such a descent."

"And was Adam's fall a mere bad example, Nicholas?"

"Rome wouldn't be about enjoying your words, Father."

"Nor shall they, Nicholas, except as you are disloyal. But the cow, do you not sense . . . this difference?"

Nicholas folded his hands but still his tongue darted as if it were an animal. His mouth twitched and his head nodded. "A creature of darkness. Return her to darkness. If you can't bring yourself to kill her . . . then take her to Seth."

"But if she is something else, more than or less than a cow, it is a sign of change of order. That she transformed herself in some way, with some inner force. It is that inner force I want to know . . . perhaps she descended from humanity—"

"By her own *doing*?" I blurted, startled as I was.

"Yes, Generous, either ascending or descending."

"A wonder, by her own doing!" I had been told not to interrupt, but the concept was astonishing. I who had seen so many astonishments.

Nicholas turned on me. "You also, Generous? Know you that man has fallen and cannot find grace except through God through the offices of the Mother Church, not by one's own doing."

Abbot Thomas stood, towering above us both. His shadow loomed. "Human nature is sound and able to attain the Kingdom by free will. All men can answer God's call with yes or with no. Surely, Nicholas, your learned colleagues to the south don't think that grace comes only through Rome to the elect and that the list of elect is predestined? And surely they do not profess that whatever man does in his life means nothing if he has not already been chosen? Surely they would argue that God is, above all, just and everything He creates is essentially good? No?"

"You twist my words, Father."

"No, it is you twisting the Word. You are talking of fatalism under the cover of grace. Aren't there good and holy men outside the Roman Church? In the forests? In the deserts? Saints without and before the office of the Roman Church? What price did you pay with your soul to be appointed a Bishop by the Pope?"

"The Church encompasses all time, future and past."

Thomas would not stop to hear him. "Is it not possible in this cow we bear witness to a miracle—not a singular event, but a new form of intelligence that we must breed and nurture?"

"Breed her lower, you will ruin the strain—whatever your Irish dreaming thinks it is. Higher, you will have a monster."

"Forgive me, Brothers," I begged. "About the cow. Could we not send her to the poor folk on Mull? Perhaps she belongs there. And if not, could she join the herd, just as a cow and let time—"

"No, Scribe and Brother. No." Thomas's color was rising and the anger growing. He had no time for my foolishness. Nor did Nicholas.

"You! You do the work of . . . you enlist the *cow* to prove your pagan heart to Rome, Thomas. This is not about a *cow*. It is about will and grace. It is a dangerous persistence, Holy Father, Thomas. They have warned. Rome considers us preparing for our own damnation as it is, with your stubbornness over the new calendar. Rome speaks of excommunication. They wish you to decline Saturday as the Sabbath and accept a fixed date for Easter."

"Ours are the calendars of the Fathers, of Abraham, Jacob, and Isaac!"

186

Nicholas folded his arms across his chest. Thomas marched about the room and spoke. His voice woke the sea monsters, so loud it was.

"This brotherhood excommunicated? By them? Upstarts. It is *their* sacrilege to say that the Christ died for only some of us but not for all of us. And what of God Himself? God lives in *our* blood, not in Rome's. Listen to me, Nicholas, for they have filled you with lies in exchange for your skull cap. There is no sinful nature. The glories of a man's constitution are his reason and his free will. Excess is the only sin. It is His purpose to make man a Creator. That and that alone is the thrust of evolution!"

"I warn you, Thomas, don't use this excuse of a cow to prove your argument against divine grace, whatever tricks the cow can do, however bright her eyes and soft her parts."

"Holy Fathers," I begged, trying to keep these men at peace for I thought they would kill each other. "It is a dimply ripe little beast who has lost her way, as we all might if we continue this. Take the beast to Mull to the poor crofters there—"

But Thomas would not be stopped. He flung a fist against his chest. "The Creation itself is grace. Grace comes from in *here*. From my will to be pure. And I'll mount every man in Ireland against that Church of yours if it dares come to these holy lands and drain us of our will . . . every man and every dead man we will raise against them. We will not be controlled." He slashed about the tiny room. His cowl burned, so hot was his anger, and he slapped at it and I also. "I give you the cow. But the calendar dates . . . those who wish to follow your new dates will observe holy feasts according to Rome. Your Passover date will not be ours, for ours is a moon date and yours is a fixed date. Your Sabbath is Sunday? Ours will remain Saturday. Those who wish to follow the ancient dates of our Fathers, which recognize the progressions and the changes in the Heavens, they will follow me. We will have two camps in Iona, sad to say. Your people must follow both sets of dates. Mine only the true one—"

"Both? That will be confusing and expensive."

"If they live under this roof and rule, they will do both."

"It is not necessary yet, Thomas. Rome is not insisting—"

"It is necessary and now. I want an open scission between this monastery and Rome. I want the choices clear. And the cow, Nicholas. Reeks of sexuality, she does, does she? Not as much as you reek of Rome. There still is a strong whiff about you. Some good and salty sea air will clear it off."

"It is after midnight, Thomas."

Thomas clapped his hands and I brought him his seal skin and gloves against the wind and snow. "Come, Brother Nicholas. We will take the cow this moment to Mull. One scission between us is enough. And if the cow doesn't belong there on Mull . . ."

And I, Generous, said, for which I regret: "Someone will have a good meal or a good cow."

Nicholas continued to press his point. "If it is clear then she doesn't belong on Mull and *those* poor souls send her back, then will she go to Seth?" Nicholas rubbed his ring, licked it, polished it with a silken hem.

"You are more anxious than I to be rid of her. I wonder why, Nicholas. Let us hope she goes to Mull and remains. If she is truly other than ordinary, it will be made clear to us in some way. Generous, Good Man, ready the coracle and bring an extra seal skin for Nicholas's thin and Latin blood and have Justus fetch the cow from the Tree of Life where she is tied." Mercurial as the Irish are, Thomas grinned at Nicholas, who did not understand the suddenness of the Irish nature. But I understood, having been its victim for years since I left Saxony. "And a seal skin for the cow."

Nicholas's color rose. He twisted his Bishop's ring angrily.

Thomas put an arm around him. "If the cow is gone, then we are destroying the evidence for free will. Are we not?"

"We are destroying many evidences, Father. Your relationship to the cow, for example."

Thomas had been joking. Nicholas, I could hear, was not. I know so much of everything but there are meanings and connections that elude me. I can only go on collecting. Ah, CuRoi, if you were here. You would understand all this. Poor CuRoi.

I peed the ice from the side of an excellent coracle and had it ready.

So wicked black the night it was not easy to find in one place all of a man's fingers, my six-fingered task greater than that of others. There was brought by Muncas a lamp of oil. The little cow was stood in the coracle, steady and sweet and trusting she stood. Nicholas rebuked the uproar of the waves in loud song, and rebuked the geis against crossing to Mull, and Thomas pushed off. With strong arms, Thomas rowed past the Isle of Sorrows, past the Isle of Storms to the far shore of the Sound. Where the granite coast of Mull folds into cliff, there the little cow leaped neatly ashore and allowed herself to be led from the beach and there she stood as the men turned the coracle from her and toward Iona.

For sure and for certain the monks congratulated themselves that the beast belonged on lonely Mull. But it wasn't half way across they were, rowing steadily, that the cow was aswim behind them and climbing into the coracle and tipping it over and the lamp out and Nicholas not able to swim, athrash and asplash shouting for Thomas and Thomas's voice, watery, steady, strained. And both of them, the

Druid Nicholas and the Druid Thomas, for that they are, holding on to the long fleece of the little cow who pulled them, Glory to God, across the Sound to Iona with much wheezing and snorting and praise and prayer from Thomas. But save them she did and when the three of them thrashed ashore and shook the sea from their bodies as dogs, for are we not the Dogs of God, it was, shame to say, Nicholas Wry-Mouth who said, "A Devil. Subtlety and jugglery. Mark it, Generous."

He caught his breath in great gulps. "A supernatural cow. Tie her to the boundary stones. Give her to Seth before we all come to grief." I wrapped them in plaids and seal fur. Thomas betook himself on his knees to give thanks for the saving of their lives, but Nicholas spoke further his bitter words and would not kneel until Thomas, judgment without fault, swung his crook mightily across the back of Nicholas and knocked him to his knees. And when they had given a thanks, uneven as it was, Nicholas stood and muttered that the beast should be tried for craft or eaten.

Thomas laughed. "Better, Nicholas, we try each other's craft—that of the Fathers against those of your Romans. Aye, Nicholas," he teased. "Better than trying the craft of a goodly cow. Outsmarted, you are, Nicholas. And out-swum. And kinder she is than you, for it was she who saved your life and you who want to kill her." The laughter of the Abbot was happy and heartful. But after he wrapped the wet cow in his own plaid, he turned to Nicholas with a scowl. "For insolence, Nicholas, Bishop or not, forty minus one."

It is a hard rule we live by. But the grace of God rests manifestly on Thomas and his judgment is without fault. Nicholas scurried to his cell, already bent in pain.

So in this way were Nicholas and Thomas delivered from the sea and bad fortune overcome.

Thomas alone took the cow. He led her into the moon-light, spoke to her, and I behind as if vanished. Thomas laid his hand on her back. Her head, heavy with exhaustion, dropped and rose. They walked together as if they had always. My oil lamp threw a luminosity about them, a circle of light that set them apart. It was the first time I had seen the sweetness between them that would soon be the talk of the monastery.

"In the night, Wee Cow, all things are black. Cows and monks and men are all the same. But we are too much the same, you and I."

She stopped on the path and turned to him. His hand rested on her head and she pressed against him. "Yes," he continued in his timbrous voice, and one would think, in grace, the animal understood. "Gentle and murderous. You killed Eldred. The arrogance of us. You a dumb beast . . . and I a prince in the house of Kings."

And then with heavier hand on her back, his face frozen in the moonlight, hard as the stones, deep as the shadows, he led her to the rath, called out for Justus, and gave him the lead. If poor CuRoi had been with me, he would have blown out the lamp to see if the aura of their own light remained. I did not dare. But still, something it was trem-bling between the two.

"The weather changes, Justus. She must be in the barn. Calm the other cows with extra timothy." Thomas patted Justus roughly on the shoulder, for each man was treated as he was wont to understand. "And walk in a large circle past the cell of Nicholas. His is a bad enough night and will be a worse one. He needs no further irritant."

"Father . . ." Justus stood rubbing his head, his beard at his chest, all awkwardness. "Father . . . I . . . am one of . . . I may become . . . Nicholas has spoke to me about baptism in the name of Christ."

"In the name of Rome? You also?"

As it is with the truly Irish, the blood mood of the Abbot shifted swiftly as the north wind on an open sea. Swelled he was with anger and power and rose above poor Justus. "Then, damn you, walk the cow through his very cell. From sunrise to sunset these are my lands and my tribes and I am King on these isles as far as you can see and I say bring the cow to the barn. My sword trembles."

Justus fell on his knees and, pulling the cow's lead, backed away on his knees, still and well he might for the rage was in Thomas still. This is true for I witnessed it and more.

— GENEROUS

With a tight hand Justus led me, with a dry mouth he spoke. "There, there, little lady. There, there." It was what they all said to me, a promise of a distant solution. "Here," they said when I misbehaved. "There," they said to soothe me.

"Oh and you'll be splitting the island soon, little lady. Thomas against Nicholas, Rome against Iona. Now, here, hurry along. You aren't a demon," he assured himself. "You're just a pretty wee bit of a thing out in the night and soaking wet. And yet the Wise Men, Nicholas and Thomas . . . no!" Justus dismissed his suspicions as he always would. "I'll play music for you in the barn and you'll be a gentle one and quiet and forget your wickedness. Aah, God, hear Nicholas. And over you. Aah, God." We walked far from Nicholas's cell but the crack of chain on flesh filled

193

the night. Justus pulled me faster, near dragging me to the glow of the barn. "You are only a cow, little lady. Only a cow."

The cows still saw me as other than cow, a stranger. They rose immediately in defense. As I was led past them, they wheezed and kicked wildly at their stalls and strained their locks. Eyes rolled in fear. Justus lowered my head into a stanchion, locked me in the stall, and tossed handsful of timothy at the herd to calm them. Still they stood, great sides twitching.

The barn was as it had always been—warm, reeking, shining. Around me the vast shapes of cows steamed and gurgled. Glimpses of night lights flashed on the stainless steel of the milk machines, the feeding bins, the overhead pulleys, the stanchions, the sluiceways. The hiss and piss, the stench, the stinking sweet manure, the sourness, was the same now except some of it was my own. Below my head was my feeding bin, above that a wall, in that a diamond window and on the window sill a broken amphora encrusted with sea creatures and filled with dry geraniums. My own father had drawn the window into the plans for the barn. Through his window, with his eyes, I could see a slice of sky, star-studded, and moonlit earth and the path to his house, cut into the land as a wound. Does he know? Did he know? Do you know, Father?

My reflections in the feeding bin examined me. Cloven and hairy my feet, heavier than I had expected my face, and in the cylindrical sheen of the metal, my nose flat and fleshy, but my eyes wet and wonderfully languorous. I wondered if my mother felt seductive when she wore her leopard skins. As a cow I was prettier by far than the others. As Celeste, I was grotesque. Oh God, Celeste, where are you?

Justus carried his cithara into the empty stall beyond mine

and ran his fingers over the strings, playing a sadder song than I have ever heard. The creak of stanchions, thrash of tail, the heavy thud of cows settling and shifting in the hay, all interwove with the music, and became heartbeat.

I watched the red numbers bleed from the moon-faced clock at the far end of the barn as the night swept over them. Justus peed in the sluiceway, shook himself off daintily. The bells tolled the death of the hours and the monks sang elegies into the night. Sunset to sunrise belonged to Set. Dong. Bell, Son of El, dong, dong, make a tinkle, the holy tool knocking up the hours from under the skirts of the priests, reckoning the length of the lives of men and cows and mine by the moon. Swallowed by the neck of night, they were, the bloody numbers, Two, Four, Nine, Three. Beth, Daleth, Tet, Gimmel. Each of them an elemental living story of the Universe. They shift and another story is told. Stars regroup as fireflies. Would I lose count of the days and my own story? I was afraid and thrilled for the self I had been, the self I was and the self I would, God willing, become. And so all of my selves passed the first night in the barn.

At daybreak through the diamond window and the interfaces of my new eyes, I saw the hut of my father and the door swinging in the wind and thought, as the sun rose and lit the face of the sky and the back of the sea, about our lists and tapped somewhere deep in my memory and found them, fatter than they had been, and the sun rolled into my mouth through the window, red and warm and round. I swallowed it. It was cinnamon and sweet. Slime dropped from my jaws. I was warm all over and tingling. Sin of Amon. Sun of Amon. The sun was in me. I felt it in my heart, in my belly, rolling into my knees, a living ball, belly, Ba'al, son of All, the circle, sun, ball, wall, watch the W, the resistance to the ball. Wordless, I was lost in words. My mind leaped on four feet. Not a cow's mind but a mind unconnected. Mad? Free? Hot little words, lists like my father's lists. Ball, bell, belly, ding dong, balls, dong dong, mortar, pestle, mother, father.

On the first morning, Muncas Bent-Neck came, blocking the light with his great body, and the cows, unnerved by him, rose up in one swift motion as he, in a neat isostasy, sat down on the stool in my cell. Muncas breathed deeply, laboring with his own slow thoughts. Soon the cows lay down and I felt Muncas's hard bony skull pressing against me and he leaned on me and cried into my fur for his far country and his little mother and a clever mind and a small body and a straight and graceful neck.

Poor Muncas changed the water in my pail, freshened the hay, and sat cleaning me and crying as he pulled burrs and burdock and balmed my tits, this one for Bridget, he blessed, and this one for Michael and this one for Columba and this one for Christ and he uprooted with his four touches something in me, that primordial orchid yearning, and I tore at the wall with hoof and horn for I could not bear his touches. And I ripped and howled until with a new pitch of anger I stood squarely on his bark-skinned foot, so heavily with my own sharp hoof, he grunted and shoved me against the wall and held me there until Justus came and pulled us apart. What was it Muncas had released in me?

There was only myself to answer and only silence, but, as if beckoned, Thomas stood beside me, shuffling his Wellingtoned feet and pressing a handful of hay to my nose. "There, there, there."

Do you mean by there to keep me in place, away from you, or to send me to another place?

"We'll soon know where you've come from and take you where you belong."

Wiser men know less about themselves and would give

their hearts for such answers. If I asked Thomas the correct
questions, I could convince myself that he understood me.
I slipped from the stanchion and rested my head on his lap.
Justus, cleaning a nearby stall, stopped to watch.

"A lonely one, isn't she?" he asked Thomas.

Yes, I answered. Thomas laughed falsely.

"The good Lord put us all on earth to help with the loneliness," Thomas replied in rote and closed his eyes, signaling
that he wished to be left alone. I closed my eyes. Thomas,
I think, made me more lonely by his being on earth. His
hands moved along my head, scratching and smoothing. I
heard Justus start up the feed pulley far from us. Thomas
must have heard also for he quickly bent to me and spoke
very softly.

"Are you sent to tempt or are the Devils my own?" He
lay his head against my side. "Many women I have known.
And war's cruel harness. Carnal, I have been lustful, but . . ."
His voice dropped in horror. "But never a beast. Why?
I think . . . I must—" and then he broke off for there
was the sound of Wellingtons sucking along the concrete
floor.

"Aah, Justus." His voice changed as he stood. "Keep this
wee one separate from the others. See that they let her
eat . . . and don't hurt her. And . . . talk to her a bit. I think
she likes the talk."

"And don't they all? Will she be joining the herd, Father?"

"No, not yet. And will you, Justus . . . ?"

"It's not a certain thing, Father. Nicholas has spoken again
of baptism."

"I've been dunked too . . . changed nothing. And Father
Nicholas, as much as he knows about the power of water,
can't keep his head above it. So much for his eternal life. It
is our call to retain the mysteries, Justus. Your chord was
once a war wail. It may be again."

"Protect us from that, Father."

Thomas strummed at the cithara and looked over his shoulder at me. "Play us a bit, Brother."

And Justus took it up with such sadness and Thomas blowing his nose, rather than weeping aloud. And when the notes quivered in the barn above us and in our heart-strings and the strings were still, Thomas said, "An odd lot we Irish are, Justus. Sad in song, happy in war."

"Father Nicholas tells us that the Romans think of us as barbarians."

"Hah! And does he tell the Romans we are the sacred caste of Wise Men who keep the mysteries?" Thomas slammed a gate. "There will be war wails yet, Justus, mark my words." Thomas sained Justus and the barn and left.

All morning up and down the length of the barn other monks milked cows and whispered to them of longings no confessional had ever heard. And the cows stood still nodding and sighing and, I believe, admiring.

And so I was in the barn. A in B. It was the only way I could remain at the monastery—as a cow. And I had the love of the Abbot, perverted as it might have been although I was not in a position to judge.

During those first weeks when Thomas came to me he came in silence and sat with me in silence, as if silent, we were alike. On warm days, he would lead me from the barn, his cool silver hand on my back, and we would walk into the meadows to a lonely beach half-circled with massive pillar stones and caves. Thomas would climb under the shade of two great pillar stones, capped by a third. He sat on warm sand, spread his writing tool, quill, ink, vellum, pocketsful of biscuits for me, bread for himself, beer for both of us, and he would lean against a pillar while I knelt before him with his holy book on my horns. No one disturbed us nor knew where we were. The chai formed by the three stones rose blunt against the horizon—a text of life in stone—strong and rough and powerful.

Those were beautiful days, the sky brilliant blue, the air full-bodied and sharp, the sea wine, potent, all bursting with existence. Thomas studying, copying, looking up to smile at me when he turned a page, blessed my silence with his own. He crumbled pieces of bread on the rocks and poured drops of beer into their cavities. Everything was alive and listening. I thought in those days that all existence must be knowledge.

But then the weather turned cold. Thomas no longer came for me, if that was indeed the cause, but certainly he no longer came. I would find there were other causes. It was Justus who patiently led me out behind the herd to graze at the sea. The air turned thin and febrile. The other cows stood apart from me, eating dulce and sweet tangle, their hooves buried in the waters. When the bells called them to the barn, they moved, one after the other, slowly, sullenly, swaying, up the beach over the shoulders of the dunes, over the fields to the barn, and I followed. The monks sang as we passed the abbey. And in the barn at night I waited angrily for Thomas. He never came.

I would look through my father's window and howl and kick and carry on until Justus or another would murmur "There, there" to me. "There, there." It became a promise. And I would lean across my stanchion and look up at the moon and think about my change and ask the moon how long, you who reckon the length of life, how long will I be a cow?

The monks still looked for me, the novice, CuRoi, lost in the nests and caves of Iona. They would not let me forget myself. They still sent John Joe out to spy into the lands of the crofters, suspecting, I am sure—for I have heard the talk in the barn—Archie and his wife. The brothers still stood at twilight—I had seen them—on the Mountain of God and looked toward the Beyond and watched for me. I heard them calling my name. "CuRoi. CuRoi." And I railed against my powerlessness. I had never heard a more terrible sound. "CuRoi, CuRoi." I thought I would soon die if I had to hear it much longer.

ITIS SOON TOLD.
I, GENEROUS, CHRONICLER, WRITE OF THE TROUBLES WITH ROME.

A great hundred salmon netted by the fishing brothers. A gift of three and two score barrels of maize from a penitent on Tiree. The passing on of a King of the Eastern World by his own hand. A light snow, early, under a hunter's moon. The calling together of holy men to fix dates. A condemnation of our calendar by the holy men through the Pope. A letter of protest by our Abbot to the Pope. A messenger from the Pope. Long nights of discourse with the messenger. The going of Nicholas to Rome and Carthage. The return with holy books and much thanksgiving. A time of plenty, of two Sabbaths a week, of laxness and with smoked fish on the table every day of the week except fast days,

Wednesday and Friday. Apples on holy days, venison roasting on the wooden griddle and then, sadly, beef. Ill feeling between Nicholas, Bishop, and Thomas, Abbot. Three clan Kings argue the Pope's cause with Thomas. Five clan Kings from Ethiopia argue the Pope's cause with Thomas. The burning of a weapon of butter and twigs by Nicholas on the night before the Passover in defiance of the rule that all fires be out until the first night of the Passover. The celebration of Easter by Nicholas and his followers on the Pope's declared day. The celebration of them also of Sundays. The complaint by Hilary the Cellarer that storehouses are emptying through Saturday and Sunday celebration. A prayer from this poor scrivener that the Lord give the young Abbot strength to defend his rule and this our island, Iona.

— GENEROUS

Through the fall and winter I grew. I swallowed the pale yolk of winter sun, the great golden doubloons of moon, the stars, the grass. I swallowed each catastrophe of sea, each knot of seaweed. I turned all into flesh, bone, blood, hide. I swallowed the earth. Grass shrieked, seaweed popped and spat the salt of Typhon in my mouth. Everything there was transformed into me. I loved my size, my increase, the strength of my limbs, the voluptuous swing of my self as I walked, the silken beauty of my fur, the dip and roll of my great shoulders, the gorgeous arrogant drape of my tail, my eyes swimming before me in the feed-bin mirror. The earth churned in me. It became me, a higher being. I redeemed it. I resurrected it. One and the same—my cow passion, my Thomas passion. I lusted to exchange and to rut. And wondered what lusted for me, whose table I would adorn, whose stomach would resurrect me into a higher being, who would contain me. I exulted in my B-ness, my container-being.

Tons of grass, tons of timothy, dulce, nettles, tangle, silage, haylage became my monumental self. I was safer hiding in my hide. I stood for hours in the fading sun, in the winter chill, in the warm barn, and when there was nothing to eat, I ate words.

Those I ate with the same passion. I spewed out their husks but the souls and the heat of them stayed within me. Force, farce, gag, choke, joke, I stuffed myself. More than my Dark Horse Copy Books could contain, I now held. My labor was heroic.

Words flew up at me. Others passed into me and sprung into my head, seeds of something, reservoir that I am. Glorious florid rich deep cunts of words that opened and opened again, curlicues and waves like paper flowers, bursting blossoming deeper and deeper to their core. Each letter had its meaning, each letter a number, each number a star, a planet, and each new configuration a new fate. Door, rood, odor, adore, ajar. I ate them. I licked them. Some slammed into my nature. Some slid in, some dropped in. They unlocked my jaw: muck, much, mulch, Molchu, mocc. They bore through my skin: violence, silence, coracle, oracle, miracle, lyrical. They flew into my nostrils and buzzed about in my head. They were whole diseases, viruses, answers and cancers that took my ever-increasing body for their lives. Through me, they evolved. Through me, they were resurrected. I hungered for knowledge. I hungered for earth.

In the months following my change, I fully expected a flash of light and a clap of thunder to return me to my womanhood. As the autumn stretched on and nothing happened, I decided, for lack of any other solution, to try prayer.

I had not yet done so, feeling it profane in the filth and, in the light of the vast unrequested change which had already overcome me from nowhere, stupid. But I thought to pray and did so. At first I could not decide whether I ought to pray for an entire shape or a part at a time. The rule in the world of prayer being humility, it seemed fitting to pray for a part. But I could not measure if my hesitation in this decision were humility or simple distrust and, utterly impaled on the horns of the problem, thought of little else for weeks until at last I decided to pray for a foot.

Which I did fervently, committing my precious hoard of words to sentencing, watching them drift out and up to an empty sky and by the end, for a fortnight, I did indeed have a small growth and ultimately a small pink delicate toe and half moon nail hanging loosely on the ankle above my hoof, which was noticed immediately and identified by Justus and cut off with a tiny bronze chisel by Thomas who pocketed my part and walked away quite by himself, lost in a thought, so by himself that Justus had to shout to him many times, and then run after him down the length of the barn to return the ancient chisel to Thomas. Prayer worked but not well enough. I shed my belief in it with no more than the cool distant flick of the tail with which I shed flies.

I knew my error. Growth is not transcendence. I had added a toe when I ought to have changed the hoof into a foot. For I had to change the cells, take them back to primitive, undifferentiated, undistinguished, and force them into new roles. And since I am, we all are, semi-conductive—and now with all this fur, even more awake to the electric winds which shift beneath me—I took myself over to the electric clock and let the numbers of time bleed into my blood and concentrated on that new foot with five new toes, on the hoof becoming jelly and then separating and spreading and then tightening into shape. I slept beneath the clock and dreamed of feet. My reward for all of this was an extra teat which alarmed Justus and myself no end and also went the way of my toe.

"Do you think she's ill?" I heard Justus ask Thomas after the operation. "That this . . . that this is a *condition*?"

"Oh, it's a condition, to be sure," answered Thomas looking back at me with an arched eyebrow, and, I was certain, raising his voice for my benefit. "We won't worry about it until it reaches the organs." My heart stopped. As did my experimenting. My change simply could not derive from the external.

It was after the dispatch of both toe and teat that the old cow Thirty-three, who had been the love of Abbot Isaac, was placed, certainly by Thomas's direction, in the stall next to my own. I thought they put her next to me because we were both at making such noise, she wheezing, I wind-sucking and kicking, but it was possible Thomas had thought she would calm me, perhaps even that she was more accustomed to human beings. I dared to think that Thomas really knew and then I put the idea aside.

Thirty-three alone accepted me. She stood by me often and licked my face of fleas and flies. And I, after much self-examination, licked her also. She tasted sour and salty. As the winter deepened her wheezes grew worse. They were great and pained brays and bellows, a huge sucking of the windy bag shattering the night and her body shivering, sinking, and collapsing only to fill again and wheeze again. I was so young then. She was almost gone by the time I understood she was weeping and for many nights after that, when she wept without stop, I lifted my head from my stanchion, flung it over the side of our stall, and laid it close against her side, riding on that ill-fated ship, the rib timbers straining under my head, the form rising and sinking terribly, the eyes glaucous, and I watching her and comforting her, I hoped, with my own misbegotten presence. In the mornings, Justus would reprimand me for loosing myself from the stanchion, shuffle his feet and scratch his head, lock me absentmindedly back into my stanchion, say, "There, there," and dismiss the anomaly.

And I would watch the sun rise and set, shifting the angles of its inclinations through the abbey window and out into the heart of each living thing. Angles of inclination, the stars, angels of my yearnings. I understand the seasons now. The summer sun sums. Growth plus growth plus growth. The cross that fixes, the sign +. And then the sun falls. The sign + turns and falls on its side and becomes the sign × and the fruits burst and multiply. And in the sterile winter quinter, watch the Q's, watch the W's, the very elements of life return to their quintessence, divide, divide, divide. Life goes underground to the seed-bed. The monks sing the hours along, notch by notch on the Great Wheel. Justus sings the seasons. We wait.

Seven notes on Justus's cithara. Stout-ribbed, ass-eared Justus, his mechanical ears are metronomes to his music. He plays to the cows and takes his songs from the skies. Through the night his music of thirds and fourths sings to the threes and fours in the abbey's window, spiraling in and then out to the fields, and the plants listen and spiral upward. And the cows listen and there is harmony in us all. Guitar, cithara, et cetera, all the rest in harmony. Between the seven plucked notes I hear the vowels. I have heard those sounds when the wind whistles its secrets on the harp of my horn. Zing. And I have found the vowels of my cow soul and howled them into the night, vowels of sorrow for my loss, of passion for the orchid thing, of intellect, of heart, the vowels of the chakras I sang, strumming on the instruments of my own parts, plucking at my own chords. I sang but it was not yet the right note.

Since Thomas had convinced me that tampering with change might damage my organs, I found another pursuit with which to fill my endless days—be-thinging bread. I created its squeeze, its heat, its soft, its yeast smell, its crust, one by one, until the frequency pulse of the parts became the whole and the pulse of the bread itself clicked in my head. Hallucination, my father had said, was the same as perception. The bread existed in my head somewhere in the quantum continuum between the real and the unreal. It would take hours to be-thing bread and, if for a moment I thought of the word bread, the vision vanished. I believe it was the way cows thought ordinarily, without words, below language, in some kind of infrared original breath of response to frequencies, to the pips and waves, as my father would say. And then one day by the sea, be-thinging bread mentally, three loaves bounced actually in the waves just beyond me. I blinked and they were gone. The next day I concentrated on a rotted fence post to create fire, and indeed the frequency of the thought of fire churned into my head and the post sprung alight with flame.

In great fear I lurched from the post. Afraid to try anything else, I remained content to send fat little brown loaves of honey bread out to sea.

Try as I might, dare as I might, I could not be-thing Thomas. He was too complex and far too distant. Caught up in the tempest between Rome and Iona, Thomas now came to the barn rarely. It was faithful John Joe who began to take me for long and silent walks. And Generous came also, led me toward the sea, muttering all the while against Nicholas and the scission and mourning for the power of the old Abbot Isaac which had kept peace in the monastery. The intrigues and hatred were just as he had predicted so long ago when I had sat with him copying. Monks whispered to each other now and looked furtively behind themselves as they prayed. Nicholas watched Thomas out of small eyes. Thomas, Nicholas. Justus forgot his notes and let his fingers wander aimlessly in the strings. Milk production fell. Printouts and suggestions and shipments of vitamins came from the computer center at Cornell. The abbey grew poor. Relics were missing from the columbarium. Everyone was guilty. No one confessed. Hilary reported the storehouses empty from the celebration of double holidays, Roman and Irish, and complained to everyone that the scission would be the ruin of the monastery. Nicholas called Thomas antique. Thomas called Nicholas a traitor. Some brothers I heard whispering to the cows, wondering why they could not simply, faithfully, justly, add the name of the Christ to the list of Gods, rather than be forced to choose only the Christ. Nicholas I heard say to Justus, "Through him, Brother Justus, believe, we will bury death and do away with Seth entirely, and all that he represents so that nothing will be seen nor known of him any longer." And even Justus argued. "To oppose Moses is to oppose Jesus," he said softly. But Nicholas denied Rome's opposition to Moses. Nevertheless, we heard that the stone face of the High Cross of Moses had been mutilated and I knew that the poor monks were trapped in the maw of either/or and if/then. Poor monks. I was not surprised that Thomas had little time for me.

John Joe and I would walk along the paths above the Strand of the Martyrs, between barbed-wire fences afloat with buntings of wool. Shame to say, John Joe walked without his shoes and leaped from one hot pile of my dung to the next. Before us, the angular granite of Dutchman's Peak stood as clear as the hand in front of John Joe's face or veiled in rags of sea cloud. I would graze and John Joe would sit at the edge of the cliff looking out toward the distant island and whispering, "Sun, Moon, Alleluia." He did not start flapping his arms until one day when four young men in four paper-thin kayaks paused in their rowing, doffed Scottish tams in tandem, and resumed their rowing. They vanished into the final fold of the Atlantic. John Joe fixed his gaze on that point. It was then John Joe began to flap his arms.

I thought of him in flight, the feathery tatters of his jacket awash in the wind, the Stonehenge of a mouth gulping air, the small frail bird-body beating against the great sky. Each of us has our moons, each of us reaches out beyond the boundaries of our own existence. John Joe would be a sorry bird. But flap his arms he would and whisper, "Sun, Moon," and throw stones over the edge of the cliff, echoing back from the sea rocks, and his laughter bouncing all around us. It was borders and edges John Joe liked, a laternal creature, stroking the earth, braying, flapping endlessly, pebble eyes fixed on that final fold as he ran back and forth at the edge of the cliff. Some days he would climb upon my back, hold my horns, kick my sides with sharp heels, and we would race along the edge of the cliff. I forgave him for kicking my sides. He wanted both of us to fly. His arms flapping, my fur rising, earth exploding beneath my hooves, I myself imagined slipping over the edge and flying to Dutchman's Peak, or Tiree at least, if not Heaven.

And one day, riding me, he kicked suddenly so sharply I bolted and did indeed fling him over my horns and tumbling down the cliff he was and I knelt and looked over the side and there he was waving at me and speaking words, speaking the psalms.

"Happy the man," he began hesitantly, slowly, and by the time he was half up the loose-flanked cliff, "who never follows the advice of the wicked or loiters on the way that sinners take," he called out clearly. "Or sits with scoffers," he shouted at the top of the cliff. "But finds pleasure in the law of Yahweh." He climbed on my back and grabbed my horns and kicked me squarely in the ribs. "And murmurs," he exulted faster and faster, "His law day and night." I bucked him off.

Words! John Joe, I am mad with envy. I ran from him. He chased me. One after the other, he shouted the psalms. The Songs of David had never been so joyous. John Joe's hands bloody, his face flushed with a grace unimaginable, he climbed me again and kicked my sides and held my horns and turned me down the dirt path, and the bunting waved in our wind we went so fast. "The way of the wicked is doomed, is doomed." As fast as I could. The Amadan was exalted. His voice cracked and rose and he howled, "From the ends of the earth I will call to You. From the ends . . ."

An odd sight we were as I pounded into the courtyard, my fur afloat behind me, he shouting, "Praise Him with the blasts of the trumpet!" Others responding, "Praise the Lord!" And all the monks came forward and stared and praised and finally Muncas went forward to grab him and four of them contained John Joe as he shouted, "Praise Him with

211

drums and dancing!" And then there was a moment between laughter and gasp, between fool and fanatic, and
Muncas could not contain John Joe. "And with clashing
cymbals!" Nor could John Joe contain John Joe. "Praise Him
with clanging cymbals!" And they dragged him inside the
kitchenings to throw cold water on him and slop and him
waving his arms wildly and shouting alleluia, "Let everything that breathes praise Yahweh, Alleluia, Alleluia, Alleluia." And some of them answered him and some did not
for it wasn't yet altogether clear if he were mad or blessed
and then he farted twice, three times, fiercely in great drum
rolls, and his feet treading the air and arms flapping, and
Thomas yelled into the melee to Muncas, "Let him go, Muncas. Let him be. His soul is already dreaming."

And lifting off the ground, in a barrage of farts, John Joe
Amadan, shouting, "Sun, Moon, Alleluia," burst through
a kitchening window and flew into the clear sky.

Thomas, deeply troubled, fell on his knees. We all did,
even I but no one noticed for all watched John Joe until he
became a spot over the Paps of Jura. Prayers were spoken
for his demented soul.

Until Hilary whispered, "Someone lit a match to the gas.
And truly, a bubbling jet of gas John Joe has become and
hadn't he lit his own match with his voice? Scraped the
sound of himself against himself and lit a fire that took him
to . . . Heaven?" All agreed with Hilary.

"The Amadan's destination is questionable," Thomas
warned the brothers.

I, witness, was beaten with a broom and sent out of the
kitchenings. I found my own way back to the foundation
of the barn. Poor John Joe.

A stunning and immediate event it was that had no cause,
no continuation. It was the immediate rude moment of many

212

immediate moments, simultaneous, a blip of a niche and gone, an event of a different order, an event of the crack.

What did you yearn for, my friend, John Joe? What do I yearn for? Why do I want to be more than me? The bee is as bee as a bee can be. Only men who do not dream would cry for John Joe. Something up there he yearned for, something he might have found. My father would have said to fly up into the clouds is an act of a half-souled Roman. The full soul yearns for depth, not height.

And sure enough, from the same dis/order into which he disappeared, another sudden event for John Joe. He returned in a carapace of ice, blue inside, fell from nowhere into the farm pond, his happy, frozen, somewhat astonished face, lifted to the sky. Had he reached the moon? Where have you been, John Joe? And why have you come back?

I stepped into the pond and licked feathery icicles from his elbows and the strands of jacket wool came off on my lips. The feathers of ice dripping from him as he lay were the feathers of the dead. I knew them from my father's house.

John Joe lay at the bottom of the farm pond until, once again, all gathered around the Amadan and pulled away the ice and flesh and then he was carried to the sea and set adrift. And sank as quickly as the cabbages of our child-time make-believe.

Find a cause for such an effect. Find an effect for such a cause.

As if even sorrow could not bear loneliness, another was taken from us. The great cow, Thirty-three, keeled over and crashed to the floor of her stall. We were all led away. The scent of her roasting filled the air for nights and sickened us. When her name tag was hung about my neck, and her stall consecrated with bags of salt, I became Thirty-three, a member of the herd. Perhaps it was, after all, given that I should be a cow, that I should deny my yearnings, that I should learn a lesson in creatureness, in compromise. What terrified me was that, like John Joe's icy carapace, contentment was hardening around my being.

One long day, the sky hollow, the sea dark, a great gull skimmed the horizon. Night-ice had formed at the shore line and broke now into plates and the sea wind drove the plates against each other, a thousand chimes at my feet, they rang like the breakfast gongs on the *Prince George*. We ate wrack torn loose by storm from its sea hold.

The gull startled the sky, slicing through it, and lit obstinately on my back. Through the day obsidian talons dug into my hide. At first I thought he was my punishment for the murderous bird-collecting. When I tried to dislodge him with my tail, he would hop forward, and backward when I swept at him with my horns. He would circle and alight again. At last, as the bells rang the day out, he flew off and as he flew the black form again skimmed the horizon and I remembered the gull from my other life dropping ice cold at my feet, the day I stole my father's scarlet vestment and tried to fly in its wings.

The plates chimed, ice against ice. The sky grew heavy with coal-black clouds and the idea pierced my being and the hold of my contentment was cracked.

There is not Heaven, not if, not then, not therefore, not reason, but an inner space of air and dust and cold and waste and shit and soul.

There is a place from which gulls drop ice cold. It is the crack, the Nick of Night, the Pythagorean comma in the pentatonic scale. It is the same place from which women become cows and cows become women. It is nightworld, nocuous, noxious, the sterile pestle of the moon, the phallus of the nightworld, the place of pestilence that pounds the earth anew. No hand dropped that gull, no superior vision determined it, no ordinary human power simply brought up to a higher octave caused that moment. *There* is a place with no law, no universal principle, no unified field theory, nothing, no connectives, no metaphor, no perspective, no causes, effects, no visions, no verse. The unmanifest. Mani means hand. There is no hand. *There.* In and of itself, without intention, without meaning. And those of them who think that *there* must be a single interior, larger, deeper, all-encompassing, less observable law, stand around and scratch their bald heads and call "CuRoi" into the wilderness, for I must have gone *someplace*— to an "is" place—and say as they said when my father set himself afire: "But how, but why, who in the world could have done such a thing, what is the cause?" There are only questions, no answers. Watch the moving W. *There, where, here, now here, nowhere, is not.* And that place, that is the place I must find if I'm to become a woman. And how will I?

 Through Thomas? Damn Thomas.

I had not been with him for weeks and I would wait no longer. I loathed him and yearned for him. With the crudities of my nose and tongue I approached the subtleties of the barn-door bolt but Justus caught me at it. "Beware, Wee One, the Carver catches the night-strayer." At last one night

Justus's whiskered chin dropped gently onto the frame of the cithara and I took my tag in my mouth to quiet it, slipped the bolt, and ran into the night to Thomas's cell.

Candlelight gleamed through the keyhole. I called with a soft gurgle. Smiling, wordless, he let me in, threw more turf on the fire, leaned his book against my strong horns, and read while I stood still, quivering in places and wondering if he were showing me anything more or even less than hospitality. His face had deeper cuts and darker lines, sadder lips, tighter and thinner, pressed with time, too taut those lips, too controlled.

Night after night he allowed me into his cell and once I was there he would ignore me except if I were to move or the book slipped to the stones. There was no further talk of desire, no yearning, no remembering. "Look at me, Thomas, look in my mouth. Look and see if the name of God is written on my tongue as it is written on the side of Adam and on the wings, Thomas, of Gabriel and on the Seal of Solomon. Look!" But he would not look. I loved him more and trusted him less. I studied him; he studied his holy book. I could as well have ripped him through with a horn as licked him clean.

One night I was not invited into the cell for five Ethiopian Kings sat with Thomas. Great black men they were, with sad wise eyes, long tapering chins, and full heads of glossy, curled hair. Jeweled dog collars they wore and blazing swords. "Not Rome," I could hear Thomas's voice repeat again and again. "Not Rome. We will lose our Kingdoms and our sacred clans. We will lose our Cain, our laws! We will lose the Old Gods. We will lose Sirius." Steaming crocks of venison and eel pies were carried in to them and loaves embedded with nuts and raisins, as many as their sword hilts were with gemstones. Finally, Thomas's voice rolled over their own and when there was no longer discourse but only Thomas's blessing, they departed deep in the night from the Strand of the Martyrs in a shining cylinder of a ship. Thomas rebuked the waves. The sea rested and the ship slid from us. Turning, seeing me, Thomas registered no surprise but smiled that enigmatic smile, almost listless, I thought, and laying his cool silver-cased hand on my back, led me to the barn. I did not know to what I had been privy. I thought then that Thomas might have been more than our Abbot, indeed a great King of the clans, a high King, a King of the Western World.

Not long after, I followed Thomas to the Strand of the Martyrs, brilliant in the clear moonlight, where he sat, dark and bent. When the wind shifted suddenly from the north and veiled the night in snow, I butted against him. "Off with you. Off. Off!" I climbed the cliff. The snow enfolded him. Heavier and heavier it fell. Occasionally he stirred and brushed his shoulders. And when the storm reached a howling crescendo, a silent coracle and a man whose head touched the sky, a great dark figure wrapped in a felt domino, his lower face covered, his long head nimbed even in the snow, a living saint or a God, radiant and dark he was, stepped ashore and embraced Thomas.

"Heaven rests upon your hands, Thomas, the earth is under your feet. Yours is mercy; mine prosecution."

"Thy rays penetrate into the ocean, Seth, thou cause the seed of women to take shape and make moisture in man. I have Seth, a name of the Lord, before me."

"Without your sunlight, Thomas, the seed does not grow."

The men embraced. I clung to their words: seed and light. They kissed each other on the lips and Thomas seized the phallus of the One called Seth and Seth that of Thomas and the testicles of Seth emitted fire and they pumped at each

217

other, milking they were the holy seed and the fire of the seed spreading around them as if they burned and each rubbed seed on the other's head and their heads shone and from the center between their eyes, a golden disc, spitting forth light as they spat forth seed. They gripped each other's forearms, and when the ritual was complete, nodded and separated. The golden discs gleamed and in the very stillness, someone stood beside me on the cliff. I leaped away. It was Nicholas, breathing rapidly, shaking incense around himself. But he had not come for me. I had never heard such as I heard that night between Nicholas and the One called Seth.

"Seth, you! Robber, Lord of Existence, Lord of the Crack, Prosecutor, Lord of Change, of Sterile Winter," Nicholas challenged from the cliff, "Typhon who creates rebellion. They shall scratch out thy name in the land and break your statues. Your festival will be miserable throughout eternity. Breaker of the Balance." Nicholas ran down the cliff toward the men, his cloud of incense following.

"I am Seth," the Dark One shouted. "I am Pan and Nick and Night and Death. I am the man of a million cubits, the God who separates, who holds the Unthinkable Life-Death, the God of the Third Eye, the God of Potency and Impotency, Conquerer of the Heart. My semen is made in my heart."

Nicholas ran in circles around Thomas and Seth. The words had been shouted since time began. And time, I knew, began before form.

"Stirrer Up of Troubles, Originator of Confusion, he who thunders on the horizon of Heaven."

"I am the God of the Seed." Seth turned to Nicholas's circle.

"You are the Murderer, the Disorderer, Enemy of Ethics,

Eater of Swine, Seizer of Souls who licks that which is rotten, who lives on offal and is in darkness and obscurity, who terrifies the weary."

"I am Life from which Death arises. I am the savior from the Realm of the Dead. I am Death from which Life comes. I am Formlessness from which Form comes. I am the Guardian of the sea, the knife which cuts the ham of the sea. It is I, Loke, God of Mischief, Chief of the Other Way, Lucky, son of An, Michael, the Man in the Moon, Sinser. I am the Father of Time, but I am not Time."

And Nicholas prostrated himself at his feet. Or fainted or was struck down, for he lay there, covered by Thomas's cloak, until the extraordinary night was done.

So. Seth.

There below the Hill of the Seat and toward the Vat, there between the black rough sharp side of the Vat and the soft bright White Strand of the Martyrs, Thomas and the Dark One sat as brothers and held each other's hands and talked in low voices, but I could read Thomas's back and it was stiff with control. Through the night they spoke, shaking their heads, yes, no. Solemnly and low they talked and although I could not distinguish a word, every cell in my body stung. This was the darkness and he the Dark One. But who was Thomas? And who was I? I moved as close as I dared for here was, if not an answer, certainly the best of questions. Closer still. Sand and snow slid away before me and at the very moment I arrived, on my knees, not my own length away from them, the God, sniffing the air, turned, stood suddenly tall, looming against the snow, his sharp face a flash of blue, a nimbus above his head, and looked directly at me. Thomas shoved at me fiercely.

"Stupid beast. Stupid beast!" He beat at me with his crook. "Loose again. Get on. Get on!" But the great figure stopped

Thomas's arm and looked at me through and through and I, immobile, felt him dry and hot behind my own eyes. Part of me knew to run, another deeper part was drawn into his moon eyes. They were gates to another reality. Someplace between this and that, Dis and Da'at, between Creation and knowledge, between time and form. When I finally loosed myself to run I crossed the sand as convincingly a bovine as I could be. I ate seaweed in clumps with sand and shell, proving myself cow, until I sickened and vomited noisily near the two men. Large string-green snakes slid from the gut of my own rebellious snake birthing them. Had I convinced them? Was I safe? And then Thomas came to me and beat me off again, yelling at me with a hoarse voice well heard by the Dark One.

"Stupid! Stupid!" And then bent to whisper, "Good little girl." And then stood to beat at me again, yelling, "Stupid disgusting woman!" He froze with his error. I scrambled up the cliff.

When Archie's boat scraped along the shore, low and loaded and clanking and points of gold coins shining from the eyes of the Dead, two after two, Seth and Thomas embraced. Archie tied the great man's coracle to his own boat and Seth stepped into the boat of the Dead. He stood facing shore, watching the cliff where I stood, his domino blowing across his body, arms akimbo, a black-nimbed cross riding the sea. And I? Was it a cow he saw on the cliff? Am I truly of his line? Not of Thomas? Not of Dog, but of Pig?

I heard Archie's oars straining toward the Other Side of the island, to the Bay at the Back of the Beyond, to the Beyond. Thomas tossed limp Nicholas over his shoulder.

No sooner were the boats around the Vat and out of sight, but Thomas hurled himself and his burden up the cliff and on top of me, tumbling me to the ground. Nicholas stirred, struggled, muttering angrily. Thomas held him down. The moon shrunk and the sky bled to white. The air was sucked from the earth. More swiftly than I had ever known it to happen even in this rough land, a storm sprung around us. The ground beneath us trembled. The sand reshaped itself into dunes, spewing and spinning and swallowing their own lives. Candle-faced demons shot missiles of tormented souls at us. Thomas's body was strong and powerful stretched against me as it was and his heart rumbled in mine. "There, there," he gasped when I shook with fear. "There, there. Oh why have you been sent to me? Who are we? What have I done?" He tucked my head into his neck.

The sea wrestled with the shore, the caverns gave warning against the storm. Bound together we were, the monk Nicholas against my belly as a calf, the monk Thomas, his breath laboring white against the granite sky, and I, hiding my head in his heaving chest. And we three, enemies, traitors, lovers, clung to each other under the power of Seth. At last, when the moon swelled again and the sand settled to earth and the earth dared breathe, Thomas, head cocked, listened in all directions. Satisfied, he pulled Nicholas and myself up onto our shaking legs and led us home.

Seth. He beat at my being. The Disorderer, Seth. Kadosh, cabosh, and now I add Kaddish, the song of Death. The gull had come not from a larger order but from the place of dis/order, the vast container, the mouth of double B, of double U, of W, that contains A. Ayn, ain't, the place of There Is Not. Dis means God, Two, double, Devil, even, the dark mirror of Life. But might it not be, I wondered that Life was the dark mirror of Life-Death, a fragment of the whole, not an opposite? Dis/order is the whole and the higher? Seth's eyes entered my dreams. They followed me in the day. And, as if connected to Seth's presence in my being, my father's lists took new life in my head. Words bloomed into secrets, secrets into words. The lists and my days began and ended with the name of Seth. Seth, Saturn, Saturday, Satan, shit, merd, murder, myrrh, martyr, mort, mortar, myrtle. I trembled under his eyes. He touched me in my sleep. He led me backward to the path of Naught, to Sidhe, the Other Side, the place of the fairies, the Tuatha, the north, the left, the old, the alternate, the Other way, the mis. And Seth, the chief of the old way, of mischief and naughty and sin. Seth, sidhe, scythe, side, Other Side, Eber, Ever, Hebrew, Hyperborean, Boreas, Boreades, bard, Jew, Yid, Druid, I went on. Seth, cess, cess-pool, cease, Caesar, Kaiser, Chazar, Cessair the Pig Goddess, Sister, cistern, necessary, privy, much, pig, Mocc-el, Michael, muck, enough, Enoch. Somehow, I knew Enoch and eunuch would become Jonah and Noah and all of this would be related to the descendants of the line of Seth, of sea, of Deluge, not of Adam, not of blood, not of earth. My father said there were no answers on earth. I would find Seth and I would find answers.

 But the bolts on the barn door were changed and I thrice-knotted to my stanchion. Although I tried to recreate Thomas's face every moment, I did not see him again for weeks until he appeared one morning with an unhappy, sullen Nicholas, glanced swiftly at my stall, dismissed everyone else from the barn, and continued angrily the same talk he'd had with the five golden Kings, and, I daresay, with Seth. I strained at the stanchion until I heard the anger in Thomas's voice. I was well out of it, for the two monks, as great snakes, hissed and spat malice at each other. The cows they milked must have been squeezed without mercy so much strain was there between the two.

"So, then, make clear again the claims your Roman friends hold against Iona, Nicholas."

"Three, Thomas. You do not recognize the Trinity."

"God is One and behind that, the Ineffable, the Unthinkable."

"You celebrate not the Easter date but the Passover date."

"It is the date of our fathers, Abraham, Isaac, and Jacob. Saturday, Nicholas? Are we then to give up the true Sabbath, Saturday? Seth's Day? Are we then to give up Seth and Saturn?"

"You do not baptize. That is the third claim against you."

"Resurrection comes through illumination, not from a dip in the sea. Not until a man be born again of seed and light is he truly born again . . . having met death, then he returns to life. There is no other way, no other path. What are you teaching the poor folk? Are you the new Moses in the wilderness, that you have come to rewrite the original laws—our Cain?"

"I have been so ordained by Rome."

"These are perduring laws, Nicholas. You are rewriting the Cain for political purpose. There is a course for evolution, for consciousness, for man to achieve Godhood. Leave your venal little messes out of such things. Let your friends have their palaces, but leave what must perdure alone."

"It is time for a new order."

"Not new order, Nicholas, the next step of the only order, toward a creature who defines its own future." Thomas

223

thundered. "That . . . no man can rewrite. It is inherent in the miracle of Creation. Do you hear me?"

Nicholas did not react. I felt it possible that he was more prepared for this discourse than Thomas. His voice was steady, oily. "And your claims against Rome, Thomas?" Superior.

"You deny the mysteries. You will then deny the Gods . . . ?"

"Not true."

"You shall. You deny death?"

"Did I not give proper obeisance to Seth?"

"Nicholas, you fainted. You have already lost the ability to contain his power. You are a weak man now, Rome's Bishop or not. Also I would have killed you on the spot if you hadn't given obeisance."

"I still have power. I can heal with saliva. Birds obey my commands. And men."

"Tricks. You cannot any longer receive the power of a God directly. Nicholas, he who regards not his roots, withers at the branch." A cow howled in pain. "There, there. And what will happen to the clans? The sacred caste?"

"The sacred caste?" The acid of derision was in Nicholas's voice. "Will no longer be all-powerful. Those who convert—"

"Those who convert will no longer be sacred. You will have no clans. The Dogs of God, Roch-el, and the Sacred Swine, Mocc-el . . . the Khans, the Canaanites . . . and the Caesars of Seth"—Thomas's voice softened—"and the Gods of Death? What will become of them in your City of God? Isis, Nem-Isis, Nepthys, Osiris, Seth?"

"We keep the Ineffable. His attributes, his names will be incorporated into new mysteries. Christ has destroyed the underworld for all time, cleaned the Augean stables of the shit of death, harrowed Hell."

224

"You deny the nightworld? Nicholas!"

"As Christ is resurrected, all men are. He has gone to
Hell for all of us. He has suffered so we may not suffer. . . ."

"All men must resurrect themselves, must resurrect
the God in them. God does not resurrect men. Men resurrect
God. I am of the blood, Nicholas, of the seed of the Fathers . . . and—"

"I dare you say it, Thomas. I dare you."

A tyranny of silence. And then Thomas's voice, awful it
was. "The holy line lives in the true Kings." Even the barn
shivered under the great truth. "Rome has no Kings, no
blood."

"You will burn for that."

"The line will continue." He choked and cleared his throat.
It was frightening. "Somehow."

Hooray, Thomas. Hooray, I shouted silently.

"Hell is a horror and mankind is free from it." Nicholas
sounded mechanical, memorized.

"You do, you deny the night Gods, Nicholas!"

"Yes."

"Nicholas!" Thomas cried out in pain.

A pail clattered against a wall and I knew Thomas had
thrown it. His voice swelled and filled the barn. Timbers
trembled. Above my head the feed pail in the sluiceway
shook. "We who dwell in this land and in the shadow of
death have found a light and that is our illumination. You
cannot deny death or darkness. Before many years, Nicholas, I see in the waves and in the wind, you will forget this
and think of Christ as the only God. Cows will wander in
these holy halls and the nut gardens will turn to mast for
profane pigs."

Nicholas stood. I could see him with one eye. His face
was florid. He pissed in the sluiceway and shook himself.
"Your mysteries will be children's rhymes . . . hey, diddle

diddle," he taunted. Thomas stroked him across the face and the flat red shape of his hand burned on Nicholas's cheek. "Violence will prove nothing. Your time is short, Thomas."

"*These* clans are the holders of the mysteries, the advisers to the Pharaohs, the helpmates of Seth, the planters of knowledge and seed, writing, building, numbers . . . to what ignorance will *your* people plunge the world?"

"Your time is short, Thomas."

Then, and only then, Thomas came to my stall and rubbed my back thoughtfully. "There are no new mysteries, only one that repeats and repeats, Brother Nicholas. Convert all the Druids, give them new books and robes and Bishops' rings. The mysteries will not vanish. Time passes, Nicholas. The sun always returns." He kissed my ears, pendant they were, pricked they became. "There is working against you and yours, Nicholas, the ever-deepening note of evolution and no matter how long is the finger of your Church, that note they cannot pluck. One does not change the initial conditions. The initial conditions *may* themselves predict and incorporate change. It is that sort of change that is upon us. A good and true change."

Nicholas left with a sloshing milk pail. Thomas sat on the stool and stroked me evenly and lovingly. "Ah, what did Seth see that I cannot? Will it be given to me to see you as you are?" Poor Thomas, he is shield. I need sword.

At Christmas, the cows were mantled with dried columbine and clover. We ate buckets of sweet timothy. The monks chanted to us, sang the songs of the turning of the year, and the year turned. I watched the clock bleed, heard the tool of God's Son swinging again and again against the hard prison of its bell and the dark presence fluttered near me, Que, Quo, Qui, WWW.

Out of the axiomatic sea, from the theoretical sky, the pale gray nose of the *Prince George* moves toward me, deducing itself from the indistinguishable. Who is your mother, *Prince George*? Who is your father? You come out of nothingness and force yourself into existence in no logical sequence, with no cause. The boat blasts.

The waters part, splitting Heaven and earth, and from the crack between comes the sun, rising on the nose of the *Prince George*, and the boat pushes the red ball of sun up into the infant sky. Willfully it comes while the wind weaves a gray coat on the sea and the light masks the dark and shapes itself and the mountains and turns the sea blue, the boat white, the island real. And I under the swift clouds of morning a cow. As my gold spool once unrolled itself, a bolt of gold unrolls on the sea, spreading before itself toward its future. Larger and larger you come, *Prince George*, filling the harbor with your sound, the sky with your shape. White gulls pull you along toward the spit, the horizon knife-sharp now, your hulk heavy, flat, smoke belching. You blast, once, twice, and the waters around you fold and fan along your bow. Where did you come from? What time do you have? Do you see me? What do I look like? Am I truly a cow?

Each week I witness the birth of the *Prince George* and each week I agonize for still I want to leap across the boundary stones, run to the harbor and see it, see the women whose laughter springs across the island, the tour guide with his booming voice. The breakfast gongs on the ship rise to my meadow. They are the same notes as the chanting of the monks. "Going going going gong. Gong, going going going." Someone strikes metal with drumstick. "They are dining on Baccarat," my father told me when he heard this sound lift itself to our cottage. "And nymphs in bikinis tend the ropes and dust libraries equal to Alexander's and the wood is polished every day with a cloth so fine it floats." That is what my father told me and then locked me in the cottage and bound my legs to keep me from the boat, to keep me from bursting on the stones. To keep me. What is true that he has told me? What is false? "Nothing," he said, "can be contradictory, if it is." Perhaps *he* wasn't. Perhaps everything that *was* for him came from his mind, and his mind was false. Perhaps we have contradictory sets of non-contradictions, many universes, some not compatible, and we must live within them all, mingling and feuding and telling lies. You will burst if you cross the stones, Celeste. Perhaps I don't have to contradict the world, I simply have to contradict my father. Today, I'll cross the stones.

Carefully, I will put one foot on them and then the other and then back away and leap over them as if they were the moon. Today I shall see the tourist boat. If I burst I shall become a coat and a meat pie a little sooner.

I pull my tether with my teeth and I am free. The air is warm and placid, the tail of summer flicking for the final time, the ground already hardened from the cold nights. I pass the millstream, over the cobbles of the ancient causeway, one after the other, clacking I go. At the stones, I leap and I am whole and, leaping, I shed more of the winding cloths my father's mind wove for me. Leaping, the ground is the same sandy hardness on this side as it was on the other side and my feet are satisfyingly there where I put them. I am whole. Bastards, liars. And off I go to the garden of the Viking-razed nunnery and there I wait for the tourists to end their Baccarat breakfasts and begin a walking tour of the island in their time, which I've entered, and to read the inscriptions and wonder at the nunnery so close to a monastery and ignore me for I will be for them only a cow. And I will examine the women.

The nunnery is a melancholy shell. The inside and outbuildings are ruins. Long-tongued gargoyles hang from the remnant of column and rafter, crude-fingered gargoyle hands pull their mouths open to suck in the souls of the dead. From the niches where marbles once stood, weeds grow and eggplants creep on vines along the ground around gravestones, and nasturtiums spring from the cracks in the benches where the moist bottoms of old nuns once spread in prayer. I rip out the nasturtiums and chew them, crisp stem and salty bud, and wait, looking over my shoulder now and then until I hear the boom of the tour guide's voice, Saxon-trimmed, his voice, as that of Generous. He comes, leading a docile group including one small boy child who carries a blue toy, pieces of which drop behind him.

"It may surprise you that on this island, so long ago, a domain of men only, now a nunnery . . . please watch the stile, Madam."

"Oh, shit." Madam tears her dress as she steps over the stile into the ruined garden.

Others examine me. "Oh, what a small cow." "She looks like a dog. Are you sure it's a cow?" "Yes, it's a Hebrides cow although most are ginger," the guide reassures them. "It's really rather lovely." "It is?" "I think it's misformed." "Well, the horns are. . . ."

Madam has long red-brown hair, a thin arching nose, and four fingers on her right hand. She places a metal band on her head, metal circles under her hair, and pivots around the courtyard. Her hem is down with threads dangling. How does a woman lose a finger? The other tourists watch her. The boy is close to me.

"Papa, can I pat the cow?"

"No, no, come away. She might be dangerous."

The woman in the torn dress dances around me. Music is in her.

The tour guide continues. "There is a tradition on this island that somewhere beneath it dwells a snakelike beast. There, above the doorway, you will see a snake carved in stone. These pagan stones come from an even earlier time when there was a great monastery on the island and were used for the foundation of the nunnery . . . are you coming with us, Madam?"

"My hem. You see. Go ahead."

"You won't see the monastery ruins?"

"I've seen the monastery." She smiles a thin archaic smile, reminding me of someone I've seen before. Who it is, was, I have no idea.

The boy drops more pieces of his toy, stops to pick them up. His father pulls him along, grumbling. "I'll buy you another, now come along. Here, here." I wish for my father, a father. I'll buy you another brother, another life. Now come along. We'll dine on Baccarat and you'll wear a bikini, Celeste. I turn away with sloppy eyes.

"Ladies and gentlemen, notice the gargoyles. Storks delivered the souls of babes. Gargoyles were the drainpipes into the afterworld."

The woman sits on a nun's bench and crosses her legs, searches in a large sack, retrieves a . . . a needle and thread. She is about to sew her dangling hem. Does she know that each stitch taken on a garment worn is a tear shed? I wish I could tell her.

Her skin is creamy skin and her dress full, very much like the monks' robes. She is not beautiful. There is something uneven about her face but it is alive and transparent, cut with deep feeling, perhaps with information, with high spots

230

of color and liquid green eyes and humor and her mouth turns up in a smile even as she examines her dress, her hem, and bends to thread the needle between middle and thumb finger and squints. This is all familiar to me. She can't see the needle clearly, which means she is at least as old as Cook, but lovelier, softer, pinker. I move closer. She smells of rose tea. I dare not imagine what it is of which I smell. Through her hair as she bends her head to sew, I see a baffling thing: a pair of delicate twisted ears at right angles, twisted into points with fine blond tufts, and inside them, in the dark cilia, when the sunlight strikes them, the faces of babies. These ears I have seen before.

Nonchalantly, I chew. Her dress is covered with little white horned cows, sleeves, bodice, all of it, dozens of cows. I walk around her. Cow, cow, cow. Cow, cow, cow. She looks up at me. "You're losing your nasturtium."

Quickly, I swallow the flower and drop my head into her lap and she points to the cows on her sleeves, on her belly, and to me, and laughs. Her laughter rolls across the garden and into the chapel walls. I see it rolling until it hits the niche of doves and they gurgle and burst apart and carry it off to Dun Hi. An angel, her laugh, an elemental force. And then she pats me and places the metal band over my own head, soft ends over my ears. "I always have trouble with these myself." She stretches the band out as far as it can go and suddenly every tiny bone in my head sings with her music, rearranges itself with her music. This is what my father meant: my bones are conductors. As they change form they receive other sounds at other frequencies. I am astonished at the music. It rushes into my entire being. I feel desire. I am filled as a body with music. My bones ring. My blood dances.

When the tourists' voices fade, the woman speaks, almost apologetically, as if she were late for prayer.

"All nasturtiums go on at once. We've simply organized ourselves in a linear way."

She means carnations and she means me.

"Incarnation, carnation, reincarnation. Pet milk, powdered milk. Add water and become whole." She tests me?

"I think that way." Who is she? She seems to hear me. I continue. "I think in circles, word to word. Of course I never really *arrive* anyplace," I attempt. She nods her head.

"Linear expectations, shame, shame." She lays her sewing on the bench and stands before me. "You leap from rock to rock. The moment of transcendence is in the leap, not when you touch the rock. Words are springs to take you from the nature of things to the spark. So, why did you choose cow?"

"Choose? I chose only to change."

"Do you mean you didn't *think* about cow?"

"Not with any intention."

"Perhaps others did," she said with concern.

"No."

"You mean you were in the *crack* and you *just didn't follow through?*"

"I suppose."

"*Someone* filled that hole. Don't take it lightly." And then she pressed a button to turn the music in my ears louder and pushed me from her and said noncommittally, "Strauss. Move. To the corner," she commanded. "Back and forth, one and two and three. To the other corner. Back straight, pick up your feet. To the right corner. Breathe out if you're tired."

My lungs are bellows. I am on fire. Who is it she reminds me of? Is this what my father meant by bursting? She holds her four-fingered hand up to me. Six-fingered Generous? Two-fingered I? The music stops but my head is full and my heart pounding. Someone in the mirror of my dead aunt's truck.

"Okay, baby."

Baby? My mother. "Are you my mother?"

She smiles at me. It is a knowing smile, an amused smile, slightly crooked, very arrogant. I shall never forget it. "Do *I* look like your *mother*?" I hang my head. "Baby, double B, didn't you learn that? Double B. Double V. House of God, container of Aleph, turned on its side, God's mouth?"

"Yes." I had not been taught about Beth as mouth. W, I knew, was teeth.

"Okay. Okay. You're supposed to *know* that. . . ."

Supposed to? "I know that for every stitch you take on a garment you are wearing, there will be a tear of sorrow."

She looks up sharply at my wisdom.

"Then I shall not weep," she answers and pulls her cow dress over her head transforming herself into something soft and muscular and silk with underneath things as fine as my father wove. And sits again cross-legged and continues to sew her hem with tiny stitches. Supple she is and flexes her toes and calls me to dance.

"Right together. Front, side, front, side, back, slide left, front, back, slide right. Point, left, cross, right, cross." What she tells me to do I do, sometimes with two feet, sometimes with four, sometimes with great sweeps of my horns. A part of me floats and flies and for moments I am not a cow.

"Dance for the dead," she calls, "and let them hear your heart. Dance for the doves. Dance for your father."

When she finished sewing, she laid the dress on the nuns' bench and climbed on my back and drove me by my horns and we danced while she called the steps, the heat of her

233

fruity body burning against my back, her knees pressing into my sides. She lay forward with her head between my horns. I was dizzy with her scent. And I moved with larger, longer, braver steps. I crashed into a gravestone. A piece of wall crumbled behind me, the music changed to the *Vienna Woods*, she whispered, and still we flew, she holding tight, turning me now and then, calling steps, and the music in my bones and my eyes blinded with tears and sweat. Who is she and why does she understand me?

"I am who you may be. Your larger whole," she shouted over the *Vienna Woods*. Trees bent. Who *I* may be?

I stopped and she fell forward and had to grasp my neck to keep from tumbling over my horns. And then she slid from me and turned in circles across the nunnery floor. From a niche a flight of doves burst: white, blue, white, white and blue and dark purple, circled, lifted, landed, lifted, landed, the white first, the purple last, circling. They were the music themselves.

"Listen, cow, listen. Kore, kowrie, cow, wealth, wheel, vache, vaca, vache en roulette, baca, vacant. Think of these things. Yod is hand is penis is the manifest. Yes? Yod goes to nod. Nod is Naught, not, the unmanifest, naughty."

"You knew my father, didn't you?"

"And the young Abbot. Well." She placed her hands on her hips and stretched into the loveliness of her body.

"I don't understand how. . . ." I hated her.

"I manifest, you see, through thought, not time. I'm off the wheel," she said, pivoting. "Over the moon."

"And I? What am I to do?"

She pulled her mended dress over her head, mumbling from within as she adjusted herself. "You're part of my morphogenetic field. You just chose the wrong chreode. For

234

now . . . for now, know yourself internally and trust no one." Her head was free of the fabric. "And your Abbot . . . don't depend on him at all."

The tour boat blasted its round-up call and I pressed her rather brutally against a nunnery wall. She was amused. "Where is the finger you are missing?"

She laughed.

"What is your name?"

"I have no name. I am not distinguished. Surely your father has explained the Real Articles to you? The pre-possessors? The pre-nouns? What may very well be my name?"

The tour boat blasted a thousand times in my body and the voices of the party floated toward us. She stood watching me until I released her but she did not move from the nunnery wall. She waited, tapping her foot. She was my father hanging his fingers in the air over his loom, waiting for me, and then, suddenly, I knew why I was being kept alive.

She nodded and reached to stroke my throat.

"The finger is in your dewlap and you are to preserve it against everything and everyone, against change. It is the measure of the Universe. You are the cow that came up from the sea."

She held her forefinger before my eyes. "Look. The length from the nail . . . so . . . to the knuckle is one measure. Yes? From the knuckle to the next knuckle another measure. The relationship, the proportion, between the measures— it is the proportion of the Universe. It is harmony. It is music. It is architectural beauty. It is mathematics. The finger you have is the perfect model of that proportion. Lesser creatures vary from the perfection." She rubbed her fingers over my lips. "Truly you are the cow that came up from the sea."

"And you?"

Her hands drifted over her cow ears. "I am a colloquy of flesh and death with good legs and a bad ass. And soon I must go for there is a mudslide in Santorini and many unprepared souls are in need of escort. . . ."

"Before you leave . . ."

"Yes?"

"In the tale Generous told me, the cow who came up from the sea was to reshape the world. How?"

"Hardly. You are to keep it in balance." She stroked my dewlap once again. "In balance."

Single file, the tourists reappeared, the child searching the ditch as his father dragged him along. Nicholas, disguised as a croftshusbandman, followed them and when he was near me, roped my horns and set to drag me away.

I had no idea Nicholas could also go beyond the stones. In my life so far, I calculated, as I dug my rear heels deep into the ground and howled at Nicholas, only the woman and Generous had not lied to me. Generous because he was stupid. The woman because she was I. Or was she? Along the stile a small piece of child's toy in the rough shape of an anvil, sky-blue, lay on the ground. I saw it at the very moment the woman did. Cow ears atwitch, she bent for it and tossed it to me. "Shape yourself," she called to me and left.

I swallowed the piece.

Shape yourself.

I seethed with sentiment—jealousy, pride, pleasure. But when the sentiments settled in the bottom of my cup and I could sort one from the other, I knew quite clearly that there was something very wrong with her information. She also made me feel considerably uglier than even I had yet felt.

All that winter her smile, still thin, still archaic, hung above my stall on the pulley bars. It was arrogant, amused, amiable, mythic. Trust no one, she had warned me, and I did not trust her. If the measure is given, how can I shape myself? If the proportions are exact, how am I to reshape the world? That is ridiculous . . . that I would reshape the world. If all things are to be kept in balance, how can things change? Balance is not the principle of change. It is the death of chance. Novelty is in the crack of things between end and beginning. It is from the wounding that change will come, from the yearning of the incomplete soul. From the pining? Of course. Balance is stability and I have to get out of the stable.

I rehearse my father's questions. So, what is the principal cause of change, Celeste? What is life, Celeste? What brings change to form and form to change? What is the meaning of the measure someone has stuck in my unwilling throat, Father? What is stable? What is not?

If I pray for order, then I cannot shape myself except within that order and I will be forever a creature. Under the hay I have the anvil, my great-aunt's mauve shoes, her beastie ears. I don't care how the stars work, rigid in their clocks and their paths. I don't care for that order and yet I bear it in my throat. I dismiss the measure. I need to be Creator. I need disorder. The barn clock bleeds and time does not return. I need to go through time, not hang in static balance. And then, beyond time, even beyond Thomas.

Thomas came occasionally, apologetically, to feed me a

handful of sweet hay or a biscuit, warm from his body. I would not look at him. Once, he held my head in his hands and pushed the hair away from my eyes and looked directly into my eyes and I stood still shivering until he dropped my head as if it were on a string and turned on his heel and left. If the woman appears in thought, not in time, perhaps he never touched her as he touched me. I imagined his passion and it gnawed at my heart.

So. I must move from the stable. Instability is disorder and it is Aleph, the Alpha, the A, just as my father told me—the power. I had once touched that power in the roots of the tree so long ago when I was changed from a girl to a cow but I had sung the wrong note or none at all or someone else's note and was shaped into this stomach, this involuted brain that I am.

According to the good Dr. Prigogine's text, which must still lie on the shelf in my childhood room, at the point farthest from equilibrium, self-organization to a more complex form is possible. And at that terrible moment when I became a cow, I had been far from stable. I had been in the very crack of change. I ought to have held on. When the structure is most unstable, it is time for change. And there is something within me, the A, beyond structure, which can make change. I had given up too soon. Chaos/disorder may be an order of consciousness itself, and I had been in it then. So I had given up too soon and went sliding down the wrong chreode chute. But there will be a right moment. I will go beyond the stars and their orbits. I will be in the crack again, the W, double B, and I will sing the message of change to my form. Form is only a tense, a sense, a lens. I will shake my kaleidoscope and rearrange it all. The question is, for me, now, whether the power of consciousness to formulate itself can succeed against the rigid orbit of the planets—will against repetition.

So. All that winter, I dreamed of Seth but danced under the woman's smile. In the meadows, I danced in one orbit, stopped, swung into another orbit. I was the star. I could feel inner things thudding against each other as I changed orbits, just as my father's silken planets thudded against each other when he changed their courses. In the barn, I danced down the central aisle, one foot in shit and one foot on concrete, a situation, I thought, metaphorically accurate for us all. And in my stall, I wore out my bed of straw each week with my dancing. Justus was amused and changed his music to suit my steps. The other cows windsucked and kicked when I danced and while a few tried to learn the simplest of steps, and succeeded, what was really important they could not learn: how to change the rhythm. Justus plucked the constellation Lyga and it rose above the sea. Justus sang the notes of the stars, their shapes and sounds. He sang Apollo and the letters of his swan form and drew the constellation in the northern skies. It is his harmony. "Change the note, Justus," I call. "Change the note and watch the new stars rise." Justus repeats his notes. Et cetera. Et cetera. Seth calls but I am afraid.

I watched, that winter, the thin stripe of storm-brewed horizon turn from red to purple to blue to black. I watched the rose window turn in those colors. I watched the storm shadows on its face. It was a melancholy winter. I ate well, God knows, and I stank. Ice clung to the rock faces of the Paps. Viking gales whipped across the foreshore over stunted hazel. One week before the end of the year, the snow in thaw, the air foolishly mild with sun, the sea cobalt and capped with white flames, that night, monks and cows quiet, I slipped my tether and went as softly as I could from the barn to the lettuce garden. Night-straying I was and suitable for beating but I went, for the gold covered the garden and hung from the trees and moon-fire crept along last year's vines and up the fences. The ground was as deep in a moment of fireflies as the sky in stars. Afraid, I hooked my tether to a small tree and held my breath as forms shifted. A strange-limbed beast became a lion, a unicorn, another cow, a cockhorse with great wings, and a towering woman in a mantle of snakes. The garden was aflame in the moonlight and I wanted to leap, to wrap myself in the gold of it. Perhaps it is better to be a cow and not to dream. Better to be here, better to be tethered. Let him think, that shapeshifter out there, that I am merely a cow, I, hide, hiding, without questions, without thoughts, with the measure, without a past. I am safe as a cow. Despising myself, I moved slowly back to the barn and locked myself into my solid stall and watched the finger of the moon as it drew itself toward the rose window.

It is safe in my stall. To strip oneself of all the B, the containers, the stable, the resistances is too terrifying. To move to the edge of great non-linear dissipate instability, far far from equilibrium where shadows are cockhorses and fireflies are stars, is to face death. Here I live in the land of certainty with the stars in the Heavens, with rules and roles. But *there*, there is no certainty. Even Generous, with his slow and stubborn pen, keeps the lists of the uncertainties, keeping them out of the way, hidden, as if they were relics of a time past, long gone. Boy born with two heads. Rooster lays eggs. Sky rains frogs. Ships with crews in the air. He knows there are great uncertainties. Even as we live in certainty and light, there are shadows. Little wonder so many have received Nicholas's Roman baptism . . . there are no shadows for Nicholas. No Seth in the darkness waiting.

The finger of the moon touched the face of the rose window and suddenly, as if in answer, a thin film of flesh covered the bones of the abbey and the bones of the abbey became rounded and soft, and the towers became . . . what is it . . . knees. And the crack of doors, a human, fleshy ass, and the rose window—the great seat of birth—burst open with the light of birth as a living eye. A cathedral of flesh, the abbey became, her belly the roof of it all. I raced from the barn but stopped at the Tree of Life and hid, somehow, in its shadow. (Aah, Nicholas, you fool.) There I saw her navel, the nave, her arms outstretched into the apse, and her head as altar. Her woman part opened in the red-gold of light. I saw her and knew I looked upon a woman with her knees in the air, giving birth to living light. What had been the soft gold reflection on the glass, now became her own fire. I watched. Stars rested on her fingers and glinted on her kneecaps.

And then she stood and shook stiffness from her limbs and the transparency of flesh became solid and she walked along the Street of the Dead down toward the sea, past me, knelt, dropped her long dark hair into the pool of sea, and washed herself. And then she stood and spun over the fields, her robes of moonlight twisting about her, twisting until she became a triangle of light, five parts four, four parts three, shimmering, and the moisture from her hair dropped as dew on the fields. She lay down again where the abbey had been, lifted her knees to the sky, stretched out her arms across the fields, opened herself, her woman part, and was stone again. Doors, towers, window, stone. The moon rose above her knees as if it had been born from them. I saw the miracle, that night, only once, but I knew then that the true light came from the darkness and it was to the darkness I must go. I could not hide.

I had watched the abbey dance. I had seen the meaning of the abbey, dancing, deconstructed, alive. Thomas says there are things which perdure. Surely not order, not construction. Surely not he, nor I, nor the measures of things. Each new creation, it must be, is stirred with a different spoon, or many spoons at the same time. I have only one of those spoons; there are others. There must be. Do I stay here as a cow, content, and pass on my line of cow? Am I to become a dish as the dead Kings become? Am I to run away to the darkness with the spoon? With the measure of things as they seem to be?

I raise a rainbow over the sea as the abbey sleeps and the day begins. "Rainbow," I say, and it collapses, sentenced, too numinous for words. I must get on with myself.

 Spring came slowly. The sun hesitated. But the days themselves lengthened and the raucous sounds of sheep mating rode on the galewinds and the cows climbed each other, grunting, wanting the bull. Thomas came one cold morning, rattled through the amulets and keys in his pockets, looked away from the questions in my eyes, and gave me a biscuit. Ah well. As I ate he roped me and led me out. We walked, he and I, I exulting to be near him, moving to rub against his side. Far across the machair we walked, to a new pasture. He let me stop now and then to rip at the heather, bitter and too elastic it was, adapted to the winds, more root than movement, as the lives of the monks. A fine mist lay on everything and a light new snow blew in from the northern sea. The waves, chalk lines against the blue,

242

arched and drew the seventy-two-letter name of God on the cobalt sea. I was indecently happy to be with him.

"The world is the sea," Thomas intoned behind me. "Swollen with the waves of pride, driven hither and thither by the winds of vainglory and capped by the foams of lust." And truly, with his eyes, I could see the chalk waves arch their backs and break and pound and crash into each other only to slip away as soft foam at the edge of the shore. "Pride, vainglory, and lust," he repeated as if exorcizing himself and warning me. I found his zealousness unpleasant.

We stopped in the middle of the meadow. Thomas bent and with his hands opened an imaginary curtain and there near the foreshore in the midst of the white air I saw a hillock and then, drifting, a nightmare, massive, a black mountain against an angry sea: the new bull.

Thomas let my rope slacken. Two other young cows, half the size of the bull, moved about him, rubbing his sides and turning from him, teasing, as he turned to them. The bull was perfect and black, with no white tufts, a bull of sacrifice, surely. Steam rose from his haunches. Around him, wherever he had been, the ground was broken with his anger and power. Three animals danced a hot and desperate dance, no waltz, warlike, a battle of orchid creatures.

Why has Thomas brought me here? Surely the other cows would please the bull. I looked at Thomas and his face closed like the rood curtain.

The air pulsed with the presence of the bull as ultimate necessity, a focus of matter and death. Thomas had led me here to die into cow. You know me, damn you, Thomas. I am Celeste. I am only a cow for a little while.

He patted me on my nose and pushed the hair away from my eyes and then led me up the incline to the bull. As he backed down the hill, he pulled the two small cows away with him and I was left.

The bull sniffs at me, sucks my smells into himself, grazes me with his terrible, sharp horns, touches me with his side, his nose, his heat, and the black robe of his shadow suffocates me in a torpor of fear. Sure-footed, four-footed, my nose at his shoulder, I could wound him with my horns but he would break my back if he mounted me. I have to mate with him because I am a cow and the Abbot wants me to and he is the only one in the world who knows, except for the lady and God knows where she is, that I am more. In the monotonous world of trajectories and deterministic change, I have to mate with the bull. But there are other worlds where there is no legitimate model, where the laws break down, where there is no key, no measure, no spoon at all, where I, just as the *Prince George*, can deduce myself from the axiomatic sea, the theoretical sky, where I can write my own story. I circle the bull as he circles me and examine every inch of him. Phobos, Panic, Chaos, Havoc, all the old Gods, dance on my back. But I can think and I think and find this: the bull is designed for mounting cows, not for running down hills. His front legs are shorter than his rear legs. I know in a mind-moment that I must make the bull run downhill. I will race to my father's house, circle it, and then step aside, and the bull will go tumbling head first, horn first, down the path, into the ground with his horns. Every stone on that path is mine.

He will fall over himself, tumbling, twisting, planted. Involuted his nature will be, much as mine had been involuted from man to animal, his from animal to plant. I will involute the beast, his horns as roots, his feet blossoms. And as I circle him I allow myself, force myself, to rub against him, matching breath with breath, pawing with pawing, sniffing with sniffing, snorting with snorting, horn sweep with horn sweep until he can not separate himself from myself, and then when he is without barrier—I have seen the orchid creature at work—I run.

So, Thomas, warn me about pride, vainglory, and lust, and lead me to the bull. My future is determined by the spot of infinity within me, not the measure. My pattern is drawn from the ethereal polar planes. It is there I must reach. I shall create this moment, a small God myself.

The sun broke through the whiteness and caught a glint on Thomas's nicked face. Bastard, I say to him. Weak bastard. And I run. The bull, totally within my field now, runs after me, with me. Over the machair and into the open sky, the snow and wind driving me forward, from the breeding pasture to my father's path. Thomas and the other monks, indistinct, who have come to watch my indignity, call in agitation to us. "Hoo! Hoo!" The bull labors after me. His shadow surrounds me, pulls at me, thickens the air, slows me. But I keep the waltz in my head, in my body, in my legs. It leads me and lifts my legs. Every bit of grass counts, every rock, every notch in the ground is important. I turn this way, he that. Wind from the sea blows us upward. His machine breath lifts the hair on my back. This rock, that stump, rock to rock. He stumbles. I try to think what it is in his head, but there is nothing except my smell and his orchid creature.

Damn your soul, Thomas. You led me to this to free yourself and to punish me, to reduce me wholly to my lower cow-self as I have reduced you to your lower self, to punish me for your own pleasure, to punish yourself and to preserve the balance. Damn you and damn your balances. And still I love you and still I pray that somewhere at the end

245

of this torment, my father, the woman, John Joe, you, will be waiting to save me. Part of me knows there will be no one. These are my rewards. Thomas, you have loved me and touched me and held me gently in your arms and been breathless at my beauty and suppleness and entered me and rocked the sea. And now you turn the brute of the bull on me. All of me imagines the crack of the bull as he tries to mount me, the terrible arching sea wave of my back breaking as he plunges. I'm at the edge of the crack, the farthest possible spot from equilibrium, the place of change, and I welcome the fear. There will be that instant, that time to change, that comma between end and beginning, cause and effect, and, in it, I will become woman. Come, bull. Come faster, come closer.

There is no order now except my own. I am my own golden spool rolling out the thread of my destiny. If there is no legitimate model, order, surely then there is no key, no measure, no spoon, and the finger sewn into my dewlap is worthless. Come bull, drive me forward. All this trouble over a key, over an orchid creature, my father maddened, with the same eyes as the bull, the Abbot. God, he has me. He mounts but I knock a rock loose at his hind feet and he slides away.

So. What is the cause of form? My cow form is the cause of this moment. Is this disorder? Is order perception and nothing else? Is this order? What carries the message of change to form? Instability opens the door. A is the instability. I am its shaper. The blue anvil of sky sits in my throat with the ridiculous finger. As I run, all that I am is shed behind me and I am left only with instability, with A, un-contained. And B, bull, stable, moves after me, a shadow of my B self. Not for me the stable. I have to be at the edge if I am to change. But how far can I go? I am exhausted.

The snow is heavier, flying at flat angles behind me. My sides burst. My legs so wooden I cannot lift them and yet I do. What can I think of? Niece, nice, Nike, niche. Aunt, ain't, haunt, haint. I am beyond lists. I falter. If I can only move him to run downhill. My father's house is a large feathered bird adrift in the wind before me. I round the house but the bull, startled at the feather-thatching, does not follow me and there he stands before me as I come back to the path. He is snorting and pawing, his parts large, red, threatening, and I have no choice but to dive forward over the cliff, down the flinty edge toward the Other Side. You should know this, Thomas, what have you done to me. Damn your soul. May you suffer ten times what I will. Behind me the bull crashes and rolls, gravel slips past my feet in rivers, a huge noise behind me, thundering, he rolls up against me, a boulder he is, knocking me over but his horn has ripped into his leg and the blood pours down the hill before us and his other horn is buried in the gravel and he cannot stand with his agony. His legs are in the air and his hooves bloom into carnations.

I stand still watching his green eyes roll in the darkness of him like little seeds in the earth. Another symmetry break. "We've escaped, you and I," I assure him uselessly. "See, you're a plant. Soon I will not be a cow." And I begin to laugh at the great white polar sky and feel my spot of infinity swell toward it as a heart and suddenly my laughter is smothered and I'm wrapped in a dark and velvety cloud of felt and my laughter rides outside me and it is deep and rolling and terrible and no longer mine and the bull moans as his life spills out before him and I am pulled further and further into the loose sand, into the Beyond. I glimpse the huge and hammy leg of Seth. I hear his snorting laughter. I feel his knife-tip through the domino enveloping me. And he cuts at my throat but I pull away and he pulls me back with powerful limbs and stretches his legs over my back, astride me, and bends my neck backward as if the bone and sinew would break, the flesh give way, and holds me with his crude antique hand on my throat and he searches in my fur for the dewlap, for the finger. Of course I escape him and again he holds me, flings himself onto me, forces me into the sand and I can see his bright gold eyes and his teeth sharpened into points, the mouth full of W's under a snout, and I cry out, "No! No! Thomas, help me." And I escape him again and he holds me. This is the moment. At the brink of change. Change yourself! But I fear for my body. I am rigid with terror as the rough staff of the God cracks against my head and blood runs into my eyes and I feel the flapping of cormorant wings against my eyes and the crescent knife at my throat and red hams and golden eyes and foul juices. Swollen and angry in his pride, muscled, huge. No! The knife . . . gravel slips down the hill. Seth looms in the night, his cape blowing behind him, his huge sausage part fiery and fierce, staring at me, piercing as an eye, his mouth agape. Rivulets of blood and sand are at my shoulder. It is worth nothing, this measure. It is a child's toy. Blood runs from my head into my eyes. The bull's blood covers the both of us and crusts on my legs and his hands. Change is one thing, death quite another. This is the man who strangles and cuts and chops bone and tears lungs, who cleans the Kings' bones and sends them to the kilns, the Divider, the Prosecutor, Winter. His hand trembles at my throat. I writhe and squirm and the ground and gravel slip away, and from above us, a tumbling sound of a great body and the bull, dead and warm and wet, rolls down the hill, gathering speed, faster and faster as the sand slips away beneath him, an avalanching bull, and Seth rolls from me but the dead weight of the bull throws him to the side. And I scramble away and race up the endless hill, the sand sliding away from me at my feet. The eyes of the bull are incandescent in the dark and filthy sand. Through snow and sand I follow his bloody path toward my father's house, the taste of the ashes of death still in my mouth. My change lies below me, somewhere in the crack, and I turn to see Seth, his arms spread up to me, his face fleshy, his tongue protruding, his mouth gargoyle-great. The letter Beth turned sideways, his mouth.

What was in me that led me back? The sand gave way again under my feet and I was at his black side.

"Take the measure, Seth. Give me my womanhood."

He looked down at me, his mouth gaping and deep. "Has the cow then come up from the sea?"

"And I wish the Abbot's love as well!" Glutton, I am. Lustful, I am, covetous.

He sailed, if that is the correct word, without touching the sand and led me into a hollow. I could hear great rushings of water above me. My hooves clacked on wet and slippery rock. Three hooded old ones stood above me. One with a mirror, one with a candle, one with a knife. Seth raised the knife, slit my dewlap, and took the measure. He held the candle against my wound until it was healed. I do not know how much time passed but I was beyond the cave, back on the shore, in deep silence, running after him as he sailed, his domino floating behind him, back to the sand still wet with the bull's blood. Seth turned to me. His face was Thomas's face.

He shrank, became delicate and smaller, his face from monstrous to godlike, gracious, he was, and his mouth, smiling, moist, no longer gaping, and cleansed himself in the sea and there was seaweed in his hair, and he held open the black domino for me to enter. "Thomas?" I entered. His arms swept around me and he pulled me gently to a rock and sat on it and pinned me on top of him and I felt him licking my nipples and biting my neck and stroking me and I called to the sea, "How can it be?" His body began to circle as if on hunt, clockwise. My hips moved with his from hour to hour and his body, his hips, moving from hour to hour counterclockwise and suddenly his tool descending ringing in me and the two orchid creatures moving in time and out of time and the tool dong dong dong inside the hollow vessel of my belly. The orchid creature led us on and on, stroke, time, stroke, time, Thomas, time. Tammuz, Chronos, the rigid orbits. Time sped, denser and denser it became as a star burning and at the end one almost could slip through the eye of the moon, through my belly and into the eye of the moon, away from time. Dense and heavy, stars we were. Becoming a star. Thighs. And then he flooded me with seagates opened and the Milky Way of his seed pouring in and on and over.

In his arms, I was woman. He led my hands over my new body. At last. The useless measure gone, my womanhood given. And later when I slid from his arms, his arms stretched for me, blindly. Blindly?

And then he threw his head back and I saw the seaweed in his hair and him laughing terribly, mouth agape, eyes moon-white, unmoving, and tossed me from himself, Seth did, and I on my back, a cow in the sand. No longer a woman. He no longer Thomas but the God again and with his staff he hit my rump and drove me up the hill away from him. I looked behind. Seth's cape blew around him.

"Who are you?"

He laughed into the night. "Chi-o, you are, art of light."

"Are you a shapeshifter? Are you Thomas?"

And he was gone and I was covered with blood and semen

and I wept and wished for all I had had and all I had lost.

Pine trees bent under the wind and the tops snapped above my head, crashing behind me. I walked on toward my father's house, leaving my womanhood behind me someplace in the crack. Chi-o, xo, cow, que. Am I the question? Is chi-o, chai-os? Chai is life. Is chaos the maker of the light? The art of light? The Creator of light? What was Seth telling me? What do I know?

Watch the W's. Cain is Qaheen. Is it not the holy time of When? Queen. Q goes to W. Does Guinevere mean Whenever? A sexual joke? Like Lance a lot? Que? Quo? Quando? Qui? Cow? How? These are the questions and we are the splintered answers who have utterly neglected the queenly questions we come from. Out of the light, comes time: Cain. Out of Why comes When. The Words began with Q and when the language was cut up the Q became a W, the Word found its mouth, the Creator created. So. Que did a Q become a W and how did the cow jump over the moon? And Why and What and When and Which and Who, above all Who, in its cosmic august path paused in the shadows, shaddai, of the gates of the Milky Way while the little dog laughed to see such craft and the dish ran away with the spoon. Is the Q the pig with its tail? And the W the ears of the dog turned upside down as the A becomes the horns of the cow? How long does this joke go on? Forever. I step across the trail of the bull, his place of planting, across the withered footsteps of my father at the top of his cliff, and stand there to watch my father's cottage, its feather roof adrift in the winds of my new consciousness.

And there, inside, in a room without dimension, I sleep and wake and wish to return and sleep again through the next night and day and wake in another night, still a cow and without the measure.

I hold a match between my teeth, strike it on the fire place, light a candle. My teeth chatter with the effort. The shadows of my father's house retreat. Curtains of cobwebs swing at the corners, balloon, and collapse at my movement. Under them nothing has changed. Skeletons of birds hang from the beams. The loom is half-filled with the findings of my father's disintegration and my flagstone, my books, my crayons arranged as if he'd waited for me. No, it is sentimental to think so, for my father had not even known me when I met him in the parking lot, when his feathers drifted away.

And dumbly I had contained that measure in my throat and surrounded it with the accretions of terror, loneliness, horror, loss, conspiracy, all of it and I a pawn for all of them. She said shape yourself. Of what use was it all? If I am to shape myself, I need no measure. And if I have given it away, it is well given and if I am indeed, somehow, the cow who came up from the sea to reshape the world, I am not impressed. I am here to reshape *myself*. Between my legs the warm pleasure trembles still and I drip with Seth's honey and the candle burning in the window of my father's house trembles with the heat between my legs.

I light the turf in the fire place. It is lovely. From my father's room, I take the silken bobbins and with my nose build Heaven on the floor. So. I must think. If the purpose of the measure was to reshape myself, perhaps I *have* led the world to disaster. So long ago I was my father's smallest planet following him. "I am Saturn, I lead. You are Herschel, following." I no longer follow, but am I now to lead?

If the purpose of the measure was to maintain the balance of the world as it is, then giving it away, I may indeed reshape the world. Perhaps man's course is not to conform to nature but to change it. And I take that course. And these people who bound me—my father, the Abbot Isaac, the woman with the cow ears, Thomas with his weaknesses— they wanted me to keep the measure safe. I did not do so.

I hear faint calls in the night. "Thirty-three, hoo, hoo. Thirty-three, where are you?"

Night, Nike, Victory, victim, victual, vici, vice, Sin. And Sin is Lamentation and Sin is the name of the moon. What does this mean? How is Naught changed to naughty?

Kings die. They go as victim to Seth. He conquers, vici. They are eaten as victual. They return to the crofters' kilns to become dishes for victuals. Seth has victory over them. What is it that connects the words? I hear it ringing. Nike is the Goddess of Victory. Nike is night, Victory, vici, vice. Vice is Sin and Sin is the name of the moon. I draw a 33 in the dust of my father's floor and as I orbit it, it becomes a WW, the form beyond the form, the Dis which contains the A, the breath of God. Seth is the double containment. Ah, you handsome double, you. Thomas is only the alternating God, Time, Tammuz, the God that must die, the last leaf on the Tree of Life. Thomas is Time—that which is manifested. But Seth, Caesar, Kaiser, Chazar, Pig, he is the endless container of all that is and all that is not: the Chazarei. Thomas's universe is a frozen, balanced, rigid symmetry. The Other Side is the crack from which novelty emerges. Seth leads the way to the Naught.

"Hoo, hoo, Thirty-three, come back. Where are you?"

I am in the middle of understanding. A Heaven of satin bobbins and silken planets are at my feet, so arranged that I may know where I have been and who I am. Leave me alone for a few moments more.

"Thirty-three." The voice is closer.

I piss on the fire to kill the smoke. I sweep Heaven away with my tail and the final ashes hiss at me.

So, then. Seth imitated Thomas. He imitated Time. He drew me away from Is-Not, away from novelty, away from change, away from the Land of Nod and Nicht, the WW, and turned me toward the narrow land of the manifest with . . . ah, yes . . . with his phallus. The phallus is Yod, which is the manifest. Mani is hand. He drew me back with his orchid creature, back to the manifest, by imitating Thomas, imitating life. He awakened my own creature and sent me from Nod to Yod, from himself to form, from the unstable to the stable, from the shit to the concrete. For *there* where Seth is, is possibility. It is the crack, the emptiness from which form emerges. And I was thrown out.

He gave me his phallus but not the fire of his seed, for the seed of the God is in the reservoir of his heart. He did not give me possibility. For a handful of seeds I sold my cow and climbed the Tree of Death to the giant to be re-born, but Seth shook me out of the Tree and when I ran home, my hands were empty and were hooves. All that—and I am still a cow. And soon I will be found and led to the barn.

Have I now upset the quintessential equilibrium of Is by giving away the proportion between Is and Is-Not? Perhaps now all the fine white hands beneath the sea will clutch at the oars of the world and pull it under, in a new tribute to Dis, the God of Not, a new Dis/tribution. Is that what I have done?

"Thirty-three. Hoo, hoo. Thirty-three."

But I feel no guilt. I will go back to Seth, somehow, and become a woman.

It is Thomas's voice threading thin in the night around my father's house. "Hoo, Thirty-three?"

Ah, Thomas, near equilibrium, Thomas, the laws of change are universal. But farther away there are no rules. There are singularities and extravagant fluctuations of nature. I have been farther away.

And I am such a one. I am not a new order. I am a break in symmetry. I am a naked singularity. But there may be others. *That* may be the true order—extravagant fluctuation, symmetry breaks, many orders, many singularities.

The extravagant fluctuation leaves the common room of her childhood and hides in her small room with her books and her flagstone as the Abbot, his face filled, I am certain, with an orderly graciousness that may mean my death, enters her father's house. The candle is a puddle of wax on the window sill. My heart throbs so fiercely within my hide I wish to run from it, to lock it behind me in my childish room. I will bring you to Rome, he will say when I show him my father's books, when I draw my name in the dust with my hoof. And Rome shall at last understand that the will must remain free, that grace is inherent, that the course of evolution must remain open. He will say all that. And I will say no. Ah, Thomas. If I were a woman and you had made love to me as Seth had, would it be the same?

I heard Thomas stamping his feet and clapping snow from his hands, silver on flesh. His teeth chattered. He scratched along shelves in search of matches. "So, Manuel. They still talk of you. God bless you, in whatever yawning gap you dwell."

I shivered to hear my father's name. Thomas moved into the weaving room, found the matches, returned with heavy feet again to light a fire, struggled with the wet ashes. Finally flames shot up and framed him. My stink in the ashes was noxious. Small and weary, he seemed. Bits of ice clung to his cheeks. I remembered the sea pearls on his eyelashes the day I met him. Ah, Thomas, our dreams, our dreams. And our secrets.

He spoke softly. "Pitiful, to waste such brilliance. And what name do I use, Manuel, for the son who was a daughter?"

My name!

I shall always remember that moment. I lifted my head. I had not heard my name for endless seasons. The wind's breath, I had heard, the insects, the birds, never my name. I had heard the thoughts of holly and oak and hazel, of sheep and cow and gosling, sounds on the tongues of monks, in the strings of the cithara, in the pounding of hearts and churning of stomachs. In them and in the whir of the milk machine or the barn squeak of lever and pulley, I had imagined my name. Even in a dog's faint howl. But I had not heard my name in all my time as a cow.

Thomas found my childhood notebooks and spread them on his knees, a spy, the Abbot, in my strange innocent kingdom. He lifted papers, my drawings of barns and kites, of apples and ice cream cones in my Dark Horse Copy Book with its wide white spaces, and he saw my A's and my B's, my fours, my W's, my Q's, my $2V = W$. He mumbled my letters aloud, wondering at equations, amused. Soon he would come to a page with my name on it. I wrote it with my father's hand cramped about my own. The first time I wrote my name without his hand, my father kissed my fingers.

The papers stopped.

"Imagine. Poor Manuel, if you only knew . . . if we only knew. . . ." Thomas removed his shoes, laid them on the hearth, and rubbed his feet of cold. One sock had a hole in it. I would not have thought it would.

"Celeste, eh Manuel? Celeste?"

I cannot answer. Nor would I have thought a God would have His creature suffer this way with my heart and lungs and throat bursting, I covered with the juices of a false love, and the blood of the bull on my ankles and his death on my soul. Perhaps I am no longer a creature of God. Unable to answer my own name, a noose tightened around my throat, my lungs bulging, something ripped and torn with the effort, the tendons of my great neck stretched to birth the words and the grief flooding over my heart, rising beyond the stopgaps of my cowhood. The dewlap opened? The finger gone? I wished words out of me into the room that night as I had wished the letters from my fingers into that copy book so terribly long ago.

Thomas sat before the fire, rubbing his feet and his forehead, listening to the sounds of the storm and the calls of other monks seeking me. My copy books lay in his lap. Aah, Father, all you taught me with your twisted mind and how much you knew and how much more you tried to teach me. You filled me with questions and I am a question and I have no answer.

"Celeste," Thomas repeated thoughtfully and I answered with bloody spittle and I struggled within again and at last the words erupted, deep and rumbling.

"I am here." My voice vibrated the length of my body. I cleared my throat and answered again. "Yes, I am here."

Thomas stood, dropping my copy books to the floor, stared into the dark space of my room. "Who are you? Where are you?"

There was violence and passion and hatred and love between us. I tormented him. My voice softened, grew liquid. "Here, come and see me."

"A devil." He ran for the door.

"I am Celeste."

"No."

"Thomas . . ."

"You know me?" At last he had my agony. His face tightened and snapped. He crossed himself. "Come out. I will not go in."

And so I came out, slowly, through spider-web curtains into the flicker of the fire-place light, my fur golden and glorious. Thomas flung an arm before his eyes and his shoes began to burn at the soles. I remembered that—the smell of them filling the air and a sulfurous smoke and he kneeling and hiding and calling to God.

"O Lord of Mercy, in my solitude I spoke sweet words to a cow. Only a cow. Your creature, dumb she was and gentle and a tender look in her eye for me when I walked in the fields. Patient. In my sin, I told her what I must not have. Punish me no more."

"Thomas . . ." I persisted.

"No."

His shoulders collapsed with the thrust of his name on my tongue. I had no pity. "Thomas, you did more than talk. And your talk was more than sweet, Thomas. You told me you loved me. You wrapped flowers in my bell chain and said that you thought of me as a woman. You tied ribbons on my horns and these bells. Many times. And more."

I believe Thomas then considered my death. He lifted his head, rose, and looked into my eyes. Nightwinged, I saw my death flutter across his eyes, his pupils constricting as my throat had. I knew he was able to kill me—and I him. My death crossed his eyes again and rested in the centers.

"Is this grace descending that the beast speaks? Or is it

a Fall? Do all beasts speak, Lord? Have I grown pure in heart to hear them? Does only this beast speak?"

My gums bled from the twisting of my jaws to form the words. My words were the same but they sprang from a new Heaven, a polar shift of new connections, from Seth, the polestar in my new sky. "I am not a beast, Thomas, I am Celeste, the daughter of Manuel, and I have become a cow. Form is only a tense."

And then with my teeth I twisted the knob of my father's cabinet and with my head motioned that Thomas pull the Bible and the books of architecture, which he did. He turned each page rapidly.

"The last page," I whispered.

And his words trembled as he spoke the final lines my father wrote. "My daughter has been cursed with my sins and will be given unjustly the child of my passion with . . ." Thomas paused. "The name is not filled in."

My father had saved Cook from shame and buried me. It was like him.

Thomas looked up at me sharply. "Why did Isaac . . . he must have known . . . why should he have permitted you . . . female . . . ?" And shook his head, bewildered. And read on. "And so I burn myself because I cannot face the eyes of my own child whom I have tortured for my passions. God forgive and accept my ashes." The leathery smoke darkened the common room.

"I forgive, Father. I forgive." And the forgiveness spilled from me on rivers of tears. Thomas held his hand over his eyes, pressing out the sight of a beast weeping.

"I couldn't leave the monastery, Thomas. I couldn't leave my father. And then . . . and then you came . . . and where would I go? What did I have? Who was I?"

"If this is true . . ." I watched his eyes move to if-then-therefore order. "If this is true, then many things break down: history, nature, original sin perhaps, certainly . . . ah, yes, certainly."

I scratched my name in the dust and my number, but nothing of WW, nothing of Seth. And Thomas said, "I will bring you to Rome and Rome shall at last understand that the will must remain free, that grace is inherent, that the course of evolution . . ."

He knows nothing of the cow coming up from the sea, nothing of the finger, nothing of reshaping the world. He knows and he refuses to know.

"No."

"No?"

"There is no legitimate model. I am not a legitimate model. I murdered Eldred . . . justifiably. I was the girl on the beach, Thomas," I said too slyly, "and I became a cow. Am I an example?"

He slumped on my father's flagstone.

"Don't use me, Thomas. Don't lead me to another bull."

"You are . . . formidable."

"Thomas." I walked closer to him and lay my head on his stiff knees. "Thomas, call me by my name. Say my name."

"Your name? I . . . Celeste. There. Celeste."

My name rolled through my body as the sun had. Celeste.

He shook his head over his roasted shoes—it would be my smell if the church were to burn me. He shook his head over my transformation, over what it meant, over what it could mean. And he stroked the short hairs between my horns and pulled gently at my long stiff ears. The sun rose and rolled around and around, and felt like Seth, hot and liquid.

"Tell me, Celeste. Tell me about living without language."

"I ate words."

He laughed. My heart flew to him.

"Yes. They were clean and cool and spongy like plant stems and they were . . . immediate . . . and young . . . and alive. Would it be madness to say that words were free? Alive?"

"No . . . no more than any of this."

"Nothing was determined and everything was so very intense. Thomas, you may think this the Fall, but my consciousness is intense, far more than when I was . . . well, when I was CuRoi."

"But lonely?"

"I had you." I waited for an offer in the present. It was not forthcoming.

"So you were liminal, neither cow nor woman . . . but truly yourself?"

"Yes."

"And you chose?"

"In a way."

"Well. It will look to others as if you've fallen. The Church, certainly Nicholas, would be delighted to put you to death as a demon. You would burn as my shoes burn. The question really is can you become a woman—can you change upward?"

"Thomas . . . don't question, please."

He lay down with his hands behind his head. The hole in his sock opened to an astonishingly ordinary toe and pointed to the ceiling beams. "This means that . . . this is the single ever-deepening note of evolution, Celeste, that man's consciousness will be free, that one can change, that one can choose . . . the creature becomes the Creator."

"Don't make me an example, Thomas."

"It becomes a world of infinite possibility, far beyond determinism, far beyond probability, light-years from necessity. It means that the direction of evolution is not form but free will." Thomas closed his eyes. "Must sleep . . ."

Then his eyes flew open. "Celeste, whatever you are, you are a remarkable being."

"I know. But I am not an example."

"You'll be safe with me. Nicholas . . . we must protect you from Nicholas. Celeste, one more question . . . why did you kill Eldred?"

"Eldred? He was worthless."

"But you said there was no legitimate model, against what do you pit Eldred?"

"It's a multiple world."

"That is not enough."

"He bothered me. A lot. I didn't like him."

"You have all the arrogance of your clan, and more."

"Thomas, the problem for me is the orbit of the planet Herschel versus the force of consciousness to formulate itself."

"Yes, that is the centralized church versus the free monastery. That I understand. You are deft at changing the subject and I am very tired."

"Eldred was in love with me. He would have guessed my secret."

"Well, *you* work at a higher paradigm. But too literal. As your friend John Joe flying . . . too literal. Killing Eldred, too literal. Too literal. I can be very literal." He slept suddenly, his mouth thrown open, his face softened and dimmed. The silver hand behind his head flashed in the rays of the fire. I dragged my childhood cow skin and covered his toe. Thomas stirred, smiling. I tucked my legs beneath myself, lay my head near his ear, and watched my dream fade. The eye of the fire winked and closed.

I have to redeem myself. I shall self-organize. For that, there is no model. Resurrection comes from the darkness and it is to the darkness I must again go. The A beyond A, in the B beyond B, the Augean stables. There is no harrowing of Hell. I must leap into the stables, wallow in them. It is Seth who stands at the gate to the Other Side of the Moon that leads to the Milky Way, the great BB mouth, Sinser himself.

A is breath. B is mouth. W is the teeth of the mouth that chews up existence in the great organic process, the great Prosecutor, Divider, Winter. Seth. "Oh, Seth. I am Celeste. I am here. I am Celeste."

I imagined myself with hands. I imagined Seth's hands. I imagined my body lithe and soft and silken-skinned. Seth danced under my eyelids. The jackdaws danced on the roof of my father's house, softly.

IT IS SOON TOLD.

I, GENEROUS, CHRONICLER, WRITE OF THOMAS'S DEPARTURE, THE FINDING OF THE COW, THE FINDING OF THE BULL, THE ILL FORTUNE BROUGHT UPON US.

It was our brother, Diarmat, seeking the lost bull, who found them. It was Diarmat who stood transfixed in the cottage by the sweetness of the two souls and it was Diarmat remembering the horrible power of the Abbot who had cut off his hand for witnessing Angels. It was Diarmat who backed away from what he had seen and fled in the morning to his cell and his secret. The monk and the cow he had seen, sleeping innocently as children, her head on his shoulder, saying in her sleep, "I am Celeste. I am here. I am Celeste."

And in the morning when fresh snow covered the frenzied footprints of Diarmat, the Abbot Thomas betook himself to wash the sorry cow, quench then the fire, dry her, and he, barefoot, for his shoes had fully burned, led her to the barn.

There the bloody carcass of the bull hung for its butchering.

Thrice tethered, she was, the wee cow, thin and weary.

Nicholas it was who called the brothers to convocation over the cow. In the abbey it was, before the altar. Thomas, judgment without fault, walked toward us with a face as dun as the moon behind the sun, and sat away from us. Nicholas argued mightily for the punishment of the cow who caused death.

"Once she murdered Brother Eldred. But a public murder it was and she was forgiven." Nicholas's head bobbed and shook, agreeing with himself. Other heads in the room agreed with him. Thomas sat straight as a tree. "Now she has done a secret murder of the bull, an intentional and willful secret murder by leading the bull to the Other Side. Not only a murderess, she is subtle and diabolical. It is an unnatural beast we have among us. The judgment of Rome is that the cow be killed."

"Rome?" Thomas's voice crashed against the sea-greened column and echoed through the abbey. "Deceit. Wiles. Politics."

"Rome." Nicholas answered in such strength as we had not before known and it was remarked afterward that Nicholas had deceived us with his weaknesses. "The Guardian of Grace."

Thomas stood, tapped his sword against his bench. "I am your authority. I say the cow is to remain with us. She will be in my charge if it pleases you and under my eye. The cow now works, as we do, toward self-perfection."

Others, without friendship, without trust, looked away from the Abbot. Nicholas walked among his followers, and those of us who had been long with the brothers trembled for the schism.

"We have not only a murdering cow, but also an Abbot who claims the beast struggles for self-perfection. If we are all not mad from this island and this isolation from the love of Rome, I question thusly: does one struggle for self-perfection through murder?"

"Nicholas, you are a fool. As Druids you and I have killed, Nicholas. As clansmen, you and I have killed. As warriors, you and I have killed."

Nicholas's mouth twisted. "And so killing to remove this demon from us will serve us no added harm, Thomas."

"No!"

"Father Thomas." Justus stood. "I owe legiance to you as I live in your monastery and have taken your vows and am your brother. My first legiance goes to Rome for I have joined with Nicholas and celebrate—"

"The point, Justus."

"If you would go to Rome yourself, Lord . . ."

There was murmur of approval.

"I?" A prouder man than all the Abbot is.

"And speak to them of the cow and the Fall and grace and decide then for yourself and for us . . . but speak to them."

"Nicholas?" Thomas questioned him. "Is this your idea?"

"My idea . . . my purpose, good sir, is to kill the cow and throw her meat to Seth."

"Justus?"

"Yes. Yes. Until you have spoken with Rome, the cow could live here without harm."

"Without harm? The choice then is I go to Rome or the cow is harmed?"

"No, no," others protested.

Nicholas walked closer to Thomas. "To save the cow, you are to go to Rome, on that I would agree."

"I see."

"Otherwise, those among us now Romans, those among us still Irish, all suffer the presence of the demon cow."

"You will be saving us, Father."

"She is not a demon cow," Thomas insisted.

Heads turned toward Diarmat and Thomas drew himself up sharply as if armies attacked.

"She speaks." Diarmat stuttered and choked. "She is a demon."

"Continue," Nicholas commanded.

"She says, 'I am Celeste. I am Celeste. I am here.' "

"Who is Celeste?" one asked.

Thomas answered, "Celeste is the daughter of Manuel, the Hermit, known to us as CuRoi."

No words then. The spring winds broke against the timbers, columns creaked, waves slapped the shore. Nicholas drummed his fingers on his sword, and Thomas, drawing his cloak around him, walked to the center of the room and stood firm and tall with his dark hair and the shadows on his face, his long chin, his fierce eyes.

"I go to Rome. In a month's time the seas will calm. In that time the cow is my charge and none shall touch her. And when I am gone, Muncas will keep her from harm." Then he turned to Diarmat and, with the brow of the Druid, cursed his betrayal of the cow's secret. "May the crows make a pudding of you."

The cow was taken from the barn and set in a manger built against the tor of the Abbot and none passed near her, God forbid she might speak, and a boat outfitted for the trip and Diarmat slipped on bladderlocks one day scraping winkles from the underside of a rock near the Port of the Cow, of all places, where no one could see him, fell so that a rock pierced him and his guts fell around his knees and indeed the crows came flying on the hot smell and ate of him while he was still alive but only barely so.

"Three deaths for the cow," Nicholas pronounced to the brothers assembled. "Three too many."

And so it was that Thomas sailed for Rome. Muncas took up a place beside the cow. And the cow rubbed her horns against stone, sharpening them, my poor CuRoi.

In our garden, patches of hate, patches of sweetness, patches of trust, patches of glory, patches of narrowness, patches of meanness, patches of love.

Some say the cow wept when Thomas left, others say not. One said he heard her angry with Thomas for leaving and Thomas sad. And when the coracle of Thomas disappeared around the Bay at the Back of the Beyond and prayers were made for his safe journey, it was not a night gone by that Nicholas stuffed the ears of three brothers with moss against the words of the cow, rolled a great Druid ball of butter and twigs, and exploded it before the eyes of Muncas, who, blinded and in terror, stumbled away from the burning house of the cow, and the three others, deaf to her weeping, pulled the cow from the stall, tied her legs, and dragged her to the stones and pushed her over the stones. Some say she called out to Thomas, others that she called out to Seth. She had no fear of the stones. Her fear was of Archie Splitnose. A bag of gold gladly given, Archie walking away with her lead in his filthy hand. Great the profit, great the pain. And supped sorrow, this poor scrivener, for the cow was Celeste, my CuRoi, my Royal Dog, my brightness, and fallen now into a sin so great, so black. Others understood and went to Nicholas for the baptism of the church. "We are born into sin," Nicholas warned them. "It is our shadow. Only through the Mother Church can we cleanse ourselves of sin, or we become the playground of demons as a beast is the playground of lice."

Some few of us, Muncas, Justus, and I, Generous, prayed for the Abbot's quick return. Nicholas purchased relics with the Splitnose gold. The brotherhood trembles for the return of Thomas. Why say more?

— GENEROUS

As Generous says, envy those who see but a small portion and think it all. Pity Archie.

Archie kept me hidden in a stall near the harbor. I could hear the water lapping. Daily the face of a small child, filthy, brown, lumpish, astonished, would appear in the window slit, another child groaning beneath. The child would stare, waver, fall away. Archie, apoplectic, would race from the stall, bellowing, brandishing the blackthorn stick. "Filth!" he called his own.

Consider, my father said, means to be with the stars. And Archie was no longer content with the ditches of his life. He considered me every moment he was able. He watched me by lantern, by sunlight, or sat sighing in the dark. I let him touch me once. He did as if I were fire.

"Aah, a fine thing you are. The very construction of you, the lovely tits." I drew my horn across his cheek. Scarlet blood ran down into the bald black fur of his cloak. Poor Archie. He sat on his stool once again and, from the dark wooden bowl of his face, considered me. Somewhere behind the gnarled and lumpy face and the nose split and spread in defiance of the nose tax, somewhere behind all of that coarseness, Archie yearned for beauty.

I too yearned. I scratched the days in the timber beside my head and listened to the water lapping. Surely Thomas would appear by Assumption and surely the church would honor his argument and surely Thomas would kill Nicholas for the betrayal.

Archie's wife, Erca, harangued him from the bothie near my stall. "Archie, have you done the potatoes yet? Archie? Leave the poor cow be." And he would leave, grumbling, for the ditches. Each time he closed the door, the ceiling and wall flaked to the floor. This prison, that prison, a stall for me, a stool for them, a window for light. I was safe.

Erca would sit on the stool and consider me. Smoking a crab-claw pipe she would be and stinking from the crack between those legs like dead herring caught up in the sea-weeds. Her hams slopped over each side of the stool, her black-stockinged legs swollen. Slow generations on her back, a tortoise of patchwork, her mother's patches on her mother's mother's patches. Like the dough in the garbage pail, there was something archebacterial about her: the first cloth, the first spore, the first anaerobic creature still crawling in her bowels, something that is now and was there from the beginning of life. I looked into her eyes. She painted my lips with rouge and sprayed me with scent. She cleaned me with warm water and soft linens. Ribbons she tied on my horns and braided my tail and draped my neck with amber beads and tigereye. I was child and treasure.

And when there were but three weeks until Assumption, mightily I listened to every sound at the harbor, for Thomas's voice, for Generous's greeting, for the camel's bubbly snort, even the scratch of the wicker hampers against his rough sides. On the nights Archie took the dread call from Mull to bring out the boat of the Dead, I wept that it should not be my Thomas passed on.

And then new sounds throbbed in the harbor, an increase of old ones. Ships arriving, shouts and orders, scrapings of large loads on the quay, the strain of winches, anchors, hammers on nails, a babble of foreign words. A thousand footfalls beyond my stall, a thousand voices, the clink of coin in the wife's store, high-whining engines, and, at last, Generous's voice greeting Thomas and the snort of the camel and then Thomas's voice.

"Sun, Moon," Generous called softly into my stall.

"Alleluia," Thomas whispered and the feet of the camel plodded away, drawing my heart out from me. What manner is this conspiracy? Archie sat at my shoulder, breathing heavily. I could not cry out.

That night, Assumption Even, Tishubov, I allowed Archie to touch me. I lifted my lead in my teeth and pushed at his hand with it.

"Wonder of wonders," he whispered, ran off, returned cleansed, and led me gently and respectfully—I have no other word—into the night beyond the village, there to drink the moon and suck the breeze and to call, I hoped, across the stones.

Kitchening smoke rose from the monastery. I listened for my brothers' voices singing the crops to blast on the mountain but no one sang. Would there be no harvest? The flanks of the mountain and the shoulders of the meadow were studded with bonfires, the night with the red eyes of warriors. Armies had come to Iona. I ran to my stall, Archie sliding and running behind me.

I had thought by now Thomas would have come for me. But no one came. Except at daybreak, Archie, limping, cursing, and made of his blackthorn stick a crossbar through the door and sat watch over me. The sound of men marching broke against the rocks of Dun Hi and a sulfurous smoke filled the air. Meteors flew across the sky. The red-mouthed raven beat her wings against the window of my stall, screaming. I had seen her in the pillar of my father's fire. There would be a harvest of men.

And then Nicholas's anxious voice speaking to Archie harshly of cattle raids and great battles and a harrowing and a hiding of the cow and Archie suddenly obedient, which I could not understand. And then Archie, smelling more of sweat than ever in his fear, face clean as a cheese, tied my lead to his wrist and took me out of the stall along a narrow dark path between bothies. Chimney pots cast long shadows on the ground; unnaturally light was Iona from the fires above her harbor. When I saw the boat of the Dead swaying at anchor under a new moon I bucked behind Archie. Immovable I was, he pulling, weeping in despair. "Come. Hurry. Hurry." And he pulling and I pulling until all the sky opened and it was the fiery butterball weapon of Nicholas bursting above us, a Druid's wonder. But against whom? And then from the sweep of dark, Thomas.

"My Thomas. My Thomas. It is Celeste. I am here!"

I called out and Archie fell down at the sound of my voice.

Thomas came. And an army, each of them with white wolfhounds on chains and flashing shield and livid sword and naked and rushing at us. Poor Archie on his back swinging his blackthorn stick, his rough coat wet with his tears and his fright, punished for his yearning.

"Ah, Archie, keep your small portion, Archie," I told him as his arm holding my lead was hacked from his body and I standing there with the hunk attached to me. "Keep your small portion and think it all."

And Archie dead, his last sound a whimpering, still yearning, Archie was, and I also and Thomas weeping, who cut the arm from my lead. His men were of his clan, brave and golden, ruddy, thick-necked, pure-browed, and keen to the fight and some bloody already from the sharpened sticks and iron nails and burning fat of Nicholas's weaponry and the stones fashioned from lime and Kings' brains, wicked they are, Druid wonders.

Thomas swung his glorious arms to the bonfires. "Rome's answer to your miracle, Celeste. We are to be destroyed. The Cain, the gothic knowledge of Naught, the harmonies, the proportions, the art of the light, all of it."

"I had the proportion, Thomas. You see . . . the digits—"

"Thomas! Come!" A warrior pulled at his arm.

Thomas swept him off, even roughly.

"Nicholas gains the stones, Thomas!"

". . . and Seth has the proportion now. You see, I gave—"

"Come, man, for God's sake!"

I did not think Thomas heard me. "Celeste, wee one—"

"I have brought this on, Thomas. I would fight with you. My horns are sharp."

"You will go to Seth, Celeste. I've brought up the Amadan to lead you to the Garden. Some time, wee one . . ." He bent and I knelt at his feet and he kissed my forehead. Had he heard me? The Garden? Did the proportion not matter?

Was the world about to come apart because Seth had the digits from my dewlap? What sort of arrogance had I?

Before his very warriors, now a great hundred of them massed, tiny penises adangle, armor aglow, neck muscles swelling, Thomas kissed my forehead again and then my eyes. His warriors turned their lustrous backs. Thomas dipped his head into my neck and flung his arms about me.

"I'll find you." Which one of us spoke those words? "I'll find you. Go."

So, what are the three causes of anything? What is the cause of cause? Thomas and his Pelagian controversy? The fury of Rome? I and my cow cause? Cause, it is its own cause and its own effect.

And he and his clan were off in a dead run up the hill toward the stones, toward Nicholas's Papal troop and the wolfhounds yelping with battle joy and the clan shouting, "Pharo! Pharo!" and the war wails rising and the twang of the cithara. Fires sprung from the stones. "Loose the boundaries," I called after the men. "Bring it on."

And there was John Joe, not happy that he was brought up, the same black pebble eyes rolling around the empty mouth, the carapace of ice now a carapace of flesh hanging from him for this moment only and he himself cloaked in membranes of memories, moving in long and fleshy curtains alive with his earthly past. He pointed to my self as Celeste, as CuRoi, as cow, to the cottage in Glasgow and his aunty and his aunty's garden and the purple cabbages tied to his stinking feet.

As he climbed me, his flesh was cold and sticky, as the yeast dough. Shaking he was, and steering my horns over the paths to the Beyond and when we were not more than half way there, under a cloud of fog, with the golden eyes of the herds of swine slipping toward us and away from us as I ran, John Joe pulled my head around, pointed to the living place on his sheet of skin where Seth and he sat tossing cubes, and I saw the purple sending and the camel sinking into the sand. On we went until his trembling became ague and he slumping over my back and at last, I had to turn and retrace my steps and deliver him to the stones.

The beaches and cliffs before me were filled with Irishmen and foreigners, black and white. A boatload of the Royal Race of Ethiops in flowing coral robes, beached and walked slowly, sedately toward the monastery, axes, flints, and swords glinting. Among them, Egyptians and Hebrews, with crooks and sandals.

At the stones, John Joe slid from my back and melted into the muddy ground of a trench newly dug. I saw his stomach unwind itself and become long, a separate animal, and go off, I imagined, toward a meadow in search of something to eat. Are we all then made of separate parts? Beings who themselves conspire to time-space harmony? I had thought so. My own copy books danced in my head. My father hadn't wanted me to know this. Puerile thoughts, he'd said. Except for the orchid creatures, who have agreed to nothing, we are all cooperating hierarchies. I watched, waiting for John Joe's orchid creature to emerge from the trench and go seeking its other part, but it did not. Perhaps it had died within John Joe long ago or left him in peace. Mud slid over the trench. I lingered.

On the flanks of Dun Hi, fighting. The skies at the juncture fiery with red points where metal met bone. God help my whole and lovely Thomas. God help me.

Girls in chemises ran by me. Men in bathrobes carrying the family cat and company after company of Senegalese and

Uhlans with misty gray uniforms and sabers glinting and then carriages of guns and the clink of gun carts. Horses snorting. I smelled sweat and the sweet oils of machines. Mothers flew with children wrapped in bedclothes. Carts piled high with wounded and dead rattled past me and from beneath the carts, a trail of blood dripped between boards.

And then a shout came from above me near the ancient causeway and the thundering of feet and in the moonlight, twisted faces of Rome's Carthaginians, coal-black and curl-haired. Coming at me.

"The cow!"

Covered, they were, the Pope's heroes in palm leaves of armor. Zealous and prize-hungry.

"Follow me!" I called, startling them for a moment. "Follow me for I go to the Otherworld."

"Christ has harrowed the Otherworld! It is not!" one among them shouted.

"It is Not and I go." And I turned toward the Other Side, escaping through the net of their doubt.

I heard my father's voice, scratchy and faint. "Sing, Celeste. Sing your song. The right note, Celeste, and all the rest will follow. Et cetera, et cetera, et ceteratatat."

I stopped and looked for him. There was nothing except sea and strand and the deep wet darkness ahead.

In the sand I drew then a large W. The waves licked it clean. I drew it again, deeper. The sea filled its troughs, retreated, and the moon painted the W in gold. W. It is Sin, Sheen, shaddai, the Hebrew letter, shadow, the sign of Seth, the double B of my childhood, the ultimate container of the A. The final instability, the place of non-equilibrium, the Garden of Disorder. I waited for Seth, the W shining in the moonlight. Invoked, he appeared.

I look upon Seth whose name is Enoch whose name is Lug, Michael whose name is Sin and who is eunuch. He comes from the great seed-bed of all that is not yet, from which all comes, to which all goes. Behind me is Thomas whose name is Time, Tammuz, Thames, Day, a portion only, a form, a frozen moment of manifestation, a blip. Seth is free of time. Seth is Never.

He draws a Q in the sand. The sea washes it away and the W returns. I feel no fear and for that I am afraid. Around his phallus his bush of hair is plucked in a six-point star. Blind and sterile he is yet alive beyond any life I have ever known. Seth. Ham. Pig. His semen is in his head and he bursts forth with the seed of wisdom and enlightenment. This then is the true snake in the Garden, the enlightened man whose sex has become his consciousness, kundalini. As above, below. Head to phallus; phallus to head, all holy. This is my spiritual wedding. He smiles and takes my lead. I follow him into the teeth of Is-Not, to W. My father has prepared me well.

I look upon Seth whose name is unicorn. He is the beast who lays his head in the lap of the virgin. This is the true marriage of sexuality and consciousness. This is the intelligence which precedes all form. And this is Enoch, chosen, descending into the Garden. In the fire, the skull burst from my father's head and flew off. Now, this Enlightened One descends to Naught, Nicht, Noch, Not. My father—was he one of these men? I go to the Garden then, to Disorder, to sing a new song. I follow a servant of God within whom the serpent of wisdom has risen to full consciousness. I follow to the Garden.

It is my father's house, abattoir. The house of becoming. A company of corpses hangs upside down from the rock walls. On each hand, three fingers are bound in twine to form the letter W, the Hebrew Sheen, Sin, Shaddai, the ticket to the organic process. I see. The ceiling mirrors in mirrors of ice. This is the Privy of Saturn. This is the place of pro-Cess, the pool of Creation, the house of the Fathers.

And he leads me. Am I so unnatural a being that I feel no terror? I feel wholeness and desire, curiosity and wisdom. Hierarchies, Celeste, think in hierarchies. Not opposites. So. I watch the ripple of Seth's domino as he moves through the grandeur of his columned halls and I imagine the flesh. So, Father, this is your God and Abbot Isaac's and, I suspect, through default or inclination, my own. And here is your nightworld, is it not? For this you left your gobbetroyals at the crossroads. For this you yearned. You, Father, lying in your bed, crying out, "I need a place to go. I need a place to go." It meant everything to you—a place for your shit and a place for your soul. It meant the depths and the dark. The spirit, it might fly to Heaven, but the soul it must go to its depths, to the soil of itself. Soul to soil. The U becomes I at last. The creature becomes Creator. Your abattoir is the house of ending and the house of beginning. It is the crack and I am at last here.

Down to the never-never, merd and murder, shit and sidhe, through the cracks in the quantum foam down through the wormwood wormholes, down out of history, down to the innermost sheer-cliffed immortality, down through the thundering holy ghoulish throat of it all where white monkeys with steel tongues hang upside down on rubber veins and pluck the terrible chord, et cetera, et cetera, one note, down into the nightworld of stillness, chasms of cold, colder still, we fall down to absolute cold and then suddenly heat and slime and soup and soul and the blue-slanted Sirian starlight plays on the Dark Gods of the nightworld, wearing their nightfaces, gimlet-eyed, exceedingly beautiful, numinous, august.

The old powers, the pre-possessors, the pre-positions, the pre-nouns, the Real Articles, the spellers who cast and move, forgotten, uninvited, outraged, vastly dangerous, cut up once and buried in the Word, they come. Impatient in patent-leather slippers, in checkered dominos, domini, and golden masks, the sheen of holiness upon them who turn earth to water, water to earth, flesh to soup, soup to soul, and soul to the sweetmeats, and dance and dine, they do. From Sirius, they come, from behind the moon, from the Dog Star of the Dog Days, this Ma'at/Motley Crew, the queenly questions.

This is the stable beyond the stable, the double B, the double V, the double U, the container of the unstable, the great mouth of the spirit. This is where they join, the A and the B, the Is and the Is-Not. This is the circle, circe, church. The place where the line, the Q, descends into the abyss of the W. An army of nightwinged creatures moves about me. They wear bags of consecrated salt between their eyes. My presence excites them. They murmur and touch me delicately. When the contained and the uncontained join, only then is the immanence Yahweh alive. It is here and alive.

Above, between layers of ice, the Jackal of Judgment runs in circles. And further above, the Newtonian penultimates of war: arcs, trajectories, bullets, machines.

Seth pulls at me. We go on.

The breath of Dis is a fart. Dis/order. Dis/gust, the taste of God, the pleasure of Dis, the reservoir from which all form springs. Last words fall from the right eye of the corpses.

"Good-bye. Hello. Don't forget. What is the question? Darling. Forever. Pharo! Do you speak French? Where is my regiment? Kaiser. Mother." I follow deeper. Wolfhounds yelp through the ice faintly. Thomas calls, "Forward! Pharo!" Seth, looking upward to Thomas's voice, draws me close and strokes my forehead. His other hand rests strong on my back. We watch above together.

The soles of men's feet are distinct, the bottoms of wheels, the hooves of cattle, but their bodies vanish. I see the familiar yellow of Wellingtons. Justus? Muncas? If the monks fight, the sacred clans are losing. A face flattens against the ice. It is no one I know. He stares at me, at Seth. Around me a farrago of human parts: steaming organs hang on coathooks, heads are tucked into wooden carts, pyramids of skins turned inside out, fetal, are curled into crates. Black pigs, Chazar, Kaiser, Caesar, race everywhere between us and as they move from me and toward me, they grow neither smaller nor larger. There is no perspective here. There is no interpretation. Is this the moon? If the three fingers spell Shaddai and the first letter is Sheen and that is Sin and Sin is the name of the moon—I do not know. Greyhound-thin, they are, the food of the dead, they are, these pigs. Ham, H'am, I am, Hamlet. For the tribe of Seth, of Michael, there is a geis against eating of pig for they are the holiest of totem animals of the highest of tribes. Of course the Jews eat no pork; it would be the breaking of the geis of their holiest clan. Paint-brush tails and sharp snouts, they have, the wealth of Hades, they are, the Much of the Underworld, these pigs, the Mucc of Mocc-el, Melech, Michael, the enough of Enoch.

At my feet in the next room are moving gardens of violet creatures, flowerlike, soft and fleshy, faceless with long fallopian arms. On each arm, eight elegant fingers clasp ovaries to soft shoulders. They dance toward me. They reach to my knees. One rubs against my leg as a cat, begging, promising.

I watch myself in the layers of ice mirrors as I follow Seth. I undulate. I am, H'am, simultaneous. I am, H'am, again and again within the glassy commas of delay between the octaves of ice. The violet creature clings to my leg, mewing softly, clutching her eggs.

I shall soon ask Seth.

The Jackal runs between being and becoming. He eats the offal, gnaws on the bones of the armies of life, and shits on the seeds which spring forth once again from this vast dark coil of Never into the event horizon of being. And there, just as my father said it would be, is the prester. A flash of immense snapping tail locked in the ice, and then the blue-black mouth, reeking. Hissing, in wide and steaming circles it swims, the eater of Time, with green-gold rust-iron eyes. Ah, Father, had you been here? Are these your dreams? Are you here now?

A pig with red eyes examines me. He runs off, ecstatic on the sweet smells of decomposition and the cinnamon. Seth draws me further into the coil. Here new parts wander about, searching as the rest of us do, for a higher coherency. The uterus clings to my leg. She is determined. So am I.

"Seth, change me."

"Would you rather be a pig?" Seth grins at me, the curved knife at his side grins at me. "Pig, pork, Phorcus, Orcus, Orkneys, Hocus, Pocus?" He nods his head. His voice softens. "Hebrew, Hebrides, Hesperides, Hibernian, Jew, Yid, Druid, Saturn, Saturday. Schma Yisroel Adonoy Elohenu, Adonoy Echod."

"I know that."

He nods his head. "It is I worshiped. Behind the One is the Naught. I guide the path."

"Change me then."

"Behave yourself."

I follow, chagrined, behooved. Above, men fall in halves.

A left hand clutches the earth. Its right hand reaches for it. Localities fail but below I am singularity.

The Sirian light fills the room and slants through the ice. It falls on Seth, sheathing him in further grandeur. He sits, now, looming, pulsing, brooding, blind, naked. His body is white marble, blue-veined Jurassic. The domino flows from him. I shrink toward my center with desire for him, for his seed, for his wisdom.

"Now!" he speaks but not to me.

The horns of a terrible black bull scrape the ice above. The bull looks down through the ice at me. And in the presence of Seth I tremble yet I speak out.

"I gave you the proportion, Seth. Change me!"

"Foolish little cow." He tosses a handful of fingerbones at my feet as slop. "There is no *single* proportion. There is no *single* order, no *particular* measure. The Universe is open. Openness *is* the initial condition."

"Then by all *means*, change me!"

He looks away. And laughs, stands, finds his way toward me, arms outstretched, shadow reaching me, covering me. He touches my horns and strokes me.

"What do you wish now? Wheels? Three breasts? Weak-kneed Thomas? Spotted buttocks? Your mother wanted spots. Perhaps you also. . . ."

My trembling worsens. His hand pauses from its great strokes.

"My mother?"

"So."

"Father? Are you my father?"

"I was also Manuel." He is defensive. "I have many fragments, Celeste."

"But you and I . . . on the beach. How could you . . . ?" How dare I ask? "My own *father*?"

"I was Thomas, for you. For that moment only."

283

Ice breaks above us. Warriors cascade to the floor.

"As your father, I was a failure, that fragment of me. But you loved me." Bending forward, he holds my head in his great hands. I sink to the floor. He smiles at me. "Cow was a fine solution. Totally non-linear, impressive."

I weep. He loved me. My father loved me.

"Only by great breaks of symmetry, Celeste, does evolution evolve itself into a new note, a new orchestration of everything in you from the most ancient archebacteria creeping in your bowels to the mind that reflects on itself. A new note, Celeste, and everything must be poised for the tuning. You understand?"

I nod.

"The tenth cube, the Ka'aba, it is the plug of the flood. I am Lug. I stand at the gate of the Naught."

I nod.

He lifts my head upward. "You are here to sing, Celeste? Your note?"

I nod again.

"See." In the ice a large yellow Wellington bounces, falls, another joins it. A face drops closer until it is sharply clear. Muncas? Dear strong Muncas? Muncas sniffs at a poppy and rips it out of the soil between us and as he does, something carmine is ripped up out of me.

Muncas's great hands splay out on the ice. He smiles and offers me the flower and then his face explodes into a bloody liquid disc, a sun, and my spine is filleted. And from a crack in the ice the vast black bull, who might be Muncas, slips through whole, shovels me up with his horns, tosses me to the ceiling, and impales me as I descend. Seth turns his back, calling out as he climbs the stone, "Invent the future!"

And the grass flies from my gut and blood rockets as the bull runs in circles around and around the coil of hall and the gimlet eyes of the nightcreatures become one long carmine streak of fear as I am circled. My grass arcs and falls. I mourn for it as I spin, am spun.

Seth calls out. "The future is not given, Celeste! It is taken, taken, taken. Take it!"

I feel myself slipping away. Cells reach, yearn, scan, clutch at each other as the hands of the halved warrior. Pain rips through me hot and furious, my father's rainbow, light caught in its own pain. I swell with it. Terror burns my heart. Something like a bladder bursts against a column. It is a part of me.

"Sing, Celeste, one note!" I hear my father shout as I am thrown against a wall near him, rammed. "Et cetera, et cetera, et ceteratatat." I spin outward. I am unbound. "Who?" I sing out. "Who?" There is no answer. It is not enough.

Flesh leaves bone. I pull my patterns into my head. There is not a part of me that is not now in my head. A leg leaves my consciousness. I draw it back in. My head is filled with radiances. The violet creature clinging to my leg tucks herself into me, mewing. I close around her. My salts, my soul, the jewel in my dewlap. I release none of them. I hold desperately to the idea of me. I am all pattern now, all dark. Have I not made bread? Have I not made a rainbow? Through the bull's crack in the ice I see a piece of blue sky, anvil-shaped. My body burns with great fevers and dark lights. Still, I am. This is not evolution. This is exaltation. Medusa, Madonna, Medea, Medua. I hear the note and I cry it out.

"Medua?" I cry. "Why?" I cry. "Medua?"

And I am answered.

I T IS SOON TOLD.
I, GENEROUS, WRITE OF THE END AND THE BEGINNING.

O swift and sorrowful spoiling. Much pain there was in the night. From within the vat of the vast woman's skull as white oxen drew it away came the wailing of a heart broken and on the beach, sawing and hewing and cutting and hacking and mutilating of holy men and swinging with our short spears until there was no telling who among us was black and who was white because of us all and over us all the color was red.

Our short swords useless against neckpieces of palm and tendon, our guts at our feet, some of us, but the power of the Abbot Thomas drove us on and the tide was with us. My brothers fought our accusers to the sea. Many were

286

made quiet. The sea ate them from the rear. Chariots, tanks, armor, swords, cannon, canon, robes, croziers, bird beaks, amulets floated and finally the thin fore line who could, made for the sides of their prodigious and wonderful fleets, wrapped themselves in Druid mists, turned themselves to seals, turned their ships upside down and the sea flooded in and there were only the hulls remaining to become cathedrals, the sails shrouds, the masts catheters.

Mothers pull sons from battlefields. Bones rest in baskets at the stones. Twisted metal, smoldering fires, broken machines, the monastery ashes, the village shattered. In the harbor, a strange and metal fleet steams out to deep water, turns upside down, and sinks. Children laugh.

Some there are who say a beautiful white-haired woman stood at the harbor waiting for the *Prince George*. Others there are who say a cow, wee-white star-speckled belly, lay dead on the shore, her hooves up in the air. Others, as myself, do not dare say.

There is a new coding now. The sound in the ripples of the foam and mud spins another great spiral imprint and the thundering voice of the Universe booms into a fiery birth, the unmanifest becomes the manifest. From dark fields come adverse forms. Disorder is the order of the Gods.

A blessing on him who would be at preserving these words against the Beast of Time and a curse upon him who would be at changing these words. Amen.

— GENEROUS

To whom it may concern:
Hey, diddle diddle,

— **CELESTE**

ACKNOWLEDGMENTS

With special gratitude to Professor Ilya Prigogine, whose kindness in allowing me to read his unpublished manuscript, *Order Out of Chaos*, was of inestimable value. And to Robert Lawlor, who taught not only sacred geometry but the most remarkable relationships between ancient wisdom and modern science. And to Sacred Architect Keith Critchlow, who taught the meanings of the true, the good, and the beautiful. To Rachel Fletcher, Geometer, who helped me to ask the right questions, and to Christopher Bamford of the Lindisfarne Association, who always had the right answers. To all these people, whom I found through the guidance of William Irwin Thompson and the Lindisfarne Association, thank you. Thanks go also to the Abbey of Iona for the use of their invaluable library, to Cornell University for their Irish collection, and to Syracuse University for making their facilities available. To Trent Duffy, production editor, and to my friends Sandra Kaplan, Jane Ogden, Sally Daniels, and Martin Kelly, for their astute and fastidious criticisms and generosity. And finally to Winthrop Palmer Boswell for her manuscripts, *Irish Wizards in the Woods of Ethiopia* and *The Roots of Irish Monasticism*, as well as her rich correspondence. To the Benedictine monks who gave me their hospitality, I ask forgiveness for a work that is purely, as relates to them, of imagination.